Now Comes Death

Other Five Star Titles
by Kinley Roby:

Death in a Hammock

Now Comes Death

A Harry Brock Mystery

Kinley Roby

Five Star • Waterville, Maine

First Edition
First Printing: July 2005

Published in 2005 in conjunction with Tekno Books and Ed Gorman.

Set in 11 pt. Plantin by Ramona Watson.

Printed in the United States on permanent paper.

Library of Congress Cataloging-in-Publication Data

Roby, Kinley E.
    Now comes death / by Kinley Roby.—1st ed.
      p. cm.
    ISBN 1-59414-287-4 (hc : alk. paper)
    1. Private investigators—Florida—Fiction.   2. Eccentrics and eccentricities—Crimes against—Fiction.   3. Inheritance and succession—Fiction.   4. Gulf Coast (Fla.)—Fiction.   5. Naturalists—Fiction.   6. Vendetta—Fiction.   I. Title.
PS3618.O3385N69 2005
    813'.54—dc22   2005006640

For Mary

Chapter 1

Helen Bradley had persuaded him, too easily according to Katherine, to volunteer for an Audubon Society breeding bird census. Snowy plover numbers in Florida had dropped to around a hundred nesting pairs. The Society wanted to locate the remaining birds and also make a general nesting bird count.

That was why on a Saturday morning in June, Harry Brock, clipboard in hand, was sweating his way north on Hobson's Choice, a three-mile strip of undeveloped beachfront on Tequesta County's southwest coast.

Harry was still in shock from being married again. And after two rough years, he knew that his marriage to Katherine Trachey was not in great shape. He was taking seriously his role of father to Katherine's two young children but, following the collapse of his first marriage, he had lived alone for sixteen years, and giving up that independence had not been easy. Katherine's problems with her pregnancy had added to their difficulties, as had her increasing objections to his working as a private investigator.

In southwest Florida, back dune thickets are rattlesnake country. But Harry now knew this blisteringly hot coast well, and he had confidently walked off the beach and into the tangled world of saw palmetto, sea oats, cord grass, and thorny brush dense enough to discourage a wild pig.

He was pushing himself through a clump of black stopper bushes when he saw a Carolina wren pop into its nest hole in a dead cabbage palm. He was marking down the sighting on his chart when a swarm of red hot needles stabbed his right calf.

While he was flailing his arms and disturbing the wren family's domestic tranquility with his language, something big and black enough to be the angel of death dragged its shadow over him with a loud rush of wings. As it shot upward, gaining altitude, the turkey vulture craned its red neck and fixed its black eyes on him in an inquiring stare.

"Not yet!" Harry muttered.

But he quickly forgot the bird in his efforts to break free from the brush and do something about the ants making their fiery advance up his leg. Swearing steadily, he thrashed his way through the barrier of sea grapes, and sprinted across the sand toward the water. Pulling off everything from his waist down, he splashed into the surf, shuffling his feet to avoid stepping on any stingrays buried in the sand, and groaned with relief as the green water of the Gulf splashed around his legs, routing the ants.

"Hey, Brock! Great buns!"

Harry gritted his teeth. He hated being called by his last name. He waded out of the water, holding up his shirttails and making other body parts available for comment as Helen Bradley strode down the beach toward him, grinning maliciously.

She was swinging a clipboard in one hand and flourishing a two-foot spike of white Spanish bayonet blossoms in the other. A strand of damp, honey-blonde hair had escaped from under her Tilley hat and clung to the side of her face. Her once-white shirt was stained with sweat and dirt. Her pants were torn at both knees. There was a long scratch on her chin, but neither it nor the hole in the brim of her hat, the result of an alligator having mistaken it for an egret, had diminished her energy.

With her blue canvas sack bouncing on her left hip, she looked like a rakish, female version of Johnny Appleseed. Which was close to the mark, Harry thought a little enviously as she hiked over the sand toward him. If you were looking for someone to go with you where no sane person had ever gone before, Helen Bradley was your woman.

Harry pulled on his trousers. "You're not supposed to pick the flowers."

"I didn't pick it, Harry, *dear*. A six-foot black racer dropped out of a sea grape onto my back. I jumped, tripped over the damned plant, and broke the stem. It's for you." She shoved it at him. "I would have brought you the snake if I hadn't missed my grab. Why are you wading?"

"Fire ants."

He took the flower stalk from her and felt more foolish holding it than he had being offered it.

Harry had never figured out his relationship with Helen Bradley. He had known her before he met Katherine, but for some reason they hadn't become lovers. But they had remained close. And, later, she and Katherine became friends. He tried to feel pleased about that, but he still wondered, without exactly wanting to do anything about it, why his relationship with Helen, once so promising, became locked in amber.

Helen was now head of personnel at Three Rivers Bank & Trust Company. She had been office manager for Boone Enterprises when Katherine had gone to work for Orville Boone. A short time later, Harry had given the law what it needed to nail Avola's biggest developer for attempted murder and other skullduggery. Helen left for the bank and Katherine went to work for the Arnell Property Management Company. Boone had gone to jail.

Harry sat down to pull on his boots and jammed the flower spike into the sand. Helen dropped onto her heels and began reading his list of sightings. He glanced at her list, saw that it was longer than his, and tried to brush sand over his check sheet. But she grabbed it and compared their entries.

"You lose," she said. "Again."

"This isn't a competition, Helen."

"Wrong, Brock. Everything is a competition."

"For you it is."

He hated the way she always beat him on these counts. He tried hard to be a good loser, but her crowing over her victories felt like something done to hurt. And it had gotten worse since his marriage. But he told himself that, given the good things about their relationship, it would be foolish of him to make an issue of it.

Helen suddenly scrambled to her feet. "Hey, look at this!"

Harry got up a little more slowly. He was pushing fifty and occasionally knew it. A dozen or more vultures had gathered and were circling over the section of back dune some fifty yards north of where Harry stepped on the ant nest. Looking higher, he saw more of them coming to the picnic.

"The first one checked me out just before I stepped on the ants. Must have decided I wasn't high enough," he said.

She wrinkled her nose. "Then he was upwind of you."

"You're no bouquet of roses."

She gave a yelp of protest. "Get a grip, Harry!" She shaded her eyes with a hand. "What's bringing them down?"

"I don't know. I didn't smell anything."

She passed up the opening with a grin and checked her

watch. "Survey's over in another forty-three minutes. Let's go look."

They set off for the back dune.

"I hear Three Rivers has an interest in this property," he said.

They scrambled up the four-foot bank separating the beach from the back dune. She paused at the top to knock the sand off her pants. "The buzz in the office is that Riga Kraftmeier brought in an interested client."

Harry recalled meeting Riga a year or so back at one of the bank's art shows. He remembered that she was beautiful but also unsmiling and silent. "What's her job?"

"Job? She's a vice president. At the moment, she's in charge of the loan department. But that won't last. She's one of the bank's major players. She'll be moving up."

Her voice sounded a little brittle to Harry.

"You having a problem with her?"

"No!" She stopped and turned to face Harry. A branch had knocked her hat forward, forcing her to lift her chin and glare at him from under the wrecked brim. "Riga Kraftmeier is a damn good loan officer. She's made the bank a pile of money. And, she's done it with a major deficit."

"What deficit?"

She pushed her hat off her forehead and answered louder than necessary. "Burdensome beauty."

They set off again toward the vultures. The boldest had already dropped onto the ground and beat up reluctantly as Helen and Harry came crashing toward them. Harry started to ask Helen what she meant by "burdensome beauty" when the rapidly-shifting wind brought him a sickening whiff of what was pulling in the vultures. Helen was pushing ahead hard. He started to speak, but she began talking loudly over her shoulder.

11

"I don't know the whole story, but something happened to Riga. Maybe a long time back. Anyway, it left her the way she is."

The wind suddenly blew strongly in their faces and Harry called urgently, "Helen, wait a minute."

But it was too late. She gave a cry, turned, and came crashing back through the saw palmetto branches straight into him, her face white as the sand. She sucked her breath in between clenched teeth, eyes wide. "Jesus, Harry. It's a man."

Harry tried to pull her away, but she dug her heels into the sand.

"No, I want to see who it is."

He followed her around the palmetto and through a screen of coffee bushes. The stench thickened. The body was sprawled on its back between two big tussocks of cord grass. An arm in a faded blue sleeve lay over a tussock of brown grass; its sunburned hand dangled limply in the air. The man's sunken face regarded Harry with apparent surprise. The wind shifted again, and Harry backpedaled.

Helen clapped one hand over her mouth and reached out with the other to grab his shoulder. Harry put his arm around her and guided her back a dozen yards to where the smell was less violent. But even as she was stumbling away, she continued to look back at the blackened face until the brush hid it from view. The vultures were coming in faster now, and only Harry and Helen's presence was keeping them off the body.

Still leaning against him, she pulled her water bottle out of her bag, drank from it, then passed it to him. "Is that who I think it is?"

He swallowed some of the warm water and forced himself to breathe deeply. "It's Truly Brown."

"I thought so!" She rested her head against his shoulder. "Did you see . . . ?"

"Yes. The top of his head's been shot off. And we've got a problem here."

She raised her head and broke free from his supporting arm as if she had just become aware of being pressed against him. She looked up at the vultures. Thirty or forty of the big birds were circling impatiently. "We can't leave him."

"Right. Have you got your phone?"

She pulled a small, blue phone out of her bag and punched in a number. Harry moved back closer to the dead man. The vultures were coming down again. Helen snapped her phone shut. She plowed forward to where Harry was standing, her face pale. The squadron of feathered ghouls was wheeling closer. She put her hands over her face.

"God, I feel awful," she said. Then she flung out her right arm in an angry gesture toward the place where Truly was lying, tears streaking her face. "Who could have done such a thing?"

Harry dropped his clipboard and pulled her into his arms. For a moment she pushed her face into his shoulder and clung to him. Then she stepped away, wiping her eyes on her sleeve.

"Sorry, Harry. Let's keep those bastards off him."

She snatched a rattling, brown cabbage palm frond from the ground and bulled into the brush in a shouting, crashing advance. The vultures dropping toward the body rose in alarmed flight. Reluctantly, he followed her.

The two deputies arrived on an ATV buggy with emergency aid equipment and a collapsible gurney strapped on the back. Harry met them at the beach and recognized Sergeant Frank Hodges. The younger officer was a stranger. Hodges, a heavy man in his early fifties with a florid face, shook hands and turned to his companion. "Deputy Freeman Weeks, Harry Brock. What you got back there?"

"Truly Brown. Very dead."

Hodges made a sour face. "Oh shit," he said, paused, and added, "lead us to him."

The three men struggled back through the brush to the body. Helen threw down her palm frond. She looked exhausted. Hodges and Weeks turned their attention to the body. When he was finished, Hodges came back, mopping his face with a large blue and white handkerchief and breathing heavily. Weeks' face was green as the Gulf.

"He's dead all right," Hodges said. "But the poor soul never had anything worth stealing. I wouldn't have thought he was important enough to kill."

"There are a lot of tracks around the body," Harry said.

Hodges nodded.

"I need some water," Weeks said in a choked voice, and headed for the ATV.

Hodges blew out his breath. "I've called in the Crime Scene Unit. I expect that later on, one of their detectives will want to talk with you two."

Helen and Harry nodded and waited for more information, while Hodges put away his handkerchief as if it was a family heirloom and carefully adjusted his hat. Behind him Harry saw a vulture, bigger and bolder than the rest, peel off from the formation and drop swiftly to the ground. Others followed.

"Truly was shot," Hodges began.

Harry broke in. "They're going for him."

Hodges turned and looked. "Weeks! Get back here! We'll lose the evidence."

Hodges scrambled back toward the body, shouting, "Git!"

Weeks came trailing back, looking sick.

"You finished with us, Frank?" Harry shouted.

"I know where to find you," Hodges called back in a distracted voice.

They had almost reached the beach when Helen suddenly stopped. "Wait a minute. Where's Weissmuller?"

For a moment Harry was at a loss. Then he remembered. Weissmuller was Truly's dog, and his constant companion: a big, brindled, battle-scarred animal with a menacing stare. He was death to cats. The County Animal Control had been trying for years, without success, to rid the world of his baleful presence.

"I don't know, but one thing is certain. If Truly was out here without Weissmuller, he didn't come willingly."

Chapter 2

"I've known Truly Brown all my life."

Helen spoke with obvious pain as she refilled their glasses with iced tea and slumped down on a blue kitchen chair.

Harry was also thinking about the murder. "There are times it's hard to be a human being."

"Who do you suppose killed him?"

"I don't know, but the people he hung out with don't sing in the choir."

"True," she said. "I'm ashamed to admit it, but I probably knew Weissmuller better than I knew Truly."

"Maybe it's just easier to know a dog."

"That's bullshit, Harry."

"Probably. But what was there to know about Truly, beyond the fact he was making do with half a loaf and wandering around in the Big Cypress Swamp with that sociopath Weissmuller, looking for Tarzan?"

"Don't be cruel, Harry. Being different is hard."

A sudden, heavy rumble of thunder rattled the windows. Mister Johnson, Helen's African gray parrot, flung his beanbag into his big, brass cage on the kitchen counter and fled after it with a squawk of alarm. Helen looked up as the sun blinked out.

"I hope this one's got some water in it," she said. "It hasn't rained a speck since January."

"Let's hope. There's a new forest fire every day." He

thought briefly that, although southwest Florida had dry spells and fires the way the North had snow and black flies, this drought had begun to be a cause for serious concern.

Helen reverted to Truly. "Did you know he had a job?"

"No. That's a surprise. Where was he working?"

She gave a half-choked laugh. "The Green Thumb Nursery, out near Fakahatchee Trace. Hannah Bridges, who owns the place, was in the bank a while ago and said he was working for her and that Weissmuller came with him every day. She said there's not an outdoor cat left in Cypress Grove."

"They were a very strange pair," Harry acknowledged.

The light was dying swiftly in the kitchen, and Helen reached for the table lamp just as a sizzling wire of yellow lightning sliced open the gloom outside Mister Johnson's window. The flash was accompanied by another, louder crash of thunder.

Mister Johnson jumped and shrieked, "Fireworks!"

"Close." Helen pulled her hand back. The air outside the windows had turned a quivering green.

For the next ten minutes, the storm crashed and slashed around the house, and Mister Johnson cursed every crackling explosion. Water began sluicing off the roof in a low roar. They sat watching and listening and talking a little, until the storm rumbled west.

"That was kind of nice," Helen said quietly. Harry agreed and stood up. Helen got up with him and asked, "How's Katherine?"

"Not great."

"The pregnancy?"

"Among other things. Maybe our deciding to have a child wasn't such a great idea."

Helen put a hand on his arm. "Yes it was. What else is

bothering her? We haven't seen much of one another lately. I feel out of touch."

"Nothing new. She's still wants me to quit what I'm doing and go into property management with her. I think she sees us starting our own business down the road. The problem is, I don't."

Helen made a face and said, "Ouch."

"Yes. By the way, did you know her mother's sick? That's some more of the problem."

"Oh, God. What's wrong?"

"Her heart. It's not life-threatening. At least not yet, but she doesn't want to give up work. So it's a problem. Her sister tells Katherine everything's okay, but that's Priscilla."

"Priscilla still lives at home, doesn't she?" Helen asked.

"Yes, and it should ease Katherine's mind, but it doesn't."

"Guilt," Helen said. "She thinks she ought to be taking care of her mother."

She hooked her arm through his as he came around the table and walked him to the Rover.

"You going to be all right?" he asked.

"I'm fine." She gave him a quick kiss on the cheek. "Ask Katherine to call me."

"I'll do that."

She waved him out of the driveway. Harry wondered whether she really was all right. She sometimes overdid the Wonder Woman routine. He also wondered why, when he had spoken harshly about Truly, she had said, "Being different is hard."

Harry reached Bartram's Hammock still feeling dissatisfied. Truly Brown's killer might not be his responsibility, but the man's death troubled him. Where was the motive? He and

Helen had worried the problem for more than an hour, and finally done no better than guess that Truly had stumbled onto gill fishermen emptying their nets or dopers coming ashore. But Helen had been unable to let it rest.

"I keep coming back to Weissmuller," she had insisted. "Truly never went anywhere without that dog, and whoever shot Truly would have had to kill Weissmuller first or gotten chewed into hamburger."

Harry had agreed. While the dog was alive, God Himself couldn't have laid a hand on Truly. But if he'd been shot along with Truly and had crawled away to die, the vultures would have been after him as well as after Truly. Harry was still thinking about the murder when he drove over the Hammock's humped bridge and stopped to pick up the mail.

He never returned to the Hammock without experiencing a lift in his spirits. But that lift was salted with the unpleasant knowledge that his tenure on the Hammock was running out. Three years ago, Emile Thibedeau had been convicted of murdering Slade Hatfield and Katherine's runaway husband, Willard Trachey. Orville Boone, who owned the Hammock and the house Harry leased, went down as an accomplice after the fact, and his commercial enterprises collapsed. The State sold off Boone's holdings to pay his creditors, but it kept the Bartram's Hammock property as buffer land for the Stickpen Preserve. The State notified Harry and Katherine Trachey, who had been living in her husband's old cabin, that they had five years in which to find another place to live.

The State relented slightly and extended Harry's lease for seven years instead of five, but still with no option to renew. Katherine postponed her housing problem by marrying Harry and moving into his place. Now she was pressing him to start thinking about where they were going to live when their lease ran out, but it was not something Harry was ready to face. For him, Bartram's Hammock was more than somewhere to live. It was the place where he had been recalled to life. The place had become his home.

Six years before the State appropriated Bartram's Hammock, along with the rest of the financially crippled Boone estate, Tucker LaBeau, in an effort to stop Boone from developing the Hammock, had deeded his farm to the State of Florida in exchange for a dollar and a lifetime lease. The State's arrangement, barring natural increase, had now frozen the human population on the Hammock at Tucker LaBeau, Harry, Katherine, her two children, Minna and Jesse, and Tucker's dog Sanchez and his mule Oh-Brother!, who, arguably, were partly human. Tucker, of course, treated them as if they were human, and there were times when even Doubting Harry thought they might be.

Harry climbed out of the Rover into the rain-washed afternoon and took a deep breath. He stared with satisfaction at the soaring, green canopy trees and their shadowed under-stories, trailing lianas and air roots in the cool shade. A quiet saffron light floated on the puddles on the dirt road. Along Puc Puggy Creek, the herons and egrets were topping off the day's catch, and the frogs had begun creaking and grunting. All over Bartram's Hammock, day was winding down. Relieved to be home, he walked back to the County road to pick up his mail.

When he reached his mailbox, he saw the corner of a letter sticking out of the usual trash. Ah, he thought, human contact, possibly a job. But the good feeling died when he read the address scribbled in pencil and saw the Maine postmark.

With a sinking heart, Harry tore open the envelope and read the brief message scrawled on a scrap of yellow paper.

Merle is dead. That's two you bastard.

Harry stared at the writing with a sour mixture of revulsion and anger. In that instant, he forgot Truly, the Hammock, everything his life was now. Nineteen years vanished. He was standing again in an abandoned apple orchard, in the last light of a grim November day, wading through knee-deep snow toward the place where Jacob Stone lay dying in a welter of blood. Merle was Stone's wife, and the man who had written the letter was his brother Gideon, who had been eleven years old when Harry shot his brother.

With his heart pounding, Harry forced the scene from his mind. He looked up just as a flock of ibis swept over his head. The sound of their wings reminded him of the vultures over Truly's body, and he gave an involuntary shudder. He crumpled the note in his fist and started to fling it away, but checked himself and shoved it into his pocket. He would burn it, destroy it utterly. He strode back toward the bridge.

He pictured himself telling Katherine about the note, but the thought of doing it pulled him up short. No. She must not learn about this. From the start, Katherine had objected to his being a private investigator. After they were married, her objections became stronger, triggered, no doubt, by his having been wounded in a skirmish shortly before they were married. "It's dangerous," she insisted. Now, carrying another child, she was even more anxious.

He leaped into the Rover and, dreading what was before him, drove home.

Chapter 3

Harry parked his Rover under the big oak at the corner of the lawn and forced himself to walk slowly toward the house, looking at things around him, taking them in, naming them, and putting himself back amongst them. Katherine's white Rava was parked just as she'd left it and run into the house. The pale gray house with its wide, screened lanai and the huge wisteria vine covering the south end of the lanai were solidly there. So were the live oaks, trailing Spanish moss from their branches and spreading shade over the house and the lawn. He began to feel better.

He had almost reached the lanai when a black and white cat trotted up to him, bushy white tail erect. He bent and ran his hand down its back. "Hey, Boots."

He went into the house and called to Katherine.

"I'm in the kitchen," she answered.

She was making biscuits. Harry dropped the mail on the table and pulled her into his arms.

"I'm glad you're home," he said.

She leaned back in his arms, her floury hands held out away from them, and cocked her head. "You okay?" Her intensely green eyes darkened with concern.

"I'm fine. Where are the kids?"

"You're not fine." She gave him a quick kiss. Her blonde hair, touched here and there with silver, was wrapped around her head in a long, thick braid. "They're around here somewhere. Jesse's been playing his clarinet and

Minna's been complaining. C'mon, partner, spit it out. You and Helen have another scrap?"

"No. Have you heard anything from Priscilla?"

She went back to the biscuits. "She called to say Dr. Whitney is talking about a pacemaker. Ma is saying no, but what else is new?"

"Why the 'no'?" The note in his pocket was burning his leg. He went back to the table and began sorting through the mail, without seeing anything he was looking at.

She stared at him for a moment, her face stiff. "You know she doesn't want the procedure. Did you get your birds all counted? Yes, the kids and I had a good afternoon. Where the hell are you?"

She began banging the biscuit cutter into the dough. Harry dropped the letters.

"I should have told you as soon as I came in. Helen and I found Truly Brown on Hobson's Choice. He'd been shot and killed and left for the vultures."

When is the truth a lie? He beat back the impulse to tell her what really was troubling him.

Katherine straightened from sliding the biscuits into the oven. "God, Harry, how awful. No wonder you're upset."

He started to say he wasn't upset, stopped himself, and hugged her instead, comforted by the swell of her belly pressed against him.

"Tell me about Truly Brown. The name sounds familiar, but I can't place him."

"You've probably seen him—a tall, scruffy man with a big dog. You wouldn't forget the dog. Look, do you mind if I go upstairs and see what the kids are doing?"

Katherine gave a puzzled frown. "Go. But hurry back. I want to hear about Truly."

Harry took the stairs two at a time, his heart pounding.

"Hi, Harry," Minna said, looking up from her book. Boots had found her and was curled in her lap, purring contentedly.

He listened to what she had to say about primates, told her what *prehensile* meant, and went in search of Jesse. The dark-haired boy was sitting on his bed, cleaning the keys on his clarinet.

"How's the practicing coming?"

"Okay. Can you look at my salt water tank? Something's not right. One of the fighting conchs has died."

They looked at the milky-colored tank together and talked briefly for a couple of minutes about what might have caused the problem. Then Harry said, "I've got to discuss something with your mother. We'll decide later what to do with the tank."

"Sure," Jesse said.

Harry couldn't stop himself from asking if everything else was all right.

The boy looked at him more sharply. "Fine."

"Okay. I've got to go downstairs."

"Tell me," Katherine said, taking the biscuits out of the oven.

Their rich aroma drifted through the kitchen. She put the coffee pot on the table and sat down, giving him an encouraging smile. Harry pulled his mind away from the note in his pocket and, unhappy with his deception, told her about finding Truly's body.

"How's Helen taking it?"

"I stayed with her for a while after I took her home," he said. "She's not feeling too great, but I think she's okay. Probably more than okay. Helen's tough."

"Not nearly as tough as you think." Katherine pushed herself up from the table and stood, frowning down at him.

"Are you getting involved in this murder?"

"No. I've got no part of it."

"Good. I'm going to call Helen."

Harry scarcely heard her. He was thinking again about Gideon Stone.

The next morning, Harry decided to talk with Tucker LaBeau about the note. He found Tucker in his garden, shucking sweet corn. Sanchez was lying under his favorite oleander bush. When Harry got out of the Rover, the hound lifted his head and barked a welcome over his shoulder without getting up.

"He's grown too old for manners," Tucker said, shaking Harry's hand.

Tucker was in his mid-eighties and a head shorter than Harry. When he moved, his collarless blue shirt and bib overalls flopped around his skinny frame like rags on a scarecrow. But, looking at his friend with pleasure, Harry couldn't remember when Tucker was last sick, despite his seven/twelve workday. His small farm looked like something off the cover of a seed catalogue.

Tucker's honeybees were humming busily around the garden. Tucker moved among them with the calm immunity of Solomon wearing his ring, but Harry's relationship with the bees was less advanced. He was about to ask after Oh-Brother! when he felt his hat lift off his head and turned to find the big mule holding it in his mouth. The mule was wearing his own straw hat at a rakish angle.

"Your memory's longer than an elephant's," he said, as Oh-Brother! returned his hat. Harry had once made a disparaging comment about the mule's hat, and Oh-Brother! had never let him forget it.

After a lot of resistance to the idea, Harry finally admitted that Oh-Brother! just might understand most of what was said to him. Tucker talked to him all the time. But Tucker talked to everything, including the trees.

"Come in and have a second breakfast," Tucker said. "I've got corn enough for a church picnic." He rattled the heavy ears in his basket. "We'll make do."

Harry grinned. As with most things, Tucker had his own ideas about breakfast. At the word *breakfast*, Sanchez clambered to his feet and fell in behind Oh-Brother!. As they passed the hen house, Longstreet, Tucker's big Plymouth Rock rooster, ran out into the screened run and crowed a greeting. He was bigger now than his predecessor Beauregard.

Bonnie and Clyde, a pair of larcenous gray foxes who thought of Tucker's hen house as their local KFC, had broken in and killed Beauregard in a daring raid, staged on the same night Orville Boone tried to burn down Tucker's house with Tucker in it. Sanchez and Oh-Brother! had caught him before he could strike a match and nearly killed him.

Once past the hen run, Tucker made a short detour to put the shuckings on one of his compost piles—objects which the old farmer treated with the care and reverence usually reserved for religious shrines. The stop brought them close to Tucker's bee yard. In a moment rich with fellow feeling, Harry, Sanchez, and Oh-Brother! nervously eyed the bees zipping around them. Tucker, however, went about the business of scattering the shuckings over the compost pile, oblivious to the menacing hum.

Tucker had bee yards scattered all over the Hammock, but these three hives were his favorites, housing Corniolan honeybees, originally imported from Yugoslavia. According to Tucker, they were butterfly gentle, but when Harry sat down on one, he discovered they could sting.

As they resumed their march to the house, Harry asked Tucker why he went to all the work and trouble of keeping bees.

"Connections." When he saw Harry was lost, he added, "They connect me to the past. When I was a boy, we always kept bees. But it goes further back than that, you know."

"Your grandparents . . ." Harry began.

But Tucker stopped him with a pitying look. "The ancient Greeks kept bees. They even had a god of hives called Aristeus, who, according to the story, taught them to curdle milk for cheese, to grow olives for oil and food, and to keep bees in terra-cotta pots."

He pulled his right ear, a sure sign he was deep into an idea. "It's a good thing to stay hooked to the past. In my view, it grows one's humanity and helps to keep you sane."

Harry shook his head. "The past is too painful," he said. "I'd rather forget it."

"Well, you can try," Tucker replied with a chuckle, "but it won't forget you."

Harry found the idea repellant and pulled his mind away from it. While they ate, Harry told him about Truly Brown. By the time they had finished eating, they were at the same dead end Helen and Harry had reached. Tucker ran a leathery, brown hand over his bald head and set the white fringe of hair over his ears floating like a small cloud of dandelion fluff. He gave Harry one of his appraising looks and said, "And you think he was killed in some kind of brawl?"

"Probably. That's a tough bunch he hung out with."

"What were they doing on Hobson's Choice? There's nothing to drink down there—not that Truly, so far as I know, was much of a drinker."

"I don't think he was. Of course, there's a certain

amount of dope coming ashore along the coast."

Tucker agreed. "Well, it's surely too bad about Truly, but if I'm not mistaken, there's something else on your mind."

Harry passed him the crumpled letter. "Merle Stone is dead."

"That would be Jacob Stone's wife?" Harry nodded. Tucker smoothed the paper on the table. "She'd be fifty-something, would she?"

"About that."

When he had read the note, he passed it back with a frown. "Looks like the little luck she had ran out. Want to talk about it?"

"No, but I think I'd better."

Tucker went to the stove and came back with the teapot. Harry winced, but Tucker filled his mug. "The letter's not signed, but I suppose it would be the younger brother who wrote it?"

"Gideon." A sudden flash of anger roughened his voice. "I try not to think about any of this. I've put it behind me. It's over with. Done."

Tucker frowned. "If I've counted right, Gideon would be about thirty."

"Yes." Harry didn't need to count. He knew Gideon's age as well as he knew the ages of Sarah and Clive, his own children. They were a few years younger than Gideon, and he had seen very little of them in the nineteen years since he had been arrested, tried, and acquitted for the murder of Jacob Stone.

At the end of the trial, his wife Jennifer had spirited them out of the Maine courtroom and out of his life. For years, Jennifer did everything the law allowed to keep him away from them. In the end, he stopped trying. Perhaps that had been a very serious mistake.

"He was eleven when Jacob died," Harry said.

"He planning to make a career of hating you?"

"Can't blame him. When I shot Jacob, I killed a man Gideon loved as a father, as well as a brother. I might just as well have shot him while I was at it."

Tucker sampled his tea and shook his head. "You know better than that, Harry."

"If you say so." Harry felt himself slipping back into the misery of the experience that had cost him his wife, his children, and his game warden's job.

"Did Merle ever try to get in touch with you?"

Harry shook his head.

Tucker paused to drink some more tea, watching Harry while he did it. "What if you hadn't shot him?"

"He would have shot me."

"Then where was your wiggle room?"

"How much help is that to Gideon, or Merle, who no longer needs it?"

"None."

"I shot the man over a damned deer."

"As I remember the story, you shot Jacob Stone because when you found him with the deer he'd just jacked, he turned his gun on you."

The picture of the frozen orchard and Jacob coming up from the fallen deer, shooting as he rose, filled Harry's mind. "They buried Jacob and went into welfare."

Tucker sighed. "And unto them who have not . . ." He got up and followed Harry to the door. "A final question. Have you told Katherine about the letter?"

"No, and don't you mention it."

The sun had burned away the last traces of the morning mist over Puc Puggy Creek by the time Tucker, Sanchez, and Oh-Brother! had walked Harry to the road.

Tucker squinted at the sky. "In my opinion, you're making a serious mistake. She has a right to know. Gideon Stone is no longer an unhappy youngster. He's a man grown. The anger in that note is dangerous. I also think you should tell the police about it."

"Katherine's got more than enough on her plate with her mother and her pregnancy," Harry replied. "I got this note because Merle died, but I doubt that I'll hear anything more from him. I'm sorry I made so much of it. We can forget about it."

Tucker started to speak, then stopped himself and shook Harry's hand. "Oh, I almost forgot, I found a partly-eaten deer carcass on the north end of the Hammock. Might be a panther or a bear kill. I was late coming home from the bee yard and didn't take the time to study it, beyond noticing Bonnie and Clyde hadn't scavenged it. That was a first."

Harry welcomed the change in subject. They talked briefly about the dead deer; then Harry left.

"Keep your eyes open," Tucker called after him.

Chapter 4

The day stretched in front of Harry like a long road with no shade. Gideon's note had shattered his peace of mind, and its message had dragged him back into that winter world of pain, guilt, loss, and misery which he thought he had put behind him forever.

The phone rang just as he walked into the kitchen.

"This here's Findlay Jay speaking, *Jay* as in scrub jay, not as in the letter *J*. You want to help me find out how thirty head of prize-winning red Durhams could have been stolen out of a fenced pasture with a locked gate?"

"Where's your spread?" If Findlay Jay had been in the room, Harry would have gripped his hand and shaken it with gratitude.

Forty-five minutes later, Harry was standing beside Findlay Jay, leaning on the top bar of a pipe gate, chained shut and fastened with a padlock big enough for an elephant stockade. Both men were staring into an empty pasture. Findlay Jay's ranch was located on the far northeast corner of Tequesta County, beyond the reach of RFD.

"When I told Norma Jean, that's my wife, what had happened to the red Durhams, she said, 'Findlay Jay, did you fall into the sheep dip again?' But it wasn't nothing like that, as you can plainly see."

"They're gone, all right," Harry agreed. Since arriving at Findlay Jay's ranch, he was getting a lot of practice at keeping his face straight.

31

Findlay Jay was, Harry judged, at least six-four and, in his western-style boots and straw cowboy hat, he looked even taller. Standing beside him, Harry thought the man, broad as a barn door as well as tall, made a pretty good shade tree. His fair skin was burned a rusty red, and his wide, blue eyes regarded Harry with a kind of pained astonishment.

"I found the tracks of at least three shod horses in the pasture and wolf-size paw marks of two or three dogs. That make any sense to you?" Harry added.

Findlay Jay shook his head slowly, frowning with concentration. "My horses haven't been in there. The only dog on the place is Norma Jean's Willie Nelson, and he's no bigger than an armadillo."

"How many keys are there to that lock?"

"Just this one." Findlay Jay burrowed in his jeans pocket and held out a heavy key for Harry's inspection.

"The fence is all solid. The gate hasn't been tampered with. The ground is marshy. There's no place where those cattle could have been driven out of the pasture without our seeing the tracks. And you're sure they were in here when you went to bed last night."

"Cross my heart and hope to die." Findlay Jay turned to Harry and did that, then held up a big hand in an Indian peace sign.

Harry turned away from the fence, struggling to keep from laughing. As soon as he could, he said, "Anything like this ever happen to you before?"

Findlay Jay looked around carefully, as if refreshing his memory. "Not recently. But, you know, there are some as will do such things."

"Anyone in particular?"

"I was speaking generally."

32

"Then I've got some thinking to do," Harry said.

At the Rover, Findlay Jay shook Harry's hand slowly. He had also seemed to walk slowly going around the pasture, but his legs were so long Harry had to trot part of the time to keep up with him. "The thing's a mystery, Mr. Brock. It surely is."

"I'll see if I can do anything about tracing them," Harry replied.

"No," Findlay Jay said slowly. "Just figure out how they was got out of there."

Harry started to protest, but the rancher shook his head solemnly. "No, Mr. Brock. One thing at a time."

Harry got back to the Hammock and found Sergeant Frank Hodges and Captain Jim Snyder standing in front of his lanai. Harry reached them just as a female red-shouldered hawk came around the southeast corner of the house, traveling like a missile, a three-foot water snake grasped in one claw. She screamed over their heads and vanished around the northwest corner with the unlucky snake twisting in her grip.

"What the hell . . . ?" Hodges shouted. He came out of his slanting crouch, his left hand clamped on the crown of his hat.

"Lady Godiva," Harry said.

"Just one of Harry's rackety neighbors," Snyder said. He leaned his long frame past Hodges' shoulder and shook Harry's hand. "Good to see you, even if the circumstances could do with improvement."

Snyder's rise in the CID had been swift and very gratifying to Harry. He liked Snyder and admired his work, but it was Tucker's unshakable conviction that Snyder belonged in some twisty cove in the Tennessee mountains, farming and running a still.

The two policemen crowded through the door and onto the lanai. Harry and Snyder had worked together on the Avola Gold case, the solving of which had gone a long way toward speeding up Snyder's promotion.

Harry settled his visitors into a couple of white wicker chairs. Frank Hodges sat down with a sigh of relief and, after taking off his hat, pulled out a blue and white bandanna handkerchief and mopped his bald head.

"It's been a while, Jim," Harry said. "Did you get the Brown case?"

"It's mine."

Harry was glad. He wanted to see Truly's killer caught, and in his opinion, Jim Snyder was the best officer in the Tequesta County Sheriff's Department's CID unit. Harry went into the kitchen and returned with a plate of chocolate donuts that brought Hodges beaming onto the edge of his chair.

"The thing is," Jim said, "Crime Scene photographed the body and its surroundings before that storm broke, and Fiona McRae, the M.E., bagged Truly ahead of the rain, but she didn't have a chance to do much else. We're waiting on the results of her autopsy."

Harry drifted into a grim recollection of Truly's body sprawled on the sand.

"You and Helen Bradley were probably the only people, outside of Truly and the perp, who were at the scene before Deputy Weeks and me got there." Hodges was speaking with his mouth half-full of donut.

"We'd like to go over what you saw as you were going in and after you found the body," Jim added, balancing his writing pad on one knee as he reached for the coffee.

"At least one person had walked around the body," Harry said. "Truly and whoever killed him must have come down Hobson's Choice from the north. Aside from the tracks and Truly's hat, all we saw was the body, but I backed us away as soon as I saw what we'd found."

"It did smell pretty bad," Hodges said. "Do you think I might . . . ?"

Harry passed him the donuts.

"Only one person?" Jim asked, when he finished writing in his notebook.

"I think so. I'm assuming the tracks belonged to the shooter."

Jim nodded and wrote some more.

"Ms. Bradley seemed to be concerned about a dog," Hodges said.

"Weissmuller," Harry said.

Both men looked at Harry with blank faces.

"The name of Truly's dog. He was named after Johnny Weissmuller."

Hodges smiled broadly. "Tarzan! That was a long reach back."

"Oh, yes," Snyder said, "now I remember. When I was a kid, I watched a lot of those old movies on television. His friends were a chimp, an elephant, and Jane."

"Jim," Harry said, "if you mention this on a date, don't make the chimp, the elephant, and Jane into a kinship group."

Jim's large ears grew pink.

Hodges laughed loudly. "That's right. My wife hates it when I tell her about old movies. Sometimes she gets real pissed off."

"Weissmuller and Truly were pretty much inseparable," Harry put in. "Helen Bradley and I think that, unless his killer found Truly alone, he or she would have had to shoot Weissmuller before killing Truly."

"You're saying the dog's got to be dead?" Jim asked.

"Weissmuller weighed well over a hundred pounds and had no trouble controlling his liking for people other than Truly," Harry answered.

Hodges had finished his second donut and seemed to be dispirited. "I don't see what good finding Brown's dog would do us," he muttered.

"If he's dead, it might tell us where Truly was killed."

"Hang on!" Jim jumped out of his chair. "If he's alive, that dog probably knows who killed Truly."

"Find him, ask him, and the crime is solved," Harry said.

When Jim and Hodges left, Harry did not go back to Findlay Jay's rustling case. Something in his conversation with Snyder and Hodges had planted in his mind the thought that if he wanted to solve his problem with Gideon Stone, he ought to try talking to him. His first impulse was to bury the idea, but he could see Tucker shaking his head and decided to let it ferment a while before trying to think about it.

Harry knew from experience that he would have more success letting the idea develop in silence than by consciously trying to wrestle it into some satisfactory shape. In the past he had created that fecund silence by painting, but the pressures of work and married life had gradually taken him away from painting. Now when he wanted a period of quiet, he took his camera and hiked one of the Hammock trails. He was almost out the door when the phone rang. He swore and went back into the house.

A woman's voice asked, "Is this Harry Brock?"

"Yes." Whoever it was didn't sound very friendly.

"My name is Riga Kraftmeier. We met briefly about a

year ago at the Northern Trust art show."

Harry's interest picked up. "I remember. You're with the Three Rivers Bank & Trust. Helen Bradley introduced us."

His words were followed by a silence. Harry had the uncomfortable feeling he had somehow offended her.

"I'd like to discuss something with you," she said finally.

"Okay."

"It's not convenient for me to discuss it now. Can you come to my house tonight at eight? I'll pay you for your time."

Harry almost said no. He did not like people who didn't like him. And the ice in her voice was freezing his ear. Then he reminded himself that Helen liked her, and Helen was generally a good judge of people. Also, he was curious about what a vice president of Three Rivers wanted to discuss with a private investigator. "Okay."

"The address is seventy-seven Pickering Avenue, Seaway. Park somewhere away from the house." She hung up.

"Well, well," he said, picking up his shoulder bag, "burdened by beauty and a lack of manners."

Chapter 5

Harry's Land Rover had long since ceased to be any particular color, except where the rust showed. The engine smoked, and the canvas top was ragged. Nevertheless, he had become sensitive about the Rover's appearance, and it didn't help that Tucker called it *The Flying Dutchman*. So, when Riga Kraftmeier told him not to park in front of her house, his first thought was that she was criticizing his transportation.

Calmer reflection, however, told him she probably wanted his visit to attract as little attention as possible. That settled, he went back to thinking about Gideon Stone and dismissed the idea of replying to the note. Trying to talk with Stone, he told himself, would be less productive than a cat's trying to reason with Weissmuller.

Harry parked beside a vacant lot on 7th Avenue and walked the two blocks to Riga's house. Pickering Street was in Seaway, an upscale section of Avola. Most of the large, low houses were single-story and backed onto canals which gave access to Ridley's Pass and the Gulf. Every house had a dock and a boat lift, but the lucky residents didn't own boats. The ferociously weeded and dead-headed flower gardens surrounding the silent houses gave the place the look of an upscale cemetery.

Riga Kraftmeier's house and all of Seaway had settled into an evening quiet. Her single-story white stucco, with its red Spanish tile roof, sat back from the street behind a wide lawn and ornamental palm and bamboo plantings. Harry found the front gate locked, and searched in the ivy for a moment before he found the bell button.

As he waited for an answer to his ring, a turtledove in one of the Canary Island palms on the lawn began its bubbling, melancholy call. The sound only deepened the surrounding silence, and Harry thought what a contrast the sepulchral stillness was to the buzzing, humming, croaking, stridulating racket of the Hammock. The front door opened, and a vigorous, white-haired woman wearing a blue dress and black shoes appeared and stared at Harry with what he took to be amazed delight.

"Arthur!" she cried in a strong voice. "Where in the world have you been?"

Hurrying across the tiles toward him, she pulled open the gate and, with tears in her eyes, rushed forward and wrapped him in a strong embrace, then kissed him on the cheek.

"Oh, Arthur!" she said. "I'm so glad to see you! Come in, come in. Riga will be so relieved."

Harry was rescued by an unsmiling Riga, who, ignoring Harry, stepped into the courtyard and said in a firm voice, "Mother, you've made a mistake. He's not Arthur. Please come in."

The woman let go of Harry and gave him a look of mingled confusion and disappointment. She allowed Riga to lead her into the house. By the time they went through the door, she was telling Riga something about a wedding dress, her strong, eager voice fading as she moved deeper into the house.

When Riga reappeared, she said, "Close the gate and come in."

She was dressed in a forest green business suit and a severely plain white blouse. The only jewelry she wore was a large cameo locket on a gold chain. Harry stepped past her into a softly lit hall. To his left was a bowl of white roses and a Tiffany lamp on a small cherry table. Above them hung an elaborate, gilt-framed mirror facing, on the opposite wall, a small, deeply-framed English landscape with its own lighting.

Not too shabby, he thought.

She led Harry down the hall, pointed him into the first room on the left, and followed him into the room, closing the door behind her. A lot of doors, he thought. The two inner walls of the room were lined with books. When he was close enough to read some of the titles, he saw that he was looking at a substantial law library. The outside wall was dominated by a wide bay window with mullioned panes. The heavy, dark wood of the bookshelves, the paneling on the outer wall and the wall at his back, and the big desk at the inner center of the room gleamed with polish.

A brass lamp with a dark red shade cast a circle of strong light on the desk. The rest of the room was quietly lit by recessed ceiling lights. For all its elegance, Harry thought the room looked more like a mausoleum than a work space, but he said, "This is a beautiful room. Is it your study?"

"No. It belonged to my father." She appeared to be irritated by the question.

The distinct, flat statement gave him no encouragement to follow up with another question.

"I want something done," she said, "and I don't want anyone to know it's being done."

As he listened, a part of his mind was recalling again Helen Bradley's aggressive remark about Riga's being "burdened by beauty." If the phrase had any meaning, he admitted that Riga Kraftmeier might bear that burden. She was of medium height, slim, with pale, gold hair that spilled heavily over her shoulders. Her eyes were an unusually dark shade of blue. As for the rest of her, Harry thought with admiration, she might have just stepped down from a marble pedestal. Too bad she was so unpleasant.

"If I work for you," he replied, "most of what we say to one another and most of the information I gather for you is privileged. Which means I don't have to reveal it to anyone other than you."

"I know what *privileged* means," she said impatiently. "Will you take the job?"

"What do you want done?" he asked.

"I won't tell you that without being certain you won't repeat it."

Mexican standoff. By this time Harry was thinking seriously of just leaving. Nothing she had said was especially offensive, but how she was saying it made him feel like something she wanted to scrape off her shoe. But he took a deep breath and gave it another try.

"Here's how to do it. You hire me for a consultation. Then I'm bound to confidentiality. But if you tell me you've been engaged in criminal conduct, I turn you in. If I don't want the job, you pay me fifty dollars. If I do, the consultation fee disappears, and we move on."

She stepped behind the desk, drew the pad of paper and the pen toward her, and wrote swiftly. Then she tore off the sheet, and passed it to him.

"Sign it," she said.

Harry read what she'd written and signed his name. "Are you a lawyer?"

"Yes. Let's get on with it."

"You understand that if you ask me to do anything illegal, and I am asked under oath about what it was you asked me to do, I'm bound to answer."

She made a point of turning to look at the rows of books behind her. Then she turned back. "I think I understand that."

Kraftmeier had made a joke. But before he could decide what to do with it, they were interrupted by a tall, deeply-tanned man, younger than Riga. He was dressed in khaki shorts and a blue polo shirt.

"Sorry, Riga, I didn't know you had company."

"Is there a problem?"

"Janet's being difficult about her medicine. As usual. She doesn't . . ."

"I'll take care of it."

"Okay, sorry for the interruption."

The door closed with its solid click. Harry looked at Riga with renewed interest. Were she and the young Adonis a pair? She ended his speculations by saying, "You're familiar with a piece of land called Hobson's Choice."

"Helen Bradley and I were doing a bird survey on it, when we found Truly Brown."

She nodded. As far as Harry could tell from her reaction, she had no interest in the information. "I want you to find out everything you can uncover about the deed history on the land and whether it's going on the block."

"Sounds straightforward enough to me," Harry said. "Who owns it?"

"The Brown estate."

That puzzled him. As far as he knew, Truly was the end of the line in that branch of the family. "For all the years I've been in Avola," he said, "Truly's lived in an old, run-down house on Bayside Drive and dressed out of Goodwill. Did he have money?"

She shifted her position and looked away from him to-

ward the window. "There's a trust. Three Rivers Bank &
Trust holds it. I may be wrong, but I think Hobson's
Choice is part of it. I want you to find that out, along with
the other things."

"Okay. But at the office tomorrow morning, couldn't
you just walk down the hall and ask someone? If Three
Rivers is managing the Brown estate, who would be in a
better position than you to learn what's going to be done?"

She turned back to Harry, her face slightly flushed with
what he thought might be anger. He had no idea why she
was upset.

"Do you want this job or not?"

"No, I guess not. You can give that fifty dollars to a
charity or keep it."

"What kind of act is this?"

"It's not an act. I don't take jobs without knowing why
I'm doing the work, or go into a situation in which I can't
evaluate the risks."

Harry got both hands on his anger and dragged it back
to its cage. He could see, from her face and the way her
body stiffened, she was not happy with his answer. She
came around the front of the desk and said calmly, "All
right, here it is: if Hobson's Choice comes on the market, I
intend to become a bidder. As an employee of Three Rivers
Bank & Trust, I have to be very careful. I must not be seen
to have used my connection with the bank to place myself
in a favorable position to buy the property."

"Wouldn't hiring a lawyer give you the same confidentiality protection I can provide, as well as a lot more
knowledge about estates, trusts, and the rest of it?"

"What I'm asking you to do doesn't require special legal
knowledge. What it does require is that the work be done
quietly and that my name be kept out of it. A lawyer making

inquiries would set off alarm bells all through the banking community."

Her explanation sounded reasonable to Harry. He even thought of something she hadn't mentioned. Riga couldn't hire a lawyer in Avola who didn't know the principals in Three Rivers Bank & Trust. Officially, no one would know where the questions were coming from. Unofficially, the whole town would know in two working days. But why, he wondered, hadn't she just told him all that in the first place? To his surprise, he found himself liking her. Well, maybe not actually liking her, but . . .

"Then I'll see what I can do," he said, putting some warmth into his voice. "Who do I talk to?"

"Ruvin Carter. He's Vice President in charge of the Trust Department and nobody's fool. When you talk to him, be very careful."

"What's your relationship with Carter?"

The iron returned to her voice. "We're employed by the same bank."

"Okay. Anything in particular I should be watching for?"

"You'll figure it out."

At the gate he said, "I'm sorry about your mother."

She nodded and waited for him to leave.

"Who's Arthur?" he asked.

"No one of any concern to you. Goodbye, Mr. Brock. Let me hear from you soon. And remember, never call me, or call on me, or leave messages for me at the bank. If you call here and my mother answers, hang up."

At the beginning of a new job, Harry usually felt pleasantly excited. Not this time. Driving to the Hammock, he went from reviewing all the dissatisfactions of his meeting with Riga to brooding again over Gideon Stone's letter.

Katherine was waiting for him. She had fed the kids and

greeted him with a wintry smile. Harry saw with a twist of concern the dark smudges under her eyes. He kissed her and wondered again with the familiar shadowing of guilt if their deciding to have this baby had been a mistake.

Beyond the extended period of morning sickness, Katherine had not exactly been sick, at least not with anything Esther Benson, her obstetrician, could put a name to, but she had not been well either. And Benson had been grumbling about her working too hard. But she didn't take direction well and, like Kipling's cat, she went her own way.

"Did she hire you?" Katherine asked when they were seated, having brushed off his attempts to find out just how bad she was feeling.

"Yes," he said without enthusiasm, "but she doesn't want anyone to know it." After they were married, he began telling her as much about his cases as he could. It troubled him a little that he was breaching client confidentiality, but he was either going to trust Katherine or he wasn't. So far, he had. He sketched briefly for her what Riga wanted him to do.

"Sounds simple enough. Why the long face?"

"Two things. First, she's got a miserable personality. Second, I've decided I don't really know why she hired me."

"Didn't you just tell me she thought hiring a lawyer would set off alarm bells?"

"Yes. But why doesn't she just ask Ruvin Carter herself? Doing that can't be unethical."

Katherine thought a minute and then put down her fork. "Maybe she doesn't want Carter to know she's interested in Hobson's Choice."

"Possibly," Harry agreed, "but don't stop eating. I want to see that plate cleaned."

"Don't stretch your luck."

"You and Riga Kraftmeier," Harry said, encouraged by her show of spirit. "Any news about your mother?"

"Priscilla called to say she and Whittier are still trying to persuade Ma to accept the pacemaker."

"And?"

Katherine stared at her plate and shrugged. Harry leaned forward and tried to keep his voice neutral. "What if you just took a few days off work and went up there to see her?"

Katherine looked up and past Harry, and shook her head. Her eyes were filled with tears.

"Katherine, I think it's something you need to do. For you and your mother."

She slid her eyes back to meet his. "I don't, Harry."

"Why not?" he asked, trying to keep the anger out of his voice.

"Because."

The telephone rang. Katherine jumped up and answered it.

Chapter 6

"It's Helen." Katherine thrust the phone at him then strode out of the kitchen. Everything about her going conveyed weariness.

"What happened with Riga?" Helen asked.

Harry had a question. "Did Riga talk to you before she called me?"

"She asked if you were competent and reliable. I said that might be stretching it, but you were a little less bent than most of your colleagues."

"Thanks for the support." It puzzled Harry that Riga would ask Helen for advice on a matter she seemed obsessively determined to keep private. "Why would she talk to you about me?"

"Hey! Back off. She's a friend."

Harry let it go. "What's her relationship with Ruvin Carter?"

"They don't have one." Helen did not sound happy talking about it. "They don't speak, but what caused the split, I don't know. But I do know I'm on Riga's side."

"Her mother's in pretty bad shape," Harry said, shifting direction. "She mistook me for somebody named Arthur. Who is he?"

"Her long-absent brother. So it's a good thing Tom's there to help. They also have a day nurse during the week."

"I think I met Tom—tall, good-looking, younger than Riga. Is he her husband?"

"That's him. They're not married, but they have a child. Cheryl is almost two. What do you think of Tom?"

"Seemed nice enough," Harry replied. "Does he have another name?"

"Tom Burkhardt. He was the tennis pro at the Hawkswood Beach and Tennis Club, until Riga saw him."

"And she promoted him to houseboy?" Harry asked before he thought.

"Tom is a sweet, intelligent, gentle man," she said, stiffly. "He's taken care of Cheryl since she was born, and he's a miracle cook and a marvelous gardener. Riga and he are getting along just fine."

" 'Though I sang in my chains like the sea,' " Harry said, wondering why she was being such a cheerleader for Riga's toy boy.

"Very funny, Brock. What happened?"

"Kraftmeier and I were in her father's study, trying to out-stare each other. Tom came in and, after apologizing for interrupting us, he said Janet wouldn't take her medicine. Riga didn't introduce us."

"Which led you to conclude she hadn't told him she was meeting you," Helen said.

"That's right. He took the hint and didn't introduce himself," Harry continued. "Riga went on looking at him as if he had tracked mud onto the rug. Then she told him she would deal with the problem. He smiled and left."

"What's got you so pissed off?" Helen asked.

"I'm not—I wasn't—" Harry snapped, and stopped himself.

Helen was right. He was mad, and he knew why. Katherine. But he needed to get over it.

"I took the job, and it stops with you. Don't ask why she hired me."

"Because she's smart, Harry. And don't forget it. Why did you agree to work for her, if you dislike her so much?"

"Maybe her dominatrix shtick turned me on."

"Why are you being so nasty?"

"Because I have never before in my life met anyone who, with less cause, was so unpleasant. Her glare did everything but turn me into a rock."

"The word *I* keeps coming up," Helen observed.

"If a skunk sprayed me, I wouldn't take it personally, but she's not a skunk, and I do."

"Oh, good, Harry. Try the possibility that the way she treats you has nothing to do with you."

"If she treated me the way a dog treats a fireplug for nothing, what would she have done to me for something?"

"Pray you don't find out." She hesitated and then went on. "Riga's father and mother separated when she was eight or nine years old. I think he was a lawyer, but that's all I know. She doesn't talk much about herself. At least not to me."

"We talked in his study," Harry said, surprised by her last comment. "It's a beautiful room and it's kept spotless, but if what you say is true, it hasn't been used by the man for twenty-five or thirty years."

"So?" Helen asked in a show of indifference. "Maybe Janet and Riga kept it as a shrine. He died at least fifteen years ago."

"Possibly, but it felt more like a mausoleum than a shrine. I don't think it's used, and Riga made a point of not sitting down, which meant I didn't either. I also got the impression she did not like being in the room."

"I was just guessing about the lawyer part."

"Riga said he was. And she's a lawyer. But she doesn't practice law. There's a lot about her that's strange."

"Is the ex-Hermit of Bartram's Hammock talking about others being weird?"

Harry acknowledged the hit. "Okay. My house is all glass, but nevertheless, Riga Kraftmeier is strange."

"I think otherwise," Helen countered, and then, as if she had said more than she intended, told him goodnight.

As he put down the phone, he glanced at his watch and was surprised to see how late it was. He went upstairs to help Katherine put the kids to bed. But his mind was still occupied with what Helen had told him about Riga. And there was something about their conversation that had left him with a niggle of dissatisfaction. He might have pursued it, if he had not met Katherine at the top of the stairs.

She was leaning against the banister, looking completely exhausted. She stared past him and said in a flat voice, "You and Helen had a lot to say to each another."

"About Riga Kraftmeier," he said. "Are the kids in bed?"

She nodded. "I got tired of waiting for you."

He usually read to Minna and tucked her in, and then talked with Jesse for a while before saying goodnight to the boy.

"I wasn't watching the time. I'm sorry," he said, putting his arm around her. "Let's go down. I'll tell you what Helen had to say about the Ice Maiden."

She hung in his arms. "I feel like that Indian in *The End of the Trail* picture. Could you make me some hot chocolate?"

"Happy to oblige." He tried to sound as if he thought it might help.

Chapter 7

The next morning Katherine woke later than usual. She came downstairs pale and hollow-eyed. Harry asked how she was feeling.

"Fine," she snapped.

She did not deal well with being late, and the kids gave her plenty of space.

"Take it easy today," Harry said as she was leaving.

"*If* I feel tired, which I won't," was her parting shot, as she ran for her Rava.

When Minna and Jesse left to catch their bus at the bridge, Harry watched them go with an uncomfortable stirring of anxiety. Reluctantly, he admitted that Gideon Stone's note had spooked him.

He sat down again at the kitchen table with a second cup of coffee, to decide how he wanted to begin his new job. While he was working on the problem, the mockingbird settled in the wisteria vine on the south corner of the lanai and began singing. Now and then, Harry leaned back in his chair to listen. Earlier, while he and Jesse were putting up the school lunches, the boy had asked him how such a small bird, with an even smaller voice box, could sing so loudly.

"One way to answer the question is to say it's one of earth's enduring miracles," Harry told him, trying to convey his own sense of the wonders surrounding them. "Another, less poetic but more useful explanation is to say it evolved over time."

"I guess I'll have to wait until I'm an ornithologist before I get the real answer," Jesse replied.

"Keep thinking about it," Harry said with a grin, amused by another miracle. Jesse had his father's looks, but he had his mother's low tolerance for flights of fancy. Minna was the poet of the family.

The kitchen windows were open and the bird's singing flowed around Harry in a full, rich river of sound. He was tempted just to sit and listen, but his idyll was interrupted by the intrusion of Gideon Stone. With a sigh, Harry asked himself, yet again, if he should write to Stone or call him.

Finding an answer was complicated by the fact that over the years Harry had convinced himself that his present life was completely separated from his former life in Maine. The emotional disconnect was one result of his struggle to break free from the guilt of killing Gideon's brother and the grief of losing his wife and children and his job. Bartram's Hammock had become so absolutely identified in Harry's mind with his new life that the arrival of Stone's letter had been as shocking to him as finding himself face-to-face with a ghost.

It also angered him. And that anger, increased by his frustration with Katherine and her condition, suddenly exploded. He slammed his hand down on the sideboard and shattered the cup he was holding. Swearing at himself for being such a fool, he swept up the scattered fragments and swore that he would not think any more about Stone. *Gideon has written*, he told himself, *and I've read what he wrote. That's the end of it. It's over and done with. Period. And Katherine and I are going to survive this . . . whatever this is.*

To mark this new beginning, Harry took a new spiral binder notebook from the hall supply cupboard and wrote

K for Kraftmeier on the top right hand corner of its red cover and told himself he was ready to go to work. Gathering the rest of his gear, he left the house, making a list in his mind of the tasks he had in hand. When he came to Findlay Jay, he said, "Tomorrow, for sure."

In Tequesta County, everything having to do with county land sales and purchases was recorded in Official Records, a division of the Clerk of Court's Office. That office was located on the fifth floor of the County Administration Building in South Avola, on the east side of the Seminole River Bridge.

As recently as fifteen years ago, the Tequesta County Circuit Court offices were housed in a sleepy two-story stucco building, cooled by slowly-turning ceiling fans with spirals of sticky flypaper hanging from them. In the quiet offices and along the dusty corridors, a few unhurried people went about their business, stopping to greet one another and exchange the latest gossip. Now, the offices were stacked in a white, air-conditioned, eight-story box made of steel, concrete, and glass. And inside, Harry found the corridors streaming with people. There were lines at all the elevators, and making eye contact with a county employee behind a counter was harder than getting a taxi on a rainy day.

The woman at the Records Desk, Harry's destination, was scowling at a *People* magazine, snapping over the pages as if disgusted by what she saw.

"I need help," Harry said optimistically.

She gestured to a sign to his right, prominently displayed on the counter. It read: "I CAN ONLY MAKE ONE PERSON A DAY HAPPY. TODAY ISN'T YOUR DAY. TOMORROW DOESN'T LOOK GOOD EITHER."

"Funny," Harry said with diminished hope, addressing the top of her head. "I want to do a title search."

"Be still, my heart," the woman answered grimly, without looking up from the magazine.

She was short and wore round, silver-rimmed glasses that had slid down her nose. Her graying brown hair appeared to be at war with her head, and her red, flowered dress looked borrowed.

He was ready to abandon hope, when she pushed her glasses back up her nose and gave him a big smile.

"You need a sense of humor to survive around here," she said and tossed aside the magazine. "I'm Fanny Townsend. Let's get at it. Who owns the property?"

"I'm not sure."

"Don't worry. We'll find out."

They did. An hour and a half later, Harry rewound the last roll of film tape on the list Fanny Townsend had given him. He left Fanny and her files, believing he knew all there was to know about the ownership history of Hobson's Choice. And because of something else he had learned while reading those old deeds, he knew who he had to talk to next.

Judge Jason Bryde had been practicing law in Tequesta County for sixty years and studying it longer than that. He had told Harry he began his legal career at the age of fifteen as an errand boy in the second-floor office of Hutchens, Bradley, and Lowe on Button Street in what had come to be called Old Avola. The Judge pronounced the name as all the natives did, reducing it to three syllables and running them together as O' Vola, with a drawl in the first *O,* to slow the thing down a little.

He met Harry on the porch steps and immediately asked

in his deep and still-strong voice, "How are Katherine and the children?"

Harry decided not to burden the Judge with tales of Katherine's pregnancy or her mother's illness and said, "Fine." The Judge nodded, took Harry's arm, and led him up the broad steps, across the verandah, and inside, talking as they went. The Judge's sprawling house stood on the Peninsular, tucked away on a tongue of heavily-wooded land between the Seminole River and the Gulf. Harry once expressed surprise at the number of big houses on the Peninsular. The Judge had laughed and said that the Peninsular was full of old houses and old money, both carefully maintained.

He waved Harry into the big, high-ceilinged room the Judge still called the parlor.

"I was just about to have tea and coffeecake, and I believe if you were to hold a gun on me, I might be able to find some potable bourbon to brighten the tea," he said, getting them seated.

The long, double-sash windows were open, and the white curtains lifted and twisted gently in the quiet Gulf breeze drifting through the house.

"I thought you were a coffee drinker," Harry said. He admired the Judge, who had served as President of the Florida Bar Association and was still an active member of its Board of Governors, and was awed by the old man's energy.

"Used to be, Harry. Now, I'm reduced to one cup at breakfast. As Amanecida loves to tell me, age is the enemy of all vices save reminiscence and sleep."

He gave a quick laugh and planted the palms of his hands firmly on the arms of his rocker. A clock on the upstairs landing began striking eleven.

"Amanecida will serve us tea eventually. She is a treasure but a stranger to haste. What brings you to the Peninsular?"

"Indirectly, it's Truly Brown's murder, but more specifically, a piece of land called Hobson's Choice."

"Aha, let's talk first about the murder," the Judge said.

They talked for a while about the killing, an event the Judge found wholly irrational and deeply distressing. "I'm not surprised to hear the police are stymied, but what do you think happened?"

"I don't know. Who would benefit from his death? Possibly someone who knew about the trust and didn't want Truly to have it. But why? I have no idea. Of course, Occam's choice would be one or more of Truly's associates, who might have heard he was coming into money and got the timing wrong. Or none of the above."

"It's usually money, although passion runs a close second. No suspects?"

"Not really. I know of someone who wants to buy a piece of land in the trust, but I don't see a motive for murder."

"Slim pickings," the Judge agreed and shifted topics with obvious relief. "Hobson's Choice," he said, and sat for a moment, rocking and looking out the window to the right of his chair, as if he were staring into the past. When he spoke, his voice was soft. "I haven't heard that place mentioned in a flock of years. Do you know where the name comes from?"

"Well, I think it's a choice that appears to be free, but isn't."

The Judge smiled appreciatively, made a tent of his fingers, and rested his elbows on the chair arms. "That's right. In seventeenth-century England, in the town of Cambridge, there was an autocratic livery man by the name of Tobias

Hobson. In the inn where he worked, he made every customer who needed a horse take the animal nearest the stable door or go without. A man of strong character. I would like to have known Mr. Hobson."

"I've been conducting a title search," Harry said, when the Hobson subject was exhausted.

"On Hobson's Choice."

Harry nodded.

"And?"

"A couple of things. Was Helmut Kraftmeier Janet Kraftmeier's husband?"

"Yes. I'm surprised you know Janet. She worked as the hostess at The Edelweiss for years and years. But that was before your time. I believe she's very ill."

Harry knew The Edelweiss. He was surprised to hear that Janet Kraftmeier had been employed there. But he did not want to tell Jason he was working for Riga Kraftmeier and did not pursue the point beyond saying he had heard the same thing.

"You must have discovered that Helmut deeded that piece of land to Gaylord Brown." The Judge raised his eyes to the ceiling, and a moment later looked back at Harry. "It must have been thirty years ago."

"It was nineteen seventy-two. Who's Gaylord Brown?"

"Myra Brown's husband. Truly's father. That's when the property got the name Hobson's Choice."

Amanecida came into the room, carrying a silver tray with the tea and cake. Harry stood up and, after she had set the tray down, he shook hands with her. He always found himself being very formal with Amanecida. She was possibly in her fifties: tall, full-bodied, with thick, black hair worn down her back. Her face was straight off a Mayan temple. In her white blouse and black skirt, Harry found her, as always, a beautiful but slightly daunting presence.

"You and your family are well, Mr. Brock?"

"We're well," Harry replied. "And you?"

"The same."

Harry said he was glad to see her again, and meant it.

"*Egualmente*. Don't let him tire himself." She tilted her head in the Judge's direction and left as silently as she had entered.

Jason pretended to be annoyed by her comment, but it was a transparent failure. As soon as she had gone, he went to the sideboard and took out a bottle.

"How long has Amanecida been with you?" Harry asked, thinking he should know the answer but didn't.

"Eleven years. She came three years after my wife died."

"Where did you find her?"

"It was more a case of her finding me." The Judge gave a short, slightly embarrassed laugh. "Rescued me, really." He passed Harry a piece of cake.

"I'd say you were a very lucky man."

"The same thought has occurred to me," Jason admitted with a smile, and poured some bourbon into his tea after Harry declined.

The tea and the cake were excellent, and when he had eaten and drunk all that decency allowed, Harry said, "You were explaining how Hobson's Choice got its name."

The Judge smiled, settled back, and folded his hands across his stomach. "The story may be apocryphal, but I'm inclined to believe it. Helmut Kraftmeier was a gambler. Back then, some high-stakes poker was played in Avola. Gaylord Brown was another plunger, but he was either luckier or a better poker player than Kraftmeier. Anyway, he and Helmut finally got into a game that lasted two days. At the end of it, Kraftmeier was cleaned out and in debt to

Brown for forty thousand dollars and change. Brown said, 'I'll take the deed to either your house or that piece of land south of Oyster Pass and call it square. Which will it be?'

"Helmut and Janet had two children by then, and however much brass Helmut had in his balls, it didn't extend to telling Janet he was taking away her home to settle a gambling debt. 'Hobson's Choice,' Kraftmeier said in disgust. 'The Oyster Pass land is yours.' And that's how it got its name."

"Janet Kraftmeier's name is on the deed," Harry said, thinking he'd missed something. "Hobson's Choice belonged to her."

"Well, well. That does cast a dark light on a distant object."

"Dark light?"

"Yes, a very dark light. Helmut left his family and went to the east coast shortly after that event. And, to the best of my knowledge, Janet never saw him again. I don't believe I knew until now that land belonged to her. Very interesting."

Harry and the Judge talked about the families until it was time for Harry to go. On the verandah, the Judge shook hands and said, "Did any of what I told you help?"

"It gave me more to work with," Harry said. He did not like being cagey with the Judge, who grinned at Harry's answer.

"Good. And when you can talk about it, I'd like to know what has you wasting a day poking around in the Public Records files when you could have been bass fishing."

Harry laughed. Releasing the Judge's hand, he hurried down the steps and turned to wave to Amanecida, who had come to the door to see him off and check on the Judge.

Chapter 8

Thunder shook Harry awake. His heart pounding, he reached out for Katherine. She stirred slightly under his hand, then rolled away from him. He watched the dark, rejecting outline of her body for a moment, savoring the relief of finding her safe and trying not to read anything serious into her withdrawal from him. Reassured by her quiet breathing, he slept again. When he woke, Katherine was clambering out of bed, and the windows were full of light.

Harry rolled over, trying for more sleep. But instead of turning on the shower as she usually did, Katherine returned to bed. She propped a pillow under her head and lay staring at the ceiling.

"What's wrong?" he asked with instant concern.

"I'm worried."

"About the baby?"

"No. About us. You."

Harry groaned in silence. He knew what was coming and tried to fend it off. "Katherine, I'm doing two divorce jobs, looking for some stolen cattle, and researching a land title. I'm probably at less risk than you are driving back and forth to the management company every day."

She ignored the joke. "That's for right now. I know you want to get involved in Truly Brown's murder, and, God knows, that won't be safe."

"Jim Snyder wouldn't let me interfere, even if I wanted to."

Harry talked with a sinking heart. Nothing he could say would put an end to her obsessive worrying, because most of it was irrational. But some of it, he admitted, was based in fact. The work could be dangerous.

"Driving a truck is dangerous," he said hopelessly, knowing she would make the connections.

"I don't want you driving a truck. I want you to get your management license and come into the company with me. Or come in without the license. Bob Arnell would hire you in a minute."

Arnell was the president of Arnell Property Management.

He probably would, Harry thought, and I would rather be staked out naked on a fire ant nest than be a property manager, or a supervisor either.

"We've discussed this, Katherine."

They were both sitting up now, arms around their knees.

"You're not taking this seriously," she said angrily.

"I like what I do," he said.

"So does Bob Arnell," she snapped, throwing off the covers and running into the bathroom.

Harry shook his head sadly. He knew that for the time being the discussion was closed, but neither her fear nor her anger was diminished. He stared bleakly out the window and asked himself if he was just being selfish in not giving in to her demands. Probably he was, but the admission changed nothing. He was not going to be a property manager.

The rain in the night had dropped the temperature a few degrees. The morning felt almost crisp, and Harry decided to clear away the big limb that a spring storm had split off one of the oaks behind the house. Over breakfast, Katherine had complained that if it lay there much longer, some big, old rattlesnake would be setting up house under its tangle of branches.

"Old Man Rabbit will hang a scowl on that," Minna said.

She was deep in *Old Man Rabbit's Birthday Party* and had added him to her populous world of fictional friends. Jesse looked up from his science book and rolled his eyes. Harry laughed, and Katherine managed a smile.

After walking the kids to the bus, Harry got out his power saw and ladder and began trimming the jagged stub on the tree.

As he worked, he thought about Katherine and about the fear underlying so much of her thinking. He assumed it could be traced back to her father's abandoning her mother, her sister, and herself when she was eight. Add that to her disastrous marriage to Willard Trachey, which ended in her being left again, this time penniless with a baby and a small child to care for.

But what, he asked himself, did that kind of understanding bring? He had not been able to convince her that she and the children and the child she was carrying were safe with him. He recalled something his mother was fond of saying. "What can't be changed must be endured," he said aloud as he climbed down the ladder, but heard no confirmation from whatever, if anything, was listening.

After he painted the scar on the oak with black paint, he dealt with the two-foot-thick limb and its branches. Despite the roar of the saw and the stink of its exhaust, he managed to wonder if there was any possible connection between the information he had uncovered in researching the Hobson's Choice deed and Truly Brown's death. It seemed unlikely. But Harry reminded himself that in his business the unlikely was a daily occurrence, and the impossible a frequent visitor. But he was no closer to the answer he was seeking. The possibility of Riga Kraftmeier having shot Truly was completely off the charts.

With the limb cut up and stacked and the brush dragged away, Harry decided to abandon speculation and see what he could learn by talking to Ruvin Carter about the disposition of Truly Brown's estate. But first he wanted to talk to Florence Herrick. In its lengthy obituary of Truly Brown, which had more to say about Myra Brown than her son, *The Banner* identified Herrick as one of Myra Brown's few surviving friends and an active environmentalist in the days before the word had much currency.

Harry hoped she could give him some useful background information on Myra Brown and the testamentary trust she had constructed for Truly's protection. He also hoped Florence Herrick might know why Janet Kraftmeier's name, and not her husband's, was on the Hobson's Choice deed.

Once again Harry asked himself if Hobson's Choice and the trust had any connection with Truly's murder. Once again, he dismissed the idea as an unlikely possibility, the principals having been dead such a long time. But there was something about that transfer that kept tugging at him. And he was looking forward to asking Florence Herrick what, if anything, she knew about the transaction.

In an effort to remain focused, he reminded himself that he wasn't being paid to solve Truly's murder but to find out if Hobson's Choice was included in the trust, and, if it was, would it be sold separately when the trust was dissolved.

He called Florence Herrick and she agreed to see him. In what he thought was a very frail voice, she gave him an address on the east side of Avola. It turned out to be Hadley Village, an upscale assisted-living facility.

Hadley Village was gated and heavily landscaped with palms, fichus, holly, mahogany, and oak trees. The shrubbery was thick and green, the bougainvillea tumbled in scarlet billows over the fences, and the lawns were maniacally mowed.

Florence Herrick lived on the second floor of a tan stucco mid-rise. She welcomed him in a quiet but firm voice. What he had mistaken for frailty was simply a quiet and reserved manner. Short and trim, with her white hair cut in a courageous bob that Harry guessed with a flash of admiration she must have been wearing like a banner for seventy years, Florence Herrick proved to be entirely different from the frail, old lady he had pictured. She wore a long-sleeved, pale-orange, flowered dress with a frilled white collar and a tan cardigan draped around her shoulders.

The small, bright apartment into which she led him was whistle-clean. Except for the tangle of books, magazines, and newspapers on the large, glass coffee table in the living room, everything was neat and well cared for.

"You will have to excuse this mess, Mr. Brock," she said, waving her hand at the coffee table as they advanced into the room. "It's the one space in this apartment exempt from my cleaning lady's resolute attentions. I make a stab at sorting it once a week." She gave a short, bright laugh. "If the spirit moves me."

The room was unremarkable, except for the number of framed photographs of people it contained. Every wall was covered with them. Harry came to a stop, amazed by their number.

"I'm afraid I have indulged myself," she said complacently. "Do you see anyone you recognize?"

"Eleanor Roosevelt, Marjory Stoneman Douglas," he replied, naming two from the group most prominently displayed on the mantle over the small fireplace.

The subjects were mostly women, and all of the photographs bore signed messages.

"You knew them all?"

"Oh, yes. I once had the privilege of calling them my friends. Of course, all but a few are dead now."

"Even Douglas," Harry said with regret.

"Even Marjory. You know, not everyone recognizes Marjory. Even many who know the name and have at least heard of the *River of Grass* fail to recognize her."

"The article in *The Banner* said you were an environmentalist," Harry remarked, letting his eyes roam over the pictures.

She shrugged. "I suppose so. Working with Marjory was so exciting I don't recall ever thinking of myself as anything other than someone caught up in that wonderful woman's vision of a Florida in which the Everglades would be preserved forever."

She stood staring at the photograph, and Harry waited for her to go on, but after a moment she turned back to him and said, "Please sit down. I'm afraid I've kept you standing."

When they were seated across the coffee table from one another, she folded her hands in her lap and asked cheerfully, "What can I do for you?"

She looked at Harry with remarkably sharp gray eyes and smiled in a way that he suspected she had once been taught to use to put gentlemen at ease without overly stimulating them.

"I'm working for a client who is interested in buying a piece of land that may be coming up for sale as result of Truly Brown's death," he said. "Were you a friend of the Brown family?"

"Yes," she said carefully. "I was a friend of Myra Brown's for many, many years." She paused and added, "I believe you and Helen Bradley found Truly's body. What a terrible thing. Terrible. That poor boy."

She shook her head in a way that seemed to Harry to express sorrow for more than his death. Harry did some quick arithmetic. When he died, Truly was fifty or thereabouts. That meant Florence Herrick had to be in her early nineties. That did, he supposed, make a fifty-year-old seem young.

"Are you familiar with his condition and his circumstances?"

"In a general way," Harry replied. "He seems to have been killed on his own property."

She sighed, as if the very name gave her pain. "Hobson's Choice. If I were superstitious, which I'm not, I'd say the place was cursed. There has been a lot of heartache connected with that piece of ground, lovely though it is."

Harry took a flier and asked if she meant Janet Kraftmeier's losing it to pay for her husband's gambling debt.

She sat up a little straighter and regarded him with surprise mixed with disapproval. "I'm astonished you know about that."

"I take it you know Mrs. Kraftmeier."

"And her scapegrace husband, who has not burdened the world for a good many years. And I say that knowing full well it is improper to speak ill of the dead, because they are no longer present to defend themselves. But I doubt there's much Helmut could say in his defense."

Harry suppressed a smile. "He lost that land in a poker game, if my information is right."

She nodded with a slight frown that might have expressed sadness. "Yes, and before the trouble it caused was over—*if* it is over, even now—I lost Janet as a friend forever. She is, I believe, no longer herself."

"No. Would you be willing to tell me what happened?"

She paused and looked at her clasped hands, straightening her back as she contemplated them. Then she looked at him. "What do you want to know? And why do you want to know it?"

"Your recollection of what happened. Mainly, to help *me* understand what happened. I have a client with an interest in Hobson's Choice. I can't give you her name. She doesn't know I'm talking to you and won't, if that's a concern. And she's absolutely a straight arrow. From here I will go to talk with Ruvin Carter at Three Rivers Bank & Trust. Three Rivers holds the Brown Trust, and Carter is administering it. Neither my client nor I have any interest in raking up mud."

Harry stopped and waited for Florence to respond. When she was ready, she asked, "How much do you already know?"

Harry repeated what the Judge had told him and concluded with, "Kraftmeier said, 'Hobson's Choice,' and Brown got Janet Kraftmeier's land."

Florence Herrick nodded slowly, frowning. She responded quietly and in a tone of voice that might or might not have expressed regret. "I never liked Helmut, but Gaylord took advantage of him. Pressed an advantage when he could easily have given him time to find the money. After all, Myra and Janet were dear friends, had been for years. And certainly Gaylord didn't need the money. Even then, he was one of the richest men in Tequesta County."

"Then why did he call in his debt?"

"Helmut was a bully and a braggart." She raised her chin

as though it required some extra determination on her part to say it. "He had rallied Gaylord about being henpecked once too often, I suppose. The fact that there was some truth in the accusation made the thrusts more cutting. Myra Brown was a strong-minded person. Living with her could never have been easy. So when the chance came to humiliate Helmut, Gaylord took it, forced him to go to Janet and beg for that land."

"Kraftmeier left home soon after that," Harry said.

"It almost destroyed Janet. She had those two children. Arthur was nine and Riga was seven. Helmut gave her the house free and clear, but there was no money. Not then, not for many years. And I think it's fair to say that Gaylord's revenge was worked out on the backs of Janet and those two children. But Janet never stopped loving Helmut."

"You said you lost Janet Kraftmeier's friendship."

She sighed heavily. "Yes. Janet blamed Myra for the loss of that land. I don't know what the land meant to her, but the loss of it almost unhinged her mind. I had never seen anyone as upset as she was. Weeping, wringing her hands, screaming that Gaylord would never have insisted on it, if Myra had stood up to him.

"Myra was away at the time, visiting friends in Chicago and the Far West. She was gone for six weeks and, when she returned home, the land had already been transferred. Myra told Janet she had no idea what had happened until she was back in Avola. But it was no use. Janet refused to believe her."

She paused and thought a moment before going on. "Janet was doubly wrong. Myra had told her the truth, and Myra had less influence over Gaylord than Myra thought. She and Gaylord had struggled long and bitterly over Truly.

Gaylord said the boy was retarded. He wanted him placed in a school in the northern part of the state, where such children were specially educated and prepared for some kind of independent life. Myra said no. It drove a wedge between them. Myra kept Truly with her, but she lost Gaylord. Oh, they went on living together, but after the Hobson's Choice affair, their marriage was an empty vessel.

"Myra became angry with Janet and told her she was a fool for having given the land to Helmut, that if she hadn't, something would have been worked out. That was the end of that friendship. And then Janet said she could not be my friend if I went on seeing Myra. I refused to give up one friend for another and lost her. I believed then and I still believe that Myra had told Janet the truth. I said so to Janet. But she said she would never speak to me again. And she hasn't."

Harry couldn't think of anything to say except that he was sorry. Florence laughed and shook her head and said there was no longer anything to be sorry about, that time had washed it all away. Harry wondered briefly if that was true, then came back to the business at hand. "The Kraftmeiers seem to be well off now."

"Yes. When Helmut died, he left Janet and the two children a lot of money. He had remarried, of course. He was still a lawyer. I believe he moved to the east coast and went to work for the sugar interests," she said stiffly. "There is money enough there—if you have a sufficiently strong stomach. And Helmut was never a man to miss the main chance."

"No children in his second marriage?"

She shook her head. Harry came to his last question. "Has the family expressed any interest in recovering Hobson's Choice from the Browns?"

"If Janet ever approached her on the subject, Myra never

mentioned it to me, and I think she would have. Although Myra, as a rule, did not discuss her financial affairs, she did talk to me about the trust. Making that trust was the hardest thing she ever did. You see, Myra never stopped hoping that Truly would pull himself together and begin showing what she called 'some gumption.' She had never admitted the extent of Truly's affliction. But in making the trust she was forced to face the truth. After she had done it, she was not the same woman."

Florence looked at Harry sharply and paused. "Are you familiar with the terms of the trust, Mr. Brock?" she asked in a slightly challenging tone of voice.

"No."

"Well, I don't remember it all, but I recall one part of it. Truly was left a monthly stipend to support him for as long as he lived. I don't know the amount, but Myra would never have allowed him to be in want. So I assume it was generous, probably more than generous. The executor of the trust was empowered to increase the stipend if he saw the need, but he could not decrease it."

"Truly never seemed to be short of money," Harry said, "but the way he lived wouldn't have called for much."

"I know," she said. "Such a shame. And now that he's dead, such an irony."

She paused and turned to look at one of the pictures on the mantelpiece. "Myra put a stipulation in the trust that says so much about her heartache and her hope. If Truly took a job, any job, at any time from her death to his own, and kept it for two years, he could inherit the entire estate without let, hindrance, or encumbrance."

Harry was surprised and said so. She smiled at his reaction. "Yes, and do you know Truly has been working?"

"Yes."

"And if I've counted right, in six months he would have been working for the Green Thumb Nursery for two years."

"Did Truly know about the option open to him?"

"Oh my, yes," Florence said. "His mother told him when she had the trust drawn up. If I know Myra, she probably told him every week until she died. After Myra's death, I reminded him of it every year. I never thought it would do any good, but I felt I owed it to Myra. And, in the end, she was vindicated. Truly finally got a job."

"Did he tell you why he went to work?"

She shook her head and laughed. "Truly never explained himself. In that, he was like Bartleby."

Harry laughed with her, trying to imagine Bartleby with Weissmuller for a companion or Truly as a scrivener.

"Do the police have any idea who killed Truly?"

"Not really. It looks now as if robbery might have been a motive. He associated with some of Avola's . . ." He stopped.

"I know, Mr. Brock. Why else would anyone want to kill the poor soul?"

"That's the question," Harry said. He stood up and was about to thank her, when something else occurred to him. "I mentioned that Ruvin Carter is administering the Brown Trust. Do you know him?"

"Yes. His father, Thaddeus Carter, set up the trust for Myra. When he retired, Ruvin, who by then had been in the bank for several years, took over the responsibility."

"Can you tell me anything about Ruvin Carter?" he asked.

"He was in a lot of trouble growing up. But he did not have an easy life. His mother was very unstable as a girl and grew worse after Thaddeus—that's Ruvin's father—lost most of his money. At one time, the Carters were very wealthy. Thaddeus' father was one of the founders of Three Rivers Bank & Trust."

Harry thanked her for seeing him. "I've enjoyed talking with you," he said.

"I'm glad I could help." She walked him to the door. "Please call if I can be of any further help. I would like to help bring Truly's killer to justice. But I suppose that's not your responsibility."

"No. But I would like to know for certain why he was killed."

"If we knew that, we would probably soon know who killed him."

Harry agreed.

Chapter 9

The next morning Harry went with Tucker to requeen a hive located in a back corner of the Hammock. On their way to the bee yard, Harry told Tucker about his meeting with Florence Herrick.

"I met her once or twice around the time I got to know Marjory Stoneman Douglas," Tucker said when Harry finished talking. "That was a good many years ago. Douglas was nearly eighty then. Florence was younger, but no spring chicken, and both of them were burning more energy in a day than I did in a week. Douglas gave some speeches over this way, and I went to all of them. Did some work for her too."

"When was that?"

"Around nineteen seventy. She had formed The Friends of the Everglades to help Joe Browder stop a development scheme to build a jetport and industrial park right in the middle of the Everglades. This battle was fought and won on the heels of a bitter fight between a developer by the name of Daniel K. Ludwig and the Audubon Society."

The two men were crossing a piece of swampy ground dotted with cabbage palms, wild cinnamon, Spanish stopper, wild hibiscus, and a scattering of Jamaica dogwood when Oh-Brother! interrupted Tucker's recollections by grasping the back of his shirt in his teeth and pulling him to a stop. The big mule was wearing his straw hat and a packsaddle, from which was slung half a hive body, a dozen supers, a sweating canvas water container, Harry's pump-action twelve-gauge shotgun, and Tucker's bee equipment.

"There's nothing wrong here," Tucker grumbled at the mule when he had checked the packsaddle and given the girth a tug.

"Where's Sanchez?" Harry asked.

Oh-Brother! was looking at their back trail. Tucker blew out his cheeks. "That's it. I was too busy talking. Sanchez has fallen behind again. Oh-Brother! was reminding me to pay better attention. We'll wait a bit. He'll be along. Time for a rest anyway."

Harry stretched and looked around. Columbine vines heavy with white and pink blossoms hung from the stoppers and the dogwood. The early sun was filling the glade with shafts of yellow light, and iridescent flies were flashing through the bars of sunshine like blue and green rockets.

"Nice place," Harry said.

Tucker nodded. He untied a pail from the packsaddle, took two tin cups out of the pail and passed one to Harry. He drew water into the pail from a spigot on the bag and set the pail down in front of Oh-Brother!. Then, when the mule had drunk his fill, he filled their cups from the bag and put more water in the pail.

"Sanchez will be thirsty. What was I saying?"

"Ludwig."

Harry checked for fire ants before sitting down beside Tucker on the grass. Oh-Brother! swung around to face them and give himself a view of the back trail. He shifted his weight uneasily, stamped his front feet, and threw up his head as if he was shaking off flies.

"Is he worried about Sanchez?" Harry had failed again to keep his resolution to stop pretending the mule thought like a person.

"No. It's that nuc he's packing for the hive we're going to queen. He can hear them buzzing. Doesn't like it."

Nuc was Tucker's shortened version of nucleus hive, the brood hive with its young queen and her small colony of workers. Harry thought Tucker had mistaken the cause of the mule's nervousness, but let it go. The mule appeared to be settling down, looking up every once in a while to check the trail for Sanchez. Tucker began talking again, sitting cross-legged on the grass.

"The Audubon Society, with help from a lot of other people, stopped Ludwig from building his oil refinery on Biscayne Bay. But right after that, there was a big push by the idiot fringe of the developer gang in south Florida to build a jetport and a huge industrial park right smack in the middle of the Everglades water flow."

"That was when Douglas formed The Friends of the Everglades."

"That's right. It cost a dollar to join, and within three years she had three thousand members from thirty-eight states. Her people raised such a storm the jetport plan was trashed."

"Were the Browns or the Kraftmeiers involved in any of that?"

"Myra Brown and Thaddeus Carter quarreled over Ludwig's oil refinery. Carter bet the farm on that refinery, and when Myra Brown threw in with the Audubon Society in opposing it, she and Thaddeus parted company. The split widened over the jetport, and that time the battle got more public. Carter lost a lot of money when the jetport idea died."

"Now Thaddeus Carter's son is managing the Brown Trust," Harry said. "Do you know Ruvin Carter at all?"

"He had a scratchy beginning, in and out of trouble as a

kid. His mother should have been put away and wasn't. I recall once seeing her on the sidewalk in downtown Avola having a conversation with a telephone pole. He had to live with that."

Harry had gone on thinking about Thaddeus and Myra and had been slow to connect the dots, but now he saw the irony clearly. "If Thaddeus and Myra Brown were at odds, why did she turn to him to set up the trust for Truly?"

"No reason not to. The trust was a business deal. It had nothing to do with personal differences over political issues. Remember, Avola was a small town. If you were a Myra Brown, the Three Rivers Bank & Trust was where you did your business."

Harry saw another connection. "Myra Brown seems to have done pretty much what she wanted. Why didn't she make her husband give Hobson's Choice back to Janet Kraftmeier?"

"I don't know. There were a lot of stories around. But one thing is sure. Janet took the loss of that land hard. All her anger that should have landed on Helmut got shifted to Myra."

Just then Sanchez came slogging into the glade, his tongue lolling and his nose almost on the ground. His head was covered with dirt and bits of leaves and twigs. He went straight for the water.

"Well, you're a sight," Tucker said indignantly. "You just couldn't pass up that armadillo hole, could you? One of these days you're going to put your head into a hole and meet a timber rattler."

The dog went on drinking. Tucker scrambled to his feet and glanced at the sun and then at Harry, making a sour face. "That's what happens when you have a dog that learned English as a second language. When he doesn't want to, he pretends he can't understand you."

The eight hives were set in a half-circle under a clump of Dahoon hollies some twenty feet in height. The trees and the hives benefited from the morning sun and the free movement of air over the low-growing palmettos. But the spreading holly branches were already casting a flickering shade across the hives. In another hour, the hollies would have them completely protected from the sun.

"Walk on. Those bees are not going to sting you."

Tucker spoke sharply to Oh-Brother!, because the mule had suddenly thrown up his head and come to a halt. Sanchez, still weary from his armadillo dig, plodded ahead of Oh-Brother!, ignoring the mule's balking.

"That's the third time he's pulled up like that," Harry said.

Tucker turned to stand beside the animal and put a comforting hand on his glossy, black shoulder. "Temperamental, aren't you? Come along and stop being a nuisance."

The mule dropped his head to press his nose briefly against Tucker's chest and snort softly.

"There's no reason to be concerned," Tucker responded. "Now, let's walk on."

Oh-Brother! stepped out briskly enough, but he walked with his head up and his ears sharply cocked. When Tucker unloaded the nuc, he showed no interest in the increased buzzing of the hived bees and went on sweeping the surrounding ground with his gaze. Tucker completed the unloading by passing Harry some gear.

"After you've put on your gear, carry the nuc over to the fourth hive in the row."

"Did you kill the queen in that hive when you were last out here?"

"Yes, and by now the bees have been without her long enough to accept a new queen."

By the time Harry was dressed and pulling on his gloves, Tucker had suited up, stoked his smoker with dried chunks of corncobs, and lighted it. He gave the smoker bellows a couple of taps. Two puffs of white smoke, like an Indian signal, rose from the smoker.

"All set."

As they advanced on the bee yard, the humming of the bees around the hives grew steadily louder and more alarming. Harry was soon moving through clouds of departing and arriving bees. Even with his suit on, Harry was uneasy. It occurred to him that wherever the cloth of the suit touched his body, as it would do every time he bent over, he would become a target of opportunity.

Tucker was eager to begin. "We shouldn't have much trouble with this. There's a heavy honey flow running now; the bees aren't hungry. They should be moderately relaxed."

Relaxed was good, but Harry wanted them comatose. He set the brood hive containing the new queen and her young workers next to the fourth hive and stepped back to watch Tucker work. Moving quickly, but without haste, Tucker sent several puffs of smoke into the entrance of the dequeened hive and turned to the nuc.

Harry was curious. "Does the smoke confuse the bees?"

"No. The smoke causes the bees to fill their stomachs with honey from their stores, in case they have to leave the hive. Once their bellies are full of honey, they become very placid and much less likely to sting." He pointed at the hive. "Lift the two honey supers off the brood hive."

Harry removed the two supers and set them on the ground. As he lifted them, he was enveloped in the warm, sweet smell of honey. Absorbed in his task, he forgot to worry about being stung. Tucker pulled off the tape covering the entrance to the nuc and sent some smoke into the brood box. Then he quickly turned to the old hive and carefully lifted three frames from the center of the hive body and set them on the ground. The frames, which hung in the brood box like folders in a hanging file, contained the comb. They were also heavy with honey and brood cells and swarming with bees.

After pausing to puff the old hive with smoke again, he removed the cover from the nuc and lifted frames until he found the one with the queen on it. Pulling that frame and another, he inserted them into the old hive with the queen safely contained between the frames.

Harry was startled. "Won't they be killed?"

"No. Because the old queen's pheromones have dispersed, her workers will not recognize the new bees as intruders and attack them."

Harry replaced the supers, and Tucker picked up the frames and gently brushed the bees still clinging to the comb onto the landing shelf in front of the hive's entrance. The bees did not seem to be at all disturbed by being tumbled around. Harry watched Tucker working with the bees and recalled what the old farmer had said about staying in touch with the past. How long had people been working with bees? Three thousand years? Six thousand? Too long, he thought with a mental shudder, and pulled his mind away from the question. The past was not a place he wanted to be.

When they were finished, Harry shed his suit and was surprised at how good he felt. Working in the bee yard had boosted his spirits.

"I felt like a kid playing," he said happily.

Tucker grinned. "Watch out. It's addictive."

Their gear packed, Tucker said, "Let's go home by way of the Point. I want to see if any more deer have been killed out there."

Sanchez had recovered from his armadillo hunt and was poking his nose under roots and into holes and generally enjoying himself. But Harry thought something was still bothering Oh-Brother!. The mule was standing at his full height, his head thrown up, his nostrils flared as he stared around him. Harry was struck by the animal's imposing stance and thought that if statues of mules were ever put up in parks, Oh-Brother! would make a good model.

"Oh-Brother!'s upset," Harry said when they were leaving.

Tucker didn't answer until he and Harry had put some distance between themselves and the two animals. Then he said in a low voice, "I didn't want to talk about it where they could hear me, but there's a panther out here, or was two days ago."

"So that's why you suggested I bring my shotgun."

"Didn't want to take mine and worry them. But I'm anxious to see if it's working the deer herd."

"Has Oh-Brother! picked up its scent?"

"More than likely. Old Sanchez's nose isn't what it used to be, but if that critter's out here, he'll soon know it."

With Tucker in the lead, the little safari turned northwest and moved out onto a thick finger of mixed wet and dry land that marked the end of Bartram's Hammock and poked out into the black waters of the Stickpen Preserve. The Preserve was a huge tract of mostly inundated land owned and managed by the Audubon Society. It contained some of the last giant bald cypresses and undisturbed wood stork nesting sites left in the country. Deer favored the peninsula for its patches of dry ground and heavy mixed growth.

They followed a trail that twisted its way through fairly open palm and slash pine woods, dipping occasionally into wetter ground where banyan, live oak, gumbo limbo, wild lime, and Jamaica dogwood crowded one another in their race for the sun. Entering one of these depressions, they stepped into welcome shade. In most of the shadowy thickets they had passed through, they had been surrounded by the calls of mourning doves. The silence in this one was complete. Not even a cricket was fiddling.

As they moved quietly ahead over the soft ground, the only sound Harry could hear was the occasional low creak of Oh-Brother!'s packsaddle and the intermittent, distant grumble of thunder. A wind had picked up and was blowing at a right angle across their line of travel. Sanchez was trotting along in a mechanical sort of way, apparently dreaming about armadillos, but Oh-Brother! was as alert as ever and stepped carefully, testing the wind as he advanced.

Tucker and Harry pushed through a thin screen of coffee bushes into an opening made by a huge live oak and came to an abrupt halt. In the dense shade under the tree, Harry saw what he first thought was a bear, reared against the trunk and looking at something in the branches directly over its head. The animal swung toward them, dropping onto all fours, and Harry saw it wasn't a bear but a huge, brindle-coated dog.

The hair on Sanchez's back rose, but he was not looking at the big dog, which gave a low, heavy growl and sloped off with astonishing speed. As it turned, Harry glimpsed a long red and white gash running from above its right eye back over its head. The animal crashed into the dense under-growth to their right and vanished. Sanchez began to bark. Tucker dropped his hand onto the dog's head and silenced him.

"What in the name of Gabriel is that thing doing in here?" Tucker asked, and started to walk toward the oak.

Harry saw that Oh-Brother! and Sanchez were staring at the oak and moving their heads as if trying to peer into the branches. "Wait," he said. "There's something in the tree."

The muscles on the mule's shoulders were quivering with tension, and his ears were laid back against his head.

"Easy," Harry told him, and stepped back and pulled his shotgun out of the pack. He pumped a shell into the chamber and came back to where Tucker was standing.

"Was that Weissmuller?" the old man asked quietly, staring into the oak.

"Yes. And he's treed something. From the look of Oh-Brother!, it's not a raccoon."

"All I can see from here is leaves."

Harry did not want to find himself dancing with what-ever was up in that oak, and he went forward slowly, stop-ping every few steps to peer into the tree. On their second stop, Harry glanced back at Sanchez and Oh-Brother!. The mule had moved out in front of the hound and was watching the tree intently. Harry would have been happier if Oh-Brother! hadn't looked so tense. He did not want to be in front of a mule stampede if things suddenly got inter-esting.

"A little more to your right," Tucker said, as they began their third advance. "I thought I saw something move up there."

They took two more steps and froze.

"Well, I'll be damned," Tucker said in admiration,

sinking slowly onto his heels, grinning broadly as he spoke to Harry, who had eased himself down beside Tucker. "Be careful with that gun. You'd be in less trouble shooting the Governor than pickling that young lady."

Standing on a low branch, looking back at them over her left shoulder, was a fully-grown female cougar, called a panther in Florida. She did not like their company and was growling to say so. Then she opened her mouth and hissed, showing them a full set of long, white teeth.

"Maybe we ought to just back out of here," Harry said, feeling inclined to give her all the space she wanted.

"Good idea," Tucker said.

They stood up slowly, but not slowly enough for the panther. She crouched and sprang out of the tree in a wonderful arcing leap. Her jump brought her closer to them and into a patch of sunlight. She touched the ground and favored them with one more snarl, before launching herself like a tawny arrow toward the scrub and vanishing without a sound.

"Praise the Lord," Tucker said, staring after her. "Isn't she a beauty?"

"Yes," Harry said, his heart beginning to slow down. "I wish they didn't have to wear those damned radio collars."

"If the state would bring in a few more cougars from Texas and release them down here, we might boost the numbers up to where they didn't have to be tracked that way. Anyway, I'm glad we saw her."

"Did you see that wound on Weissmuller's head?" Harry asked.

"I did, and it's bad. I'm going to have to catch him and see what can be done about it."

Chapter 10

All the way back to Tucker's farm, Harry tried his best to change Tucker's mind.

"Among other things," Harry said, "trapping Weissmuller would be harder than lassoing a snake."

"Nothing ventured . . ." the old farmer retorted with his elfin grin.

With growing exasperation, Harry tried another approach. "That dog is living in the woods, killing deer and running cougars up trees. What do you think you're going to do with him? He would tear your throat out as quick as look at you."

But Tucker only shook his head in his patient way and said, "He's just a dog, Harry."

"Well, I don't want to have to put the pieces in a bag so they can bury you," Harry snapped, letting his frustration get too far forward.

Tucker turned up his eyes like a plaster saint. "Leave me where I lie. The vultures are skilled morticians."

Harry groaned, admitted defeat, and limped off the field. Then he encouraged himself by saying Tucker was never going to catch that brindled devil anyway. So why was he worrying? He got home in time to meet the school bus.

Over dinner, Minna and Jesse were wide-eyed as they listened to Harry's account of his and Tucker's encounter with the panther. Katherine was more interested in what he had to say about Weissmuller. Later, when she and Harry were sitting on the lanai, she asked, "Are you going to let Tucker go after that man killer by himself?"

"I tried to convince him to leave Weissmuller alone."

"Didn't you say the dog was hurt?"

"Well . . ."

"And isn't that why Tucker is trying to catch him?"

"Yes, and also because Weissmuller's killing deer and harassing the female panther that may be trying to raise cubs out there."

Minna and Jesse had grown tired of the conversation and slipped off upstairs. Clearing the table also had something to do with their departure.

"And another point," Katherine added. "Weissmuller probably knows who killed Truly. The same person who shot Truly probably shot him."

"You might be right, but I'm not going to try to solve Truly's murder by interviewing Weissmuller, if that's worrying you. And, changing the subject, what about a large cup of Chocolate Fudge Brownie Frozen Yogurt at the Super Scoop? My treat."

Katherine considered the offer and said with a grin, "You're taking advantage of my condition. But, yes, let's go. However, you're wrong to think the Chocolate Fudge Brownie Frozen Yogurt will get you off the hook where Weissmuller is concerned. I'll round up the kids."

"Wait a minute," he said, but she was gone. "Okay, I'll clear the table."

While Katherine got the kids organized, Harry called Riga Kraftmeier. Tom Burkhardt answered, sounding affable and relaxed. The man had to be doing something right, Harry thought.

"Hang on, Mr. Brock," Burkhardt said. "She's around here somewhere."

Harry hated it when younger men called him Mr. Brock. A moment later a woman's voice asked, "Is that you, Arthur?"

There was a disturbance on the line, and Harry heard Riga say, "No, Mother, it's not Arthur."

"Then where is Arthur?" Janet demanded.

"Tom!" Riga called in a sharp voice. "Hello!"

Harry jumped and pulled the phone away from his ear. There was more shuffling and then Riga came back on.

"Yes?"

Harry could hear Tom and Janet discussing Arthur's whereabouts in the background. "Where is Arthur?" Harry asked, not altogether innocently.

It was a mistake. The line hummed vacantly. The background sounds diminished and vanished.

"I have some additional information," he said finally into the echoing silence. Then he waited.

"Am I going to hear it anytime soon?" Riga asked.

"Hobson's Choice is probably in the Brown Trust. Tomorrow, I'm going to talk with Ruvin Carter and try to find out if it will be put up for sale. Anything you want to tell me before I see him?"

"Ask him if the parcel of land will be sold separately, and make absolutely certain my name and all references to me stay out of the conversation."

Her voice had the strained patience of someone forced to explain the rudiments of personal hygiene to the village idiot.

"Okay. Do you know the ownership history of Hobson's Choice?"

The line went dead again. Harry thought about hanging

up. Then he told himself to get over it. The silence began to acquire an unpleasant personality.

"You've got about three seconds," she said.

Harry took a deep breath, tried to feel the bottoms of his feet, and exhaled slowly. It did not help. "I spent a couple of hours tracing back the deeds on Hobson's Choice. I found out some things. Do you want to hear them?"

"Why would you think that?"

"I did it on your nickel."

"Did I ask you to?"

"Yes. Do you cook your meat?"

She made a choking sound that might have been either suppressed amusement or rage. When she replied, she spoke very rapidly. "You found out the land belonged to my mother before it was deeded to Gaylord Brown. You probably found out from other sources that my father persuaded her to give him that land, which he used to settle a gambling debt after losing everything we had except this house to Gaylord Brown in a poker game. And you probably learned somewhere other than the Clerk of Court's Office that shortly after that, he abandoned his wife and children and went to live in Boca Raton with a three-dollar whore he picked up at a blackjack table at the Conochee Casino."

Harry opened his mouth to say he hadn't heard about the three-dollar whore or the Conochee Casino but managed to shut it before he did any more damage. "If you want, I'll come over, and you can shoot an apple off my head with a weapon of your choice and the option to miss."

This time she really did laugh. Not long, not loudly, but she laughed. "Just watch yourself with Ruvin," she said. "And one more thing. Are there any validity issues in that deed issue?"

"No. Everything seemed . . ."

She hung up.

The Big Scoop was on the east side of Avola on a county road with few houses, no amenities, and the occasional hand-lettered sign made from a piece of broken board and nailed to a fence post, announcing such things as Boiled Peanuts and Hog Dog Trials. But the Day-Glo green ice cream stand, on its gravel island in a swamp that brought alligators as big as culvert pipes to its back door, was famous throughout Tequesta County.

The alligators didn't care about the ice cream. What they favored were the dogs that careless owners let out of their cars for a run, while they hurried to order their double-dips with chocolate sauce, jimmies, and marshmallow toppings. Coming back to their cars, they whistled in vain for Old Spot, who in dumb-dog fashion had waded into the black water for a drink and vanished without a yelp in a swirl of water half the size of a living room.

When they had eaten their Jumbo Cups of Chocolate Fudge Brownie Frozen Yogurt, Harry stuffed the cups and napkins into one of the overflowing, sixty-gallon green plastic garbage pails set on cement blocks at the four corners of the Super Scoop. Then he inched the Rover out through the motorcycles, pickups, cars, SUVs, and racing kids crowding the lot.

"Can you believe parents would let kids out of the car in that place?" Katherine demanded in a disgusted voice as they pulled onto the road.

"I'd be all right," Minna said, "but one of those old 'gators would probably get Jesse."

"They would not," Jesse retorted, while Lucy held the football and smiled.

Harry goosed the Rover down the road with the doors open, blowing out the mosquitoes that had gathered in the cab while they were parked. Part of the *frisson* of visiting the Super Scoop came from swatting the mosquitoes.

"I'm going to see Ruvin Carter tomorrow," Harry told Katherine when he had blown out the bugs and slowed down enough for him and Katherine to hear one another speak.

"Helen doesn't like him," she said without much interest. "She didn't like talking about him."

"I hope you didn't mention Riga Kraftmeier."

"Are you interested in what she said, or not?"

"Yes, I am."

"Sorry, I'm not up to it."

"It was probably boring anyway," Minna said.

Harry kept his thoughts to himself.

Chapter 11

It rained again in the night, and Harry woke early to a shining morning. Katherine was still asleep. He dressed. Then he eased himself down the stairs to the kitchen for a glass of juice and a quiet look at the day before the kids got up. The Hammock was full of bird song, and the male red-shouldered hawk screeched a welcome at him as he stepped off the lanai onto the wet grass.

He was so busy drinking his juice and watching the hawk hunting through the oaks, that for a moment he didn't see the note. It was shoved into the top of a partly-split stick. The stick was shoved into the lawn a few feet from the lanai door. With his stomach already beginning to knot, Harry pulled the scrap of paper from the stick and read it.

Hey Asshole I'm here.

It was unsigned, but Harry knew the writer was Gideon Stone. He folded the note, threw the stick toward the woods, and went into the house. He went upstairs to the bedroom. Katherine was in the shower. Unlocking the metal case at the back of his closet, he took out his 9mm automatic, slid a fully-charged clip into the magazine, checked the safety, and stuck the gun into the waistband of his shorts. Then he went back down the stairs and out of the house. Once out the door, he drew the gun, worked its action, and eased off the safety.

Very carefully and very thoroughly, he scoured the barn, the shed, and the edge of the surrounding woods, without finding so much as a boot track that wasn't his own. Relieved, he pushed on the safety and stuck the gun back in his waistband, pulled his shirt down over it, and carefully examined the first-floor windows and the back door. They were all locked and secure. He went inside and made a thorough search of the downstairs rooms. He found no one, and no evidence of entry.

He finished just as Katherine came down the stairs, her hair done up in a towel.

"Hi," she said, still half-asleep.

"Hi," he answered, and went upstairs again to lock away the Luger.

Before going downstairs, he sat on the bed and listened to Minna and Jesse encountering the day. He also thought about Gideon and the note. But he didn't bother wondering how Stone had found the house. He knew that for thirty-nine dollars, or nothing, anyone could find anyone. Addresses, directions to find the addresses, telephone numbers, Social Security numbers, e-mail addresses, shirt size, anything. It was all for sale. He sat listening to Katherine clattering dishes in the kitchen, the kids dressing, and Minna singing, and he thought grimly about how totally accessible and totally vulnerable they all were.

Forcing himself to his feet, he went downstairs to his office and pulled Gideon's earlier note from its file. He spread it on the desk and put today's message beside it. Both were written in the same jagged scrawl on the same cheap yellow paper, probably torn from the same pad.

"Bastard!" Harry said.

"What?" Katherine called.

"Talking to myself," Harry replied, startled into remem-

91

bering he was not alone. He filed the notes and went into the kitchen. Katherine was making breakfast. Harry poured himself some coffee.

As he poured the coffee, he confronted the fact that the intervening years had not shielded him from the consequences of Jacob Stone's death. And the miles separating him from Maine had proved to be no barrier to Gideon Stone. The flash of awareness was so intense his hand started shaking. Tucker was right. The past had not forgotten him. He set down the pot and the cup with a bang and swore.

"Did you scald yourself?"

"No." He made a show of grabbing up a dish towel and wiping his hand. "The cup slipped. My hand must have been wet."

He forced his mind away from Stone and told Katherine about the hawk. But while he talked, he was also making decisions. The first was that he would not start carrying a gun. He would not think of himself as a hunted man. Furthermore, if Stone had wanted to shoot him, he could have done it this morning. And above all, if Katherine discovered he was carrying a gun, she would demand to know why. If that happened, he feared she would learn about Gideon.

The children came down to breakfast, and he welcomed them cheerfully. He would deal with Gideon. Gideon was going to go away. He would see that he did.

The headquarters of Three Rivers Bank & Trust was a five-story tan stucco building located in north Avola on the corner of Willet Lane and Route 41. The banker's office was on the fifth floor, far away from the to-ing and fro-ing of employees and customers and the ringing of phones. The two warnings he'd had from Riga Kraftmeier about Ruvin

Carter had not prepared him for what he found.

After the third-floor stop, to let off a nervous young couple intensely discussing whether or not their mortgage was going to be too much for them to carry, Harry made a silent, solitary ascent in the mahogany-paneled elevator and stepped out into a deeply carpeted foyer. Facing the elevator, a perfectly groomed young woman with silver-blonde hair sat at a pristine desk, slowly turning the pages of a magazine. At the sound of the elevator's chime, she looked up and smiled.

"Hello," she said. "I'm Tiffany. How can I help you?"

Harry gave her his name.

A moment later, Carter came out of his office.

Tiffany stood up. "Mr. Carter, Mr. Brock is here to see you."

"I see him, Tiffany," Carter said without looking at her. "Come on in, Brock."

"Is there anything I can get for you, Mr. Carter?"

"You might go downstairs and when nobody's looking, grab a couple of million dollars, sweetheart, and run it right back up here to me."

Tiffany smiled at Harry and went back to her magazine. Carter followed Harry into the office and flung the door shut behind him. "That girl," he said, when he finally stopped chuckling at his own joke, "has got the finest ass in Tequesta County, but she couldn't find it with both of her lily-white hands. I've offered to help her look, but so far she's saying, 'No.' " He laughed loudly. "Sit down, Brock. What the hell brings you up into this crow's nest?"

Harry thought he might have begun hallucinating. The powerfully-built man wringing his hand was wearing a green, long-sleeved Texas shirt, fastened with two buttons at each wrist, no tie, faded jeans, and bulky running shoes.

He wore his yellow-streaked brown hair collar-length and a Buffalo Bill mustache and goatee, both of which needed mowing.

Carter released what was left of Harry's hand, waved him into one of the two deep, leather chairs facing his seriously cluttered desk, and dropped into the other. While he pushed his legs out, balancing his feet on his heels, and groaned himself into a more comfortable position, Harry glanced around the spacious, paneled office with its hunting scenes, maroon drapes, and brass lamps, and wondered if somebody was playing a joke on him.

"I don't often get to visit with a private investigator," Carter said. "What brings you to Three Rivers and me, Brother Brock?" His delivery was as rough as his handshake, and Harry concluded that this was the real thing and no joke at all.

"My work takes me everywhere," Harry said as neutrally as he could. "I was told when I called Three Rivers that you're the exccutor of the Brown Trust."

It didn't seem likely. Harry wouldn't have let this man look after a rock.

"I am," Carter said with a grin. "If you can believe it."

"I have a couple of questions concerning the trust," Harry said.

"Truly Brown!" Carter said loudly. "By God, he was one of a kind. Poor son of a bitch. Did you know him? You and Helen Bradley found him, didn't you?" Carter shook his head. "Him and that goddamned dog. Now that was a pair!" He broke out in a laugh that was almost a shout.

"We found him on Hobson's Choice," Harry responded. "And no, I didn't really know him beyond saying hello when we met, which wasn't often."

"He kept to himself, didn't he?" Carter settled deeper

into his chair. "You asking about the trust for yourself or somebody else?"

"A client."

"And who would that be?"

The smile was still lingering, but that loud voice, Harry noted, had suddenly modulated and acquired an edge. Carter might not be as simple as he appeared. Harry reminded himself that banks took their promises of confidentiality seriously.

"My client wants to remain anonymous. But the questions I have are straightforward."

Carter scowled slightly. "All right, let's hear 'em. If I don't like them, I'll say so, and tell you to get the hell out of here."

"Fair enough. Will the Brown properties named in the trust be offered for sale?"

"Yup."

"Is Hobson's Choice included in the trust properties?"

"Yup."

"Finally, will it be sold as a separate parcel of land?"

Carter stood. "Might be. But I've said all I'm going to on that subject. You ever do any skydiving?"

"No," Harry said, getting to his feet and struggling to see the relevance of Carter's question. "That an interest of yours?"

"Hell, yes. You might want to try it. By God, it's a ride. Look, you can tell your client," he put a lot of emphasis on the word *client,* "that all this will be public information before many more moons pass."

"How many moons?" Harry asked.

"Quién sabe, amigo?" He grinned and reached for Harry's hand, and while he shook it, he shepherded him toward the door. "You think about that skydiving. By God

95

I've never done anything like it. You'll think you're born again."

The door opened to Tiffany's perfect smile. Harry escaped with relief. Tiffany walked him to the elevator. The door opened at their approach, and Harry stepped into his waiting coach.

When he turned to face the door, Tiffany said with a smile, and what Harry thought was more than a touch of irony, "Goodbye, Mr. Brock. Have a nice day."

The door closed. Harry descended, thinking P. T. Barnum couldn't have gotten him out of the tent more smoothly. And that was probably not where the resemblance stopped.

From Carter's office, Harry crossed Route 41 and drove east into a section of Avola with streets named Mechanics Way, B Street, and Diesel Avenue. On R&V Boulevard, he found the truck rental company he was looking for. Like the rest of the area businesses, Orloff's was a chunk of dusty concrete surrounded by a heavy-duty chain-link fence, with a low, flat-roofed building in its center baking in the sun. Harry thought the place was as grim as his own thoughts and quickly suppressed the comparison. The Rover and the huddled office were dwarfed by the huge red, blue, silver, and green semis and their trailers crowding the lot. The smell of diesel and hot grease thickened the air.

The red-haired, heavyset woman, with a ring on every finger and both thumbs, looked up from her battered desk as Harry stepped into the office, where she sat surrounded by stacks of invoices and other dusty piles of paper. "Whatcha need?" she demanded.

"You got a cattle van on the lot?"

"Yeah, but you can't have it. It's going out of here in, let's see . . ." She spun her chair and consulted a handwritten list on the wall behind her. "Two hours." She looked at another list hanging beside it. "I'll have one tomorrow morning. That too late?"

She turned around to face Harry.

"The one that's here will do. I just want to measure it."

She sat back in her chair and laughed. "That's a new one. Hey, Bud," she shouted. "There's a guy here wants to measure a cattle van. We charge him insurance?" She laughed again.

Harry waited while Bud in the next office laughed and then coughed for a while.

"Go measure," she said. "It's back in the northwest corner."

He found the huge, slat-sided van by following his nose. It had been hosed down, but it still reeked. Harry took out his notebook and tape and began sketching and penciling in measurements. Ten minutes later, he was back in the Rover.

Harry spent the rest of the afternoon, except for the time spent walking the kids home from the bus, trying to find an absconding tenant who had made off with a washer, a dryer, and an electric stove. Over the years, Rafe Juliette, the landlord, had given Harry a lot of trade. His Wild Turkey Condos in East Avola housed some colorful characters, known collectively and pejoratively to the members of the Sheriff's Department as Rafe's People.

Harry considered Rafe to be a major stakeholder in the county's penal system, because he regularly housed more criminals than the Tequesta County Jail. Harry knew from experience that Rafe's people moved a lot, but they never willingly moved far. Rafe called their living arrangements "domestic light." Possessed of few chattels and fewer social skills, they were surprisingly attached to Tequesta County. Most of them had been born there. Few had been beyond its borders. When they did talk with one another about their travels, they were generally discussing the various state and federal penal facilities they had visited. So, looking for one of them was deceptively simple. If they were out of jail, they were probably in the county, but finding one of them was something like trying to find a particular mouse in a hayfield.

It was dark by the time Harry found his mouse in a small room on the second floor of a ramshackle building behind the town docks. His name was Ernesto Piedra, a handsome man in his late thirties, with curly black hair and a sad, self-incriminating smile. Ernesto was full of remorse. His mouth was drawn down in sadness. His black curls trembled as he shook his head over the stove, the washer, and the dryer. *"Arrepentimiento,"* he said, had robbed him of sleep. But he had *"cometidos."* His responsibilities were of various ages and had many different mothers. Ernesto had not been sleeping well for a long time. He did not have time to sleep. He was too busy increasing his *cometidos.*

"Ernesto, Rafe Juliette wants his stove, his washer, and his dryer back." Harry feared the man's melting gaze might weaken his resolve.

"Mañana," Ernesto said, *"matinal!"*

Harry shook his head. *"Hoy,* Ernesto. *Hoy."*

Ernesto's face collapsed into an expression of great suffering. "It will break their hearts. Even now they are cooking dinner, washing and drying their children's clothes."

"It will break their hearts having to visit you in jail."

"Por cierto," he said with a sigh. *"Lo hare yo mismo."*

He did, and the matter was resolved. Rafe was out his

fee to Harry. But Harry knew he would, of course, file for loss by burglary, put the recovered items in other apartments, and make out like the bandit he was. Harry could almost hear Jim Snyder groan at the perfidy of men.

After finishing with Rafe, Harry decided to talk to Riga. She answered the door and let him in. On his way down the hall, Janet Kraftmeier stepped out of one of the rooms and said in an accusing voice, "You're not Arthur."

"No, Mother, he's not," Riga said.

She took her mother by the arm and walked her briskly down the corridor. Tom appeared and took over. Riga led Harry into her father's study.

"What is it?" she asked without closing the door.

Harry was accustomed to the routine now and ignored her unsmiling welcome. "I talked with Carter. Why didn't you tell me?"

A smile flickered at the corners of her mouth. "What did he say?"

"The land in the trust will be sold, and Hobson's Choice is going on the block."

"Will it be sold separately?"

"Carter wouldn't or couldn't tell me, and he cut off the interview as soon as I asked the question."

"Is this your gumshoe?" a harsh voice asked behind him.

Harry turned to find a tall, thin, balding man with a sallow complexion standing in the door, hands pushed into the jacket pockets of his rumpled gray suit. He regarded Harry from beneath heavily-lidded eyes. Harry found the man's sneering mouth and slouching stance repellant, but he had presence, and his arrival had clearly upset Riga. "This is a private conversation, Arthur." Her voice climbed as she spoke, and a flush spread up her neck and into her cheeks.

"I don't think so," the man said. He freed his hands and walked forward until he was scowling down at Riga. "It's my business, little sister. It's *our* money."

"I'll come back," Harry said.

"Stay where you are," Riga said. She glared at her brother.

"I know what you're up to," Arthur told her in an angry snarl. She stepped back. "You're screwing around with that crook Ruvin Carter, trying to get your hands on Hobson's Choice. That's it, isn't it?"

"It's none of your business."

Harry forgot about leaving.

"It fucking well is my business. You're still stuck in this shit!" He waved his arm at the room and advanced again on his sister. "This and that goddamned Hobson's Choice. Well, you're not spending a nickel more of our money to feed your obsessions."

Riga was backed against the desk. Harry was about to intervene, when Riga suddenly lunged forward and shoved him away from her.

Harry gave a silent cheer.

"I'll spend the money any way I want. It's my decision, not yours. And Hobson's Choice would be a good investment. Developed properly, that land will be worth four million dollars an acre."

"The money is mine as much as it's yours," Arthur said. He seemed indifferent to the push.

"But I have the power of attorney."

Arthur glowered at her. "That's only a piece of paper, Sister. Don't think it's going to stop me from getting my share." He sloped out of the room, leaving behind the static of his threat and the stale smell of cigars.

"Are you all right?" Harry asked.

Riga straightened and gave Harry a hard look. "Have you anything else to tell me?"

"Your brother carries a gun."

"Yes. He's a professional gambler. Have you read today's *Banner*?"

"No." Harry was still trying to absorb the news about her brother.

"Three Rivers Bank & Trust has printed an announcement postponing the disposition of the Brown Trust. This has to be Ruvin Carter's decision. Talk to him again. Find out what's going on."

She was obviously disturbed, but Harry couldn't tell whether it was her brother or Ruvin Carter who had upset her. He left wondering what Arthur had meant by calling Carter a crook.

Harry had called Katherine from Rafe's office to tell her he would be late and was pushing the Rover hard on the last mile of road before reaching the Hammock when headlights flared behind him. Despite the racket the Rover was making, he heard whatever was coming behind him accelerate. Harry pulled over as close to the shoulder as he could get and prayed the oncoming road warrior was sober enough to see him.

The car, a sedan, hauled up beside him. Its dome light was on, and the front windows were run down. Harry glanced sideways and saw a big, dark-haired man with a bushy beard glaring at him. He leaned toward Harry, his right hand out of sight.

"Oh, shit!" Harry said.

Harry risked another look just as the man snapped himself erect. His right hand came up holding a gun. Harry braked as hard as he could. There were two terrific explosions. Harry's windshield disintegrated as the Rover attempted to shake itself to pieces, dive into the swamp, and reverse directions all at once.

His night visitor stomped on the gas and disappeared down the road in a cloud of smoke. Harry got the Rover stopped and leaped out and ran into the swamp, expecting his assailant to come roaring back. But the road stayed empty and silent. When the mosquitoes grew worse than the risk of getting shot at, he took himself home, swearing and squinting into the wind and the bugs.

Chapter 12

Harry drove into his yard, turned off the ignition, still furiously planning to track down the bearded son of a bitch who had shot out his windshield and tried to blow him to hell. As the adrenaline gradually boiled off, a chilling thought broke through his anger. His assailant was Gideon Stone. At that moment, Katherine appeared at the lanai door.

"Brock, are you waiting for a personal invitation to come in and eat this burnt offering that used to be your supper?"

He stepped onto the grass, finally grateful he was still upright. He walked slowly toward the house, inventing and discarding stories that would explain the Rover's shot-out windshield, but determined not to tell her Gideon Stone had done it. He would say that bad luck had thrown him into the path of either a psychopath or a lunatic who had fried his brain with alcohol or drugs or both. The story was so plausible that he went into the house smiling and full of apologies for being late.

"Somebody tried to shoot you!" Katherine shouted. His funny story about the drunk/drugged old-style hippie with the revolver had not amused her. "You're telling me with a smile on your face that somebody tried to kill you?"

"I don't know if . . ."

She grabbed the phone off its hook and shoved it into his chest. "Call the police. Do it now."

Harry backed away from her. "It can wait. The incident's over. The idiot's long gone. Let's just sit down and have our supper. I've kept you waiting long enough."

Katherine grasped the phone in both hands and stood looking at her husband for a moment in silence. "Harry," she said firmly, "somebody overtook you on the public highway and tried to shoot you. You're alive only because the bastard missed. Call it in."

He made the call. He told the dispatcher what had happened and gave her a description of his assailant, but no name. When he put the phone down, he renewed his promise that he would not tell Katherine who his attacker was. He ate, but she was too upset to do more than pick at her food. Not even his account of Ernesto Piedra made her laugh.

"I hate it that you're a private investigator," she burst out at one point.

"But what happened tonight had nothing to do with being a P.I.," he protested. It was the only completely honest thing he'd said since coming home.

"I don't care. You're in danger. Even Piedra might have killed you. Then what would the kids and I do?"

Harry didn't have an answer. He tried and failed to comfort her, and while he was doing that, he began to make plans for dealing with Gideon Stone.

The next morning, after Katherine had left for work and Harry had walked the kids to the bus, Jim Snyder and Hodges turned into Harry's yard. Harry took them into the kitchen. Harry had guessed Hodges would be with Jim and had already put a plate of sugar donuts and a pecan Danish on the table, along with the coffee. Katherine had insisted on making a separate pot of coffee for them, warning Harry against making any on his own.

"Now is that hospitality or what?" Hodges asked, his moon face shining as he beamed at the table.

Before Harry had the coffee poured, Hodges' mouth was circled by a ring of powdered sugar. Jim took a nervous sip of the coffee and then smiled in obvious surprise. "Katherine made it," he said. "Of course, yours is pretty good too, Harry." Apparently shocked by his dishonesty, Snyder created a diversion by dusting his fingers and pulling out his notebook.

"Tell us what happened out there last night."

Harry described the drive-by and took copies of Gideon's notes from their folder and passed them to Jim. "I dated them."

"You got the first one back before Sergeant Hodges and I talked with you about finding Truly Brown." He spoke in a pained voice, his ears growing red. "Why am I just hearing about this?"

"It's very old stuff, Jim," Harry said.

Hodges had leaned sideways and read over Jim's shoulder without letting it interfere with his eating. When he could bring himself to stop chewing, he made a loud observation. "The first letter came on the twelfth. This is what? The twenty-first? Nine days isn't long ago."

Harry shook his head. "I mean the things behind these two notes happened a long time ago. Besides, I'm not certain the guy who took the shot was Gideon Stone." Just having these notes on the table was making him feel bad.

"No. But if he rides in a sleigh pulled by reindeer and comes down the chimney Christmas Eve, it's probably Santa Claus," Jim replied.

Promotion, Harry thought, was having a bad effect on Snyder. Before he made Captain, he was never sarcastic.

"What kind of car was this jillpoke driving?" Hodges asked.

"I think it was a Malibu, six or seven years old. Dark paint. The exhaust system was pretty well shot."

Hodges chewed and shook his head for a while. Then he said, "What do you think, Cap? Are there somewhere around five hundred Malibus like that in the county?"

"More," Jim said. "Not much help, Harry. What about tags?"

"Sorry, I was trying to keep the Rover from jumping the ditch and turning itself into a swamp buggy. Didn't see them."

Jim pushed his plate out of the way and laid his notebook on the table. "Description of the shooter?"

"Big man. I'd guess six feet. Maybe more. Long, dark hair; heavy, springy beard."

"He look like this Stone guy?" Hodges asked.

"The last time I saw Gideon Stone, he was a scrawny eleven-year-old."

"It's not much," Jim said. "We'll find out if this guy is still around, if he's got any priors. Then I'll make sure the department gets a description of him. Would you be willing to help Graham draw us a picture?"

Harry pulled himself back. "Sure."

Jim closed his notebook and got to his feet. Hodges followed, still clutching his unfinished donut.

"Look," Harry said. "I don't want Katherine to know anything about Gideon Stone. As far as she's concerned, it was a drunk or a loony who took a shot at me. I'm serious about this. It has to be kept away from her."

Jim frowned. "She doesn't know about these notes?"

"No."

"It's none of my business, but why not?"

"I don't want her stressed any more than she already is."

Both officers looked at him with renewed interest. "We don't know where this guy is, Harry," Snyder said. "We don't know who he is or why he tried to kill you, if that's what he had in mind. Don't you think Katherine ought to know what's going on here? And there's the kids."

Harry nodded. "I've thought of that. I'm walking them to and from the bus."

"We're going to have to know . . ." Snyder responded, but Harry cut him off.

"When the time comes, I'll tell you what you have to know, but it's ancient history and I want it to stay that way."

Hodges swallowed the last bite of donut. "Looks like this Stone guy doesn't know that. Maybe you'll want to think about it some more. If it was my wife . . ."

Snyder interrupted. "Okay, let's get on with it. Harry, I'll try to keep Katherine out of the investigation, but I'm not going to have the last word on this, you know."

"Not good enough. If you want my cooperation, you'll see she doesn't find out."

"I'll do the best I can." Jim dropped a hand on Harry's shoulder and smothered Hodges' attempt to say something more. "Meanwhile, and for the next few weeks, do your driving in the daylight, until we can get a lead on this joker."

"Stick your shotgun in the Rover," Hodges said.

Harry followed the two deputies out of the kitchen.

"Load it with buckshot," Hodges added, dusting powdered sugar off his tunic.

Jim picked up his hat from the chair by the front door and stood turning it in his hands, his long face drawn into a frown of concern. "Don't stand in front of lighted windows," he said. "Lock the house up well, whether you're in it or not. And despite what Sergeant Hodges says, I don't want you turning vigilante."

"I hear you, Captain." Harry walked the two officers to their cruiser. "How's the Truly Brown investigation going?"

Jim's face remained glum. "Well, I hear Ruvin Carter's getting ready to liquidate the Brown estate. Don't quote me, but aside from that, the whole thing's dead in the water. No new leads."

Hodges gave a bark of laughter. "I wonder how much of it Carter's already liquidated."

"Meaning?" Harry asked.

"Well, he spends a fair amount of time in the Oconee Casino," Hodges answered. "The word is he's a high-roller."

Jim responded with an unusual show of anger. "You want to leave that kind of talk right where you heard it. We ought not to be spreading malicious gossip about our important citizens."

"I'm just saying what I hear."

"Don't say it," Jim said. "It doesn't do you or the department credit."

"Okay, Captain." Hodges winked at Harry.

"Do either of you know Carter?" Harry asked.

Hodges shook his head but Snyder said, "I've met him once or twice. Doesn't look much like a banker, does he?"

"No. What do you know about him?"

"Aside from being a little eccentric, nothing."

Hodges rolled his eyes. Talking had eased Harry's mind enough for him to wave them out of the yard. He stood for a while, listening to the cicadas in the oaks and a bobwhite whistling bravely in the cord grass meadow across the creek. Walking back to the house, he found himself recalling

Hodges' remarks about Ruvin Carter.

Despite Jim's complaints about his rough-cut sergeant, Hodges had his head on straight, and it occurred to Harry that a picture of Ruvin Carter was just what he needed to check out Hodges' story. Without asking why, he made a segue to Truly Brown and the fact that Truly had been working and was about to put his hands on a fortune when he died. He wondered if the police had visited the Green Thumb Nursery and suddenly had the urge to go out there himself.

It troubled him that the investigation of Truly's death was making so little progress. Despite what he had told Katherine, he would like to do something to move the investigation forward. He also thought about Findlay Jay and made a guilty face. Aside from measuring the cattle trailer, he hadn't done much about the rancher's missing cattle. He would have to remedy that.

The Fakahatchee Road marked the south boundary of Cypress Grove, a sprawling and mostly undeveloped parcel of pine upland east and a little north of Avola. A lot of wholesale nurseries, tree farms, pole barn cattle ranches, and an alpaca farm were strung out along the road. The Green Thumb was a thriving retail nursery, despite its location. Harry liked nurseries in general and the Green Thumb in particular, although he had never met its owner. He liked plants, the space, and the smell of earth, compost piles, and growing things.

Even knowing that only in love and the trifecta does hope triumph more fully over experience than it does in a garden, Harry still planted flowers. One of his favorite quotations came from an ancient Egyptian gardener who had inscribed on his tomb a gentle suggestion for living happily:

"Surround yourself with growing things. Fill your hands with flowers."

Searching for someone at the Green Thumb to talk to about Truly led him to Hannah Bridges. He found the owner in an open shed at the back of the nursery, working at a wooden potting bench. She was surrounded by black plastic bags of potting soil and bulging trays of geraniums that she was transplanting into four-inch pots. The shed was well away from the graveled paths, where customers, pulling bright red wooden carts overflowing with multi-colored dreams, wandered with the glazed eyes and rapt expressions of lotus-eaters.

Hannah Bridges was a big, florid-faced woman, dressed in a spacious blue dress covered with pale yellow daisies. Over that she wore a rumpled, tan linen jacket with the sleeves rolled halfway to her elbows. She was standing on a plank to keep her sneaker-shod feet out of the mud while she worked. Her wonderfully thick, wavy, silver-gray hair spronged around her head and brushed her shoulders in a tangle of amiable neglect. She was vaguely familiar to Harry.

Harry introduced himself and told her why he was there.

"Truly Brown," she said with a rich and sympathetic laugh. "Now there was the genuine article."

Harry must have looked confused, because she exclaimed, "An original! Why are you asking about him? Are you with the police?"

"No, I'm a private investigator."

She laughed again. "As long as you're not with the press." As she talked, her hands went swiftly about the task of filling the pots. She frowned a little and said in a disapproving voice, "I didn't think much of that funeral service. I've been to dog burials where the chief mourners said more thoughtful things about the deceased than that minister said over Truly. And there weren't any flowers. Even the Neanderthals knew enough to praise their dead with flowers."

That's where he'd seen her. She'd been wearing a wide-brimmed purple hat with a bird of paradise blossom pinned to its left side.

Although Harry also thought the minister's comments about Truly had set new standards for insincerity and shallow observation, he said, "I guess he'd been a joke too long for people to adjust their thinking at such short notice."

She hummed doubtfully. "I haven't been down here long. Was it because of his Tarzan fixation?"

"That and the fact he was all-around different in the way he lived. Did you know he came from a wealthy family?"

"I'd heard some remarks about the Browns once being important people in the county. And a few weeks before he was killed, he told me he was coming into some money and might not be able to go on working for me. I said that was too bad, because I'd come to depend on him. Which was true. He was a good man with plants."

"His mother left him all the Brown estate, or most of it, in a trust," Harry said. "He was given a stipend to live on, with the stipulation that if he worked at any job for two years, he could have it all."

"How much money are we talking about?"

"You can count it in the millions, a bunch of it in land."

Her hands stopped flying from tray to potting soil to pot to the hose, and she stared hard at Harry to see if he was joking.

"He was a wealthy man," Harry said smiling at her disbelief. "Did he ever tell you what made him decide to go to work? This was the first job he ever had in his entire life."

"No. The only thing he ever talked about was Tarzan and how he intended to find him one of these days."

"Do you think he was crazy?"

She gave Harry a sharp look. "It would take someone smarter than me to know that." She paused to run her forearm across her forehead. It was hot in the shed, despite the breeze that blew with a rising and falling rhythm of its own and occasionally lifted and swirled her long hair like hay in a field. She went back to filling the pots before she spoke again. "You know, he had it all worked out about how Tarzan and Jane had come by ship to southwest Florida from Africa. How he'd been living out there in the swamps all this time." She paused again and then said in a surprised voice, "Wait. It just came to me. I think I remember him saying a while back that he was almost ready to get a real search going."

She lifted one of the pots she had filled and turned it around, studying it. "I never cease to be amazed," she said, shaking her head. "From seeds the size of ground pepper to this. Seeds, water, and earth. Or in this case, potting compound. Add a pinch of light . . . where was I?"

"Truly was going to launch a major search."

"Oh, yes, I asked him if Tarzan wasn't getting to be pretty old to be living alone out there in the Everglades. He fired right back that Jane was with him, and neither of them would ever grow old. I suppose he was right. They never will grow old."

Harry had the answer he had been looking for. Truly had gone to work to get hold of the trust money. He grinned. "Did he bring his dog to work?"

She puffed out her cheeks and widened her eyes at him. "Weissmuller! Now there was something straight out of

The Call of the Wild, only I don't think Jack London ever imagined anything to match Weissmuller."

"Didn't he scare off the customers?" Harry asked.

She laughed. "When he wasn't hunting cats, he clung like a burr to Truly and never so much as barked, although once in a while if someone made a quick move around Truly, the hair would come up on his shoulders. But all Truly had to do was run a hand over his head to settle him right down."

Harry thanked Hannah, shook her hand, and tried to leave the nursery without looking left or right. He almost made it, but a few feet from the exit a climbing rose called Morning Fanfare, with deep pink blossoms, reached out and grabbed him. When King Darius threw Daniel into the lions' den, it was nothing to what Harry was doing to Morning Fanfare by carrying her off to the Hammock. But he told himself, lust has no conscience. He might have added, and no common sense either.

Harry began carrying his gun. That is, he kept it within reach. Because southwest Florida is shorts and light top country, wearing a shoulder holster can lead to a certain amount of social awkwardness. On the first day he wore his weapon, he walked into the 7-Eleven on Sago Avenue to pay for his gas, and everyone in the place hit the floor facedown and the young female clerk burst into tears. After that, he kept the automatic between the seats in the Rover.

Katherine said angrily that she hated the gun. Helen, however, thought his security arrangements were inadequate. She had found out about the drive-by from Katherine. Like Katherine, she knew nothing about Gideon Stone, and Harry intended to keep it that way.

Nevertheless, she sided with Hodges and said he should

be carrying a shotgun instead of that pistol. "Christ, Harry," she told him. "Wake up. Stop pretending this isn't happening. The crazy son of a bitch tried to kill you."

Harry let it go. He had recruited Helen to help him take a photograph of Ruvin Carter, and although she agreed to take part, her cooperation came with a price.

"Are you starting an album of weirdos?" she asked.

They were parked across the street and half a block west of the Three Rivers Bank, where they were going to wait for eleven fifty-five to arrive so Helen could accidentally meet Ruvin Carter coming out of the bank on his way to lunch. The plan was for her to stop him to talk for a moment while Harry took his picture.

Helen had swung around on her seat and was staring at Harry with a marked lack of esteem. He had bribed her into this bit of sneaky camera work by promising her lunch at the Harborside, an upscale eatery on the inner lagoon of Fiddler's Pass. But he suspected her dislike of Carter and her desire to see Truly's murderer swinging from the yardarm had more to do with her agreeing than the prospect of a pricey meal. That and her ongoing interest in Riga Kraftmeier.

"Does this have anything to do with what you're doing for Riga?" she had asked when he had run his proposal past her.

"Yes," Harry said, stretching things.

"And you can't tell me what that is?"

"No."

"And it also involves the murder of Truly Brown."

"There's a remote possibility."

"Okay. And here's something else, but you didn't hear it from me. Riga said Arthur's got something on Carter. That troubles me."

"Have you met Arthur?"

"Once, and that's enough. He's a scumbag, and scary to boot."

Harry recalled Arthur's comment to Riga that Carter was a crook. "What's he got on Carter?"

"Either she doesn't know or she's not saying. With Riga, it's hard to tell."

"Did she tell you her brother's a professional gambler?"

Helen grinned. "On a New Orleans riverboat called *The African Queen*. Are you ready for it?"

Harry laughed. "I haven't been ready for anything in that house."

"Arthur's coming back has shaken Riga. I don't like him, and I don't like him messing around with Carter. He could get Riga into real trouble with the bank."

"And you don't know what he's got on Carter, if anything."

"No." Helen suddenly switched subjects. "How long did Katherine live in Trachey's cabin before Emile Thibedeau grabbed her and the kids?"

"A few months. Why?"

"Until you took him down, along with the two goons from New Jersey?"

"Yes. Look, shouldn't you be going toward the bank?" Harry made a show of checking his watch.

"There's time," she said. "Was that what got you and Katherine together?"

"Why are you asking me these questions?"

"Because Katherine is my friend, and you married her. Because she is my friend, I'm supposed to like it that you married her. Well, I don't."

Harry was rattled. "You hardly knew her when I married her."

"It doesn't matter."

"There's Carter," Harry said gratefully.

"Shit. You're not getting away with this. You're answering the question," she said in a menacing whisper, but she was already halfway out of the Rover. She pushed her head back into the Rover. "If you say anything to Katherine about this, you're carrion." She backed up, straightened her dress, gave her hair a toss, and strode across the street.

Harry stared after her. What the hell was that about? She reached Carter and spoke to him. Harry picked up his camera. A couple of minutes later, he had the pictures he wanted. Helen went into the bank, and as soon as Carter had gone on his way for another block, Harry took the film to have it developed.

Chapter 13

When Harry returned from Avola, Sanchez was waiting for him with a note pinned to the bandanna he wore for a collar. Sanchez had half a dozen bandannas of different colors. Every morning he chose the one he wanted to wear. Today's choice was orange. Harry gave the dog a drink and a cookie, and then he unpinned the note.

"I'll be damned," Harry told the dog. "He's caught that man-killer Weissmuller."

Sanchez grinned. While he was getting some gear together, Harry tried to persuade himself that grinning was just a trick Sanchez had learned, and it didn't mean he understood what Harry had said.

"I wasn't sure you'd help me," Tucker said as he and Harry, followed by Sanchez and Oh-Brother!, were walking along the trail to the tree where they had seen Weissmuller and the panther. "You were set hard against my doing this."

"I still am," Harry said. The pines through which they were walking were loud with locusts. Even the air seemed alive. Harry's spirits lifted. "What did you put in the trap to draw him?"

"A dead cat. I got it from the vet and dragged it around out there for a while. Then I put it in the back of the box. Weissmuller wouldn't have looked at meat, but he'd go through fire to chew up a cat."

When the four reached the trap, Weissmuller began

snarling and crashing into the sides of the box trap so hard that it rocked from side to side and groaned like a ship in distress. Pieces of the dismembered cat began flying out through the double-wire caging.

"And you're going to try to tame that thing," Harry said.

"Oh, his bark's worse—"

"Don't say it."

Tucker laughed and got a big square of canvas from Oh-Brother!'s packsaddle and threw it over the pitching cage. "Give me a hand with this," he said. He tossed Harry a length of rope.

While Tucker held the canvas, Harry wrapped the rope around the cage and knotted it. Deprived of light, Weissmuller stopped flinging himself around and settled down to a steady growling, accentuated periodically by a bellow of rage.

"Now all we have to do is load it onto Oh-Brother!'s travois," Tucker said. He and Harry crossed the top ends of the two poles forming the legs of the travois and lashed them to the mule's packsaddle. Then they walked Oh-Brother! into position with the trailing ends of the poles beside the cage.

"Now we load him," Tucker said.

"And pray the box holds." But by this time Harry was worrying less about getting the box onto the poles than he was about what Tucker was going to with the beast when he got him home.

They wrestled the box with its snarling cargo onto the poles and lashed it tight, then ran a second rope around the cage and up to the mule's packsaddle. Oh-Brother! stood with his head twisted around and his ears cocked during the loading, taking a keen interest in what was going on behind him. Sanchez trotted back and forth, barking occasionally.

"He's just encouraging us," Tucker explained. Harry nodded and immediately felt foolish. "Oh-Brother!," Tucker called when they were ready.

The mule leaned into his chest strap, and easily walked off with the travois and its growling burden. The Hammock was sinking into its midday quiet by the time they got back to Tucker's place. Only the cicadas were keeping up their racket. Harry was soaked with sweat, but Tucker looked as fresh as when they started.

"Now what?" Harry demanded.

"I've got a kennel all ready for him. I ran the concrete floor two days ago and put in the poles and stretched the wire." Tucker grinned at Harry. "Don't ask. It's horse-high, pig-tight, and bull-strong."

Harry had to agree it was. While they were wrestling the trap into the enclosure, the vet arrived.

"Heather Parkinson," Tucker said.

The slight, brown-haired woman, wearing dark glasses, blue coveralls, and a Dolphins' cap, stuck out her hand. "My practice is mostly large animals," she told Harry in a cheerful voice as she wrung his hand. "But this was too interesting to pass up." She gave him a bright smile. "Let's have a look at this monster. Is that him under all that canvas?"

"That's him."

"I'll just get that canvas off the trap," Tucker said.

"Let's get him out of there and see what's what," Heather said, and followed Tucker into the enclosure.

Harry started to protest but stopped himself. Tucker loosened the knots and peeled off the canvas. Weissmuller hit the side of the box closest to Tucker's legs so hard the heavy cage rocked up on one edge and crashed back down; the sound of it striking the cement was drowned by the dog's roar. Tucker and Heather jumped back.

"That's what's what," Harry observed through the fence.

Heather laughed and pulled off her cap and waved it at
the front of the cage. Weissmuller obliged by slamming into
the wire, snarling and snapping. She straightened up and
said to the dog, "Oh, my, look at your head. Got to do
something about that, and I've got just the Bud for you."
She came out of the kennel enclosure whistling and hiked
off toward her panel truck.

"Man's best friend," Harry said to Tucker.

Tucker nodded. "He just needs some gentling."

"This will do it," Heather said. She shook a four-foot
piece of metal pipe with a needle sticking out one end at
Tucker as she went back into the kennel, and motioned to
Harry. "You just volunteered to put a body part somewhere
near that trap when I give the word."

Harry groaned and followed her with all the enthusiasm
of a condemned man climbing a scaffold.

"Now," she said.

Harry took a long step forward toward the front of the
cage. Weissmuller lunged against the wire. To Harry's
horror, the front of the cage bulged and cracked as the
wood began to splinter. The dog's efforts to reach Harry increased.

Heather yanked her pipe out of the cage and leapt to her
feet. "Got him!" she shouted. "Everybody out!"

She and Harry shot out the door and Tucker slammed it
shut just as Weissmuller smashed his way free and launched
himself at the three of them. That is, he shook himself free
of the wire and broken door frame, snarling and gathering
himself for an attack on the fence. But as he crouched, his
legs folded and he fell forward, the ferocious growl dwin-
dling to a sigh as he collapsed.

"Saved us the trouble of dragging him out of the box." Heather said.

"Lord a' mercy," Tucker gasped.

"I'm not going there," Harry said.

Heather picked up her bag and pulled open the kennel door. "Well, let's get started on that head," she said.

The Oconee Casino, owned and operated by the Conochee tribe, was a huge, windowless stucco box, painted a rusty beige, set down in an extraordinary space just about halfway across the Everglades. Harry stepped out of the Rover onto the broiling tarmac of the immense parking lot. He squinted in the blazing light and looked around at the small gathering of tribal buildings, and beyond them at the miles of grass and shallow blue water and scattered knobs and hammocks with their dark green trees. Standing in the center of the vast, pulsing bowl, Harry felt the immense sun, the sky, and the puffy clouds were almost close enough to touch.

Harry reflected for a moment on the irony of a gambling hall sitting out here in the midst of all this beauty. But the casino was the tribe's golden goose, as well as one of the few places left where their ancient foes could still be scalped with impunity.

Harry abandoned his sour-sweet reflections on the fruits of tribal autonomy and set off for the shade offered by the barn-like structure with its huge glass doors. He had left home early and it was only midmorning when he stepped into the hall, but the smell of tobacco smoke and alcohol fouled the chilled air. It could have been any time or no time among the slot machines, blackjack tables, roulette tables, baccarat tables, and dice tables, huddled under the darkly-shadowed walls. A few customers were already at the games, and a dense quiet gripped the place.

A scattering of dealers were lounging or working at their stations. Harry stopped at the nearest one, a blackjack table, where a lean middle-aged black-haired man, dressed in a crisp white shirt, a fringed maroon vest, and dark trousers, was rearranging packs of cards.

"Hi," Harry said, and pulled a picture of Ruvin Carter out of his pocket and placed it face-up on the table in front of him. "You ever see this guy?"

The man looked at the picture. "Nope." He bent down behind the table.

The way he said it tripped a switch in Harry's head. "Would you tell me if you had?"

"Nope."

Harry went in search of the management. It had come to him a little late that not only was he on private property, but the laws of Tequesta County carried little weight here. He was in an independent nation. It further occurred to Harry that he might have made a mistake in thinking the casino management was going to be much help to him. But when he asked a baccarat dealer for the manager's office, she pointed into the darkness beyond the breakfast buffet. The darkness turned out to be a short, softly lighted hall. Halfway down it, he found an office door with a polished brass marker that read, *Ondine Jones, Manager.*

A carefully groomed young woman about thirty answered his knock. She was slim, black-haired, and dressed in a peach blouse and navy skirt.

"My name is Harry Brock."

She took the ID Harry passed her and went behind her desk, then read the ID carefully. While she studied it, Harry looked around the office, admiring the Frank Dienst black and white photographs of the Everglades framed and mounted on the walls. He recognized several of the prints from Dienst's collection *Wet Land Voices*. Dienst prints did not come in cereal boxes.

"How can I help you, Mr. Brock?" She spoke in a clear, neutral voice, returning his ID.

"I want to know if this person is, or has been in the recent past, a patron of the Oconee." He held out the picture he had shown to the blackjack dealer, but she did not take it or look at it and answered without smiling.

"I'm sorry, Mr. Brock, we cooperate to a certain extent with the Tequesta County police, but we don't identify our customers for private investigations. We believe people who come here to the Oconee are entitled to their privacy. So long as they break none of our laws, they are welcome. If they do, we have our own police force to deal with them."

Harry experienced a surprising mix of feelings when she finished speaking. He felt foolish and embarrassed. He had blundered into this place without thinking carefully. Surrounding this reaction were the quick flickerings of anger. Where, he asked himself, were they coming from?

"I'm sorry I troubled you."

"No trouble, Mr. Brock. Is there anything else I can do?"

It was his cue to leave.

The sun was blinding as he crossed the parking lot to the Rover. He thought about Ms. Jones and the Oconee and grudgingly admitted he had deserved the treatment he got and should be grateful it hadn't been a lot worse. But some of the anger, however unjustified, remained. The Oconee was a gambling casino. Move it twenty miles east or west, it would be a criminal enterprise.

Harry was climbing into the Rover when someone shouted. He looked around. Standing in the shade at the west corner of the casino was a man smoking a cigarette. No one else was in sight. Harry decided he did not want to walk over there. He started the Rover, slipped the automatic down between the door and his seat, and drove to the corner. The man slid into the rider's seat. It was the blackjack dealer.

"You know the guy in the picture?" Harry asked.

"He's not family. But I know him. You a cop?"

"No."

The man nodded. "Well, it's against policy, but I think I should tell you. He's dropping a lot of cash out here."

"How long has it been going on?" Harry asked.

"More than three years, maybe. That's how long I've been here. He in trouble with the law?"

"Not as far as I know."

"Okay. That's all I want to say about it."

"Thanks. What made you change your mind?"

"Lost a wife to gambling," the man answered stiffly. He got out and walked back around the corner of the building.

Driving back to Avola, Harry thought about the blackjack dealer's information and what he was going to do with it. He certainly wasn't going to say anything to Carter about it, and he wondered only briefly if he should pass the information along to Snyder. Carter's gambling might or might not have given him financial problems. One thing it didn't do was make him a suspect in Truly Brown's murder. But it might have something to do with Arthur Kraftmeier's calling Carter a crook. Harry felt his spirits slump. He suspected he had pursued the gambling lead to take his mind off Gideon Stone.

On Monday morning, Harry drove to Carter's office. Tiffany remembered him. Dressed in an ivory suit, she rose from the shadows behind her desk like a lotus from dark waters and took him straight to Carter's door. The banker was sitting with his feet on the desk, cleaning his fingernails with a jackknife. "Hey, fella, what brings you back?"

He dropped his feet onto the floor and came around the desk to shake hands.

"The Brown Trust. My client would like to know why the sale of the Brown properties is being held up," Harry said.

"If your client thinks . . ." Carter began loudly. Then he checked himself and lowered his voice, but Harry caught the glitter of anger in his narrowed eyes. "I'm putting my personal feelings aside for a moment to speak for the bank. Someone in this goddamned bank is trying to get a leg up on this land sale you're so interested in. Until I learn who it is and find out what their game is, the Brown Trust will not sell so much as a shovelful of dirt. You got that, Brock?"

"Am I right in thinking you see yourself threatened?"

"You bet your ass." When he went on, he was no longer talking like a good-old-boy. "Unless this disbursal occurs with complete transparency and utter probity, the bank collectively, and I personally, will be damaged. I'm not going to let that happen. Make sure your client understands that."

"How long a delay are you looking at?"

"Who the fuck knows? Get out of here, Brock."

After lunch, Harry drove out to see Findlay Jay. The rancher had just finished riding several miles of fence line in his pickup and climbed down from the mud-splashed truck wearing a wide grin and shook Harry's hand warmly. "I believe you've got some news," he said.

"I think I know how your cows were stolen, but I need to make one more measurement at the pasture gate to be sure."

"Get in," Findlay said. "I'll drive us over there."

Harry straightened up and slipped the tape measure back in his pocket. "Here's how they did it," he said. He turned his back to the fence and spread out his arms. "They backed a cattle trailer right up to this spot. This gate is a long inch shorter than the bed of a cattle trailer is high. That means they could drop the tailgate right into the pasture. Then they rode their horses down the ramp, loosed their dogs, rounded up your cattle, herded them up the ramp into the truck, rode their horses back into the trailer, called in their dogs, closed the tailgate, and drove away."

A slow grin broke the solemnity of Findlay Jay's face as Harry stopped speaking. "Lord of All," he said in an awed voice, "I believe you've treed the bear. Indeed I do. Now, if that don't leave the whole tribe walking." He regarded Harry with a look of delight, mingled with admiration.

Harry let himself bask in the glow of Findlay Jay's approval for a moment. Then he said, "What about letting me start looking for those cows?"

"Oh, I know where they are. Ernshaw Welty's got them Durhams." While he spoke, he was rummaging in the pockets of his shirt and his denims and finally pulled out a folded and crumpled note and handed it to Harry. "Here's his number. Just as soon as you call him and tell him how them cows was took, he'll truck them right back here."

"You mean someone you know rustled these cows?" Harry demanded. The question didn't begin to express his astonishment.

"Oh, yes. Ernshaw's a neighbor. There's been Weltys on that land since just after the Civil War. The Jays and the Weltys come down here from the Cumberland Gap country. Way back."

Harry thought he was having his leg pulled. "This is a

joke, right? I'm not sure I like . . ."

Findlay Jay showed sudden and deep concern. "It's no joke, Mr. Brock. Our two families have been feuding for something close to two hundred years. If I hadn't got you to figure out how those Durhams were rustled, Ernshaw would have kept them. No, it's not a joke. We're talking about twenty-five thousand dollars' worth of cattle, Mr. Brock."

"That's the craziest thing I ever heard of. Why do you put up with it?"

Findlay Jay chuckled, but Harry saw that the smile had gone out of the rancher's eyes. "Well, I've got his quarter horse, Jubilee. That stallion's got a stall full of blue ribbons, and a jump from Jubilee's going to cost you big-time. Three of my mares are carrying his foals right now. Ernshaw still hasn't figured out how I lifted the critter. It's been six months."

Harry thought that ought to be a lot funnier than he found it. There was something in the big man's voice that chilled him. "Sounds like a dangerous game to me."

"Oh, it's not so bad," Findlay Jay said. "Fifty years ago, we were shooting one another."

Chapter 14

That evening over supper, Harry told Katherine about Findlay Jay and his sense that the rancher and his neighbor were playing a dangerous game.

"You really can't help yourself, can you?" she demanded.

"What do you mean?"

Minna and Jesse abruptly stopped eating, their faces stiff with alarm.

Katherine threw her napkin onto the table. "I mean trouble draws you like manure draws flies."

"You can take the girl out of the country, but . . ."

"This isn't funny. Those bastards would kill you without so much as a blink. You don't know the first thing about them."

"I don't know Ernshaw Welty at all."

"Stop dodging. You don't know Findlay Jay either. They're poison."

Harry wasn't convinced, but he left it. Later, while he and Katherine were clearing away the remains of dinner, she said, "About my going home, do you really think I should do it?"

Harry risked a comment. "If you want to, why hold back? Your mother's ill, but you don't know how ill. If you go, it might ease your mind." He did not say that getting away from him and the Hammock might do them both some good.

Katherine put the last pan into the cupboard and re-
garded him with a frown. "You just don't understand,
Harry." Calling him by name signaled a formal moment.
He stopped wiping the counter and listened. "I left home
when I was seventeen. And I left to get away from her and
Priscilla. I felt I'd suffocate if I didn't."

"Sounds familiar."

"You don't take the past the way I do," she told him.
"You keep leaving it behind you as if it was only a place you
passed through on your way here. I don't know how best to
say it, but I owed Ma better than to leave the way I did. I
owed Priscilla more."

"Take the kids, go home, tell them both you're sorry,
not that you did anything very bad. Could you have stayed
there?"

"Maybe. Priscilla did."

"You have two fine children and another on the way because you left."

"You can have kids anywhere."

"Go see your mother. Ease up on yourself."

He put his arms around her. She leaned her body against
his, her thighs, belly, and breasts pressed against him. He
felt the tension draining out of her. She wrapped her arms
around him and rested her face on his shoulder. "God, it's
hard going," she whispered.

"It will be okay," he said, wanting to believe it.

An hour later, Harry was talking with Riga Kraftmeier.
He had put a new windshield in the Rover and arrived at
Riga's house with his face and hair free of squashed bugs.
To his surprise, instead of taking him to the study, she led
him into a large sitting room at the front of the house and
pointed him toward one of the two sofas arranged in an L

facing a glass-fronted fireplace. She was dressed in pale blue slacks and a long-sleeved white blouse. She wore no jewelry other than a gold necklace with an oval, gold locket. But it and her hair, falling in soft waves over her shoulders, were, Harry decided, all the ornamentation she needed.

Whatever Harry thought of Riga's personality, he found it a pleasure to look at her, and perhaps that was another reason why he came in person to deliver his messages. He thought about this as he sat down and was startled to find her studying him with an appraising eye, quite different from her usual cold stare.

"You saw Carter," she said.

Harry said he had, and gave her a summary of their conversation.

"But he didn't say how long the delay would be."

"No. I'm not sure I should say this, because it's guesswork, but I think he may suspect that I'm working for someone in the bank. Whether he knows or even suspects it's you, I can't say."

"How could he have found that out? Have you told anyone?"

"I told my wife, and you told Helen Bradley, and, perhaps, Burkhardt. But I am almost certain none of them would have told anyone else."

"But it would have to be one of them," Riga insisted.

Harry decided he did not want Katherine blamed. "Arthur knows I'm working for you."

She stared at him for a moment, apparently thinking. "Yes, he does."

"But it doesn't have to be any of them," Harry said. "Carter could have guessed. You were right. He's a lot smarter than he looks. Here's something else. Carter's angry. He hasn't stopped the Brown Trust resolution on a

130

whim. Something's gone wrong. I just don't know what."

"Is that all?"

Harry said it was and she stood up abruptly, her face rigid. Harry followed her to the door, wondering why she was angry, *if* she was angry. He waited until he was out of the house and then asked her if she was done with him.

"Why would you think that?" she demanded.

To Harry's surprise, she sounded hurt. "Nothing personal. I just thought my job might be finished, especially if your cover's blown."

"Is there some reason why you no longer want to work for me?"

"Of course not. I—"

"Then let me be judge of when the job, as you call it, is finished."

"Okay, but . . ."

She had already closed the door.

For the next two days, Harry dealt with paperwork that had been accumulating, and spent several long hours in the Assistant State Prosecutor's office in Avola, giving a deposition in a much-delayed fraud case in which he had worked for the plaintiff. He also decided to deliver his message to Ernshaw Welty in person, rather than do it by phone. Despite Katherine's warning, his curiosity about the man was too strong to resist.

Welty lived as far back in the woods as Findlay Jay, but the wooden fences on his horse ranch gave his place a more upscale look than the electric fencing on Findlay Jay's cattle spread. The man who met Harry in the yard of his sprawling house was short, wiry, and suspicious. His thin, weathered face was closed and his handshake brief.

"You carrying a message from Findlay Jay?" he demanded in a sharp, cracked voice.

"I'm surprised you know that," Harry said.

"You shouldn't be," Ernshaw answered. "Your name's around. And one of my hands seen you turning off the Yellow Willow Road. There ain't noplace but Findlay Jay's out there."

"I'm supposed to tell you that Findlay Jay knows how you lifted those Durham cattle."

Welty stiffened but otherwise gave Harry no hint of what the news meant to him. "How'd I do it?"

"Backed a stock trailer up to the fence gate, lowered the tailgate over it, loaded the cows, and drove away." Harry was going to say, 'Pretty slick,' but there was something in Welty's flat stare that stopped him.

"You figured it out," Welty said. His voice was flinty as his stare. "Findlay Jay's too dumb to have done it."

"Mr. Welty, when I took the job, I thought I was looking for rustlers." When Welty did not reply, Harry continued. "It wasn't until later that I found out Findlay Jay knew where his cows were. Had I known the particulars, I doubt I would have taken the job."

Welty balled his fists. "He's got Jubilee."

"I guess that's not a secret," Harry replied. "And my job's finished." Without offering to shake hands, he turned and walked back to the Rover. The hair on the back of his neck didn't stop prickling until he turned onto the main road.

On his way home, Harry stopped in Avola and bought an aquarium for Jesse. He had failed to halt the die-off in the tank that had advanced with the fatality of a red tide. In fact, the increasing cloudiness of the water, uninhibited by the filters, may have been an algae bloom. That, at least, was Jesse's conclusion, and the boy was becoming sufficiently knowledgeable about salt water aquariums to convince Harry he was probably right. Jesse's science teacher had a sample of the water and was having it tested in one of Avola's marine labs.

He and Harry had just finished setting up the new tank when Katherine called from the foot of the stairs. "Harry, Helen wants to talk to you."

"This weekend, I'll help you restock," Harry said. Jesse stepped back to look at the tank.

"And this time we quarantine every specimen before putting it in the tank," the boy added.

Harry dropped a hand on his shoulder with a surge of pride. "Right," he said. In the past year, Jesse's emotional and intellectual development had been impressive. Even Katherine admitted he was rapidly leaving childhood behind.

"I've been talking with Riga," Helen said when he picked up the phone. Then she stopped.

"Something wrong?" Harry thought she sounded troubled.

"I don't know. It seems wrong to be telling you things Riga's said to me. But I guess I'm going to." She stopped again.

Harry waited. The line hummed vacantly. "Helen?"

"I'm here. Look, Riga told me about your meeting with Carter. She thinks you're right. Carter probably was talking about her. She figures Arthur outed her, and now she's going to force the issue with Carter."

"How?" Harry demanded.

"She didn't say, and I didn't ask. But I think Arthur's really upset her. And I want you to keep her from doing anything that will get her into trouble at the bank."

"Did Riga tell you Arthur had talked to Carter?"

"No."

"Did she mention money?"

There was a pause. "I don't remember."

"Helen, do you know Riga's planning to buy Hobson's Choice?"

There was a pause. "Yes. And she and Arthur have been fighting over it. Arthur has been threatening to challenge her power of attorney."

He wasn't surprised. "Do you know what that power entails?"

"Jesus, Harry."

"It's your call," Harry said impatiently. There was something about Helen's involvement with Riga that troubled him, but he couldn't name it.

"Okay, when Helmut Kraftmeier died, he left both Riga and Arthur an equal amount of money. He left Janet the house and some money. I don't know any of the numbers. Then Arthur left. When Janet became incapable of managing her affairs, Riga got power of attorney to manage her mother's estate without consulting her brother. That meant the house as well as the cash. Today, the house is sitting on land worth over a million dollars. If Riga wants to remortgage the house, she can."

The gold ring, Harry thought. That's where some of the leverage to buy Hobson's Choice is going to come from. Or was, until Arthur showed up. "Thanks, that helps, but I wish I knew for sure whether or not Arthur has been talking to Carter."

"It sounds as if he's had some contact with him. How else would Carter have found out about Riga hiring you?"

"There's Tom Burkhardt."

"Not in a million years."

"Maybe. There's one more thing. When I asked Riga to describe her relationship with Carter, she almost took my head off. What's that about?"

"You keep poking buttons with her. When she first went to the bank, and before she met Tom Burkhardt, Ruvin made a real play for her. She wasn't interested, but he wouldn't give up and kept on with the flowers, the cards, tickets for the symphony, invitations to go out on the Gulf on his boat. He was a major pain in the ass. She didn't fully shake him until she began dating Tom."

"How did he take that?"

"Not good. I don't know what was said, but he and Riga don't speak unless they have to."

"Do Carter and Arthur have any history?"

"They've known one another most of their lives. They're pretty close in age. Helen doesn't talk much about her brother."

Harry went upstairs to read to Minna with the thought developing in his mind that Riga might be less in control of things than he had thought. Arthur might be her Achilles heel. Thwarted, would she do something foolish? He thought she might. She was a woman used to getting her own way.

Over the weekend, Harry and Jesse stocked the aquarium. He tried without much luck to get Katherine to show some interest in the project. She tried, but it wasn't really a success.

"It's okay," Jesse told Harry. "When she's feeling better, she'll like it."

Harry said, "Sure she will." But his knot of worry about Katherine pulled a little tighter.

On Monday morning, he got a telephone call from Snyder.

"Arthur Kraftmeier's dead," Snyder said. "His body was found at five this morning in the Seminole River, a mile south of Avola and a little north of Oyster Pass. And I'm calling you because I found a note from the deputy who called the Kraftmeiers, saying Riga Kraftmeier wanted you to be told as soon as possible. This is as soon as possible. Why does she want you involved?"

"Cause of death?" Harry gave himself a moment to answer Snyder's question.

"The back of his head was bashed in, and he was shot through the heart. Why does Riga Kraftmeier want you to know her brother's dead?"

"I'm working for her, and that's between you and me."

"Good try, Harry. What are you doing for her?"

"Right now, I'm not going there. Was he wearing a gun?"

"Yes. How would you know that?" Snyder's voice had cooled perceptively.

"Because he was wearing it the day I met him at Riga's house. If he wore it indoors, I figured he wore it outdoors. Had it been fired?"

"No. And that suggests he wasn't feeling threatened when he died."

"Why shoot him *and* beat his head in?"

"I don't know. Was Kraftmeier hiring you to gather information on her brother?"

"No."

"Okay. I'll talk to you later."

Harry called Riga.

Chapter 15

"Where's Arthur?" Janet Kraftmeier demanded. She was blocking the door and scowling at Harry.

Harry said he was sorry but he didn't know, which was true and not true.

Tom Burkhardt rescued him. "Come in," he said. "Riga will be here in a minute." Harry thought Burkhardt's face was registering a lot of strain and supposed Arthur's death was the cause. Burkhardt led Janet by the hand down the corridor. He stopped at a door, opened it, and said to Harry, "I'll put you in here for a moment while I take care of Janet. Then I'll make sure Riga knows you're here."

Harry looked around the small room with interest. A sewing machine stood in its case on a small table. A spindle-backed straight chair stood at an angle at the table, as if someone had just left, although there was no other sign the room had been used recently. Shelves of carefully folded cloth, pattern books, and wicker baskets lined one wall, and a small couch and a small chintz-covered chair occupied the opposite side of the room. Another mausoleum, Harry reflected.

"Come out," Riga said behind him.

Harry turned. She was dressed in tan shorts and a man's green shirt, its tails knotted at her waist. She wore no makeup, but her hair was carefully brushed. "I'm very sorry about your brother," he said.

"Thank you. Tom shouldn't have put you in this room."

She led him back up the corridor to the living room where they had last talked. "You're late." She did not sit down.

"Captain Snyder called about Arthur's death. Why did you want me notified?"

She was either unable or unwilling to answer him.

"What have the police told you?" he asked, breaking the impasse. In the room's dim light, it was hard for him to read her face, but she seemed to be in command of herself. He noted with interest that she looked less distressed than Burkhardt.

"What difference does that make?"

She seemed unable to break out of whatever was jamming her. He tried to be patient. "Because there are some things I want to be sure you know. Knowing what they've told you will help me decide how to go on."

"I'm not going to faint or have hysterics, if that's what worrying you."

"Never crossed my mind." To his surprise, she snapped her head around as if he had slapped her. "I'm sorry. That came out harsher than I intended."

She ignored the apology. "Just tell me what you think I should hear."

Harry took a deep breath. "Right. Have the police questioned you?"

"No. Why should they?"

He postponed his answer. "Did they question Burkhardt?"

"No."

"When they have the time of death, they will grill both of you. Was Arthur married?"

"No. Why should the police want to question me?" She appeared to be angry.

"Because you're the person who was closest to him. Because he was murdered. Because they are going to want to know everything you can tell them about Arthur's life. Why did he come home? What was your relationship with him?" He stopped himself.

"And because, whether they say so or not, I will be a suspect."

"You should get yourself a lawyer. If you want, I can suggest a good one." Harry expected to have his head taken off, but she surprised him.

"Who is it?"

"Jeff Smolkin of Smolkin, Barrett, and Klein. He represented Luis Mendoza some years back."

"You saved Mendoza's neck. Maybe you can save mine."

"Not funny."

"No? From the condition of Arthur's body, the police think he had been in the water between twenty-four and thirty-six hours. If they're right, he died sometime Saturday night or Sunday morning. He was found around five a.m."

"Who found him?"

"A fisherman."

"Were you here that night?"

Riga hesitated. "No."

Harry waited.

Riga pulled herself up. "I was with Helen Bradley."

"Can Burkhardt confirm that?"

"No."

"You were at her place all night?" Harry did his best to keep his voice matter-of-fact.

"From about six p.m. Saturday night until about seven Sunday morning." She avoided Harry's eyes.

The thought occurred to him that she might be lying. "Where was Cheryl?"

"Here with Tom."

"Get the lawyer," he said. "When are you going back to work?"

"Probably Wednesday. Thursday at the latest. I expect to have everything taken care of by then."

Harry nodded and wondered how she felt about her brother's death. He had questions about almost everything she'd told him, but they could wait.

"If I need you, I'll call," she said.

Harry called Helen at work.

"Have you heard about Arthur Kraftmeier?" he asked.

"Yes. It's gruesome. I can't stop thinking about it."

"Was Riga with you the night he was killed?"

The hesitation was brief, but Harry caught it. "That's right."

"All night?"

This time, Helen's answer was faster and a lot more forceful. "Yes."

Harry did not like the answer.

"Arthur was murdered. It's going to be a capital case. Do you know what the expression, 'accessory after the fact,' means?"

"You think I'm lying!" She was almost shouting.

"I'm sorry," Harry said. "Can we finish this conversation over lunch?"

"If you promise not to call me a liar."

As always, Helen was on time. As soon as they had ordered, Harry said, "There's no painless way to hear what I've got to say, but I'll say it as quickly as I can."

"Just don't call me a liar."

"I won't. Unless something unusual happens, Riga is going to be a prime suspect in her brother's murder. And unless you tell the police the truth about where you were when the murder took place and, if you know, where Riga was on Saturday night, you will be in almost as much trouble as she is."

Helen gripped the edge of the table so hard her knuckles were white. "Are you saying the police think Riga killed Arthur and that I helped her do it?"

"No. Unless there is an overriding reason not to—and I don't think there is here—the police look first at the people closest to the victim."

She started to protest. Harry cut her off. "Try thinking about it as if you were Jim Snyder." She made a face. Harry ignored it. "Arthur Kraftmeier comes back to Avola after a very long absence; he and his sister Riga quarrel seriously over money and over her power of attorney. There are at least two credible witnesses to these fights. He is shot. Who would you think of as the principal suspect, knowing as you would, if you were Jim Snyder, that most crimes of violence are committed against one family member by another?"

Helen flushed and averted her eyes. "Who will tell them Riga and Arthur quarreled?"

"I will, and so will Burkhardt."

She gasped. "You! Why would you do such a thing?"

"Because if I'm asked, I have to tell the truth. And so do you, unless you want to run the risk of being charged with obstruction of justice and possibly perjury. Were you involved in Kraftmeier's death?"

"God, Harry, of course I wasn't. You couldn't possibly . . ."

"Helen, it doesn't matter what I could or couldn't think. What matters is what conclusions the police will draw, if they find you've lied to them."

Harry watched anger, fear, and anger again, run like clouds over Helen's face. She squirmed in her chair and then flung herself back as if he had cornered her.

"Riga didn't kill her brother," she said in a defiant voice.

"Good. You've told me the truth. At least as far as you know it. Keep on doing it."

Harry came away from lunch with a knot in his stomach and no better understanding of what Helen and Riga were up to than he had when he called her. Helen refused to tell him why Riga had been with her or why Tom Burkhardt couldn't confirm Riga's whereabouts on Saturday night.

"You're not being much help," he said finally in disgust.

"Too bad," she said.

In fact, beyond saying Riga had spent the night with her, she refused to discuss the night at all. By the time Harry dropped her at the bank, she was white as a sheet and silent as a mummy.

Thoroughly disgruntled, Harry drove straight to Tucker's farm. Tucker was in his bee yard pulling up pigweeds.

"This stuff grows faster than toadstools," the farmer said, holding a handful of weeds in one hand and shaking Harry's hand with the other. Bees going to and from the hives zipped and buzzed around the two men. Tucker paid no attention, but Harry was keenly aware of their presence and tried to move as little as possible as he shook hands.

"Where's your help?" Harry asked. Sanchez and Oh-Brother! were not in sight.

"They're babysitting Weissmuller," Tucker replied. He bent down and put his arms around the bundle of weeds at his feet and headed for a compost pile. "Let's see how the patient is getting along."

"You still throwing meat to him over the fence?" Harry asked.

"Oh, nothing so dramatic as that," Tucker said.

They walked around the barn to the kennel. Sanchez was close to the fence and Oh-Brother! was standing close to Sanchez, watching what Tucker called "the patient." Harry was waiting for Weissmuller to begin roaring at their approach, but, to Harry's surprise, the big dog went on sitting under Oh-Brother!'s nose. All three animals observed Harry and Tucker's approach calmly. Oh-Brother! waggled his ears at Harry and Sanchez thumped his tail on the ground.

"I don't believe it," Harry said. He approached the fence hesitantly, but Weissmuller, his head still bandaged, continued to sit with his tongue hanging out, panting contentedly. "How did you do it?"

"Most of the credit goes to Oh-Brother! and Sanchez. They've put in the hours, talking things over with him, listening to what he had to say, and now and then dropping in a suggestion." Tucker regarded the three animals with a benevolent smile. "It's astonishing what a little sympathetic care and understanding can accomplish."

"You don't go in there with him," Harry said.

"Oh, yes. I change his bandage every day, hose down the floor, and give him his food and water. He's a changed animal. Sanchez and Oh-Brother! think Weissmuller got the way he was from being overly protective of Truly."

"What about the cats?"

Tucker sighed. "I doubt he'll ever be altogether reliable where cats are concerned. He doesn't like to talk about it, and Sanchez says some dogs are like that, and there's not much that can be done about it."

"He's probably right," Harry said, and then pulled himself up short. The change in Weissmuller might be almost miraculous, but Harry was not ready to begin talking about what the dogs said to one another. He was far enough down

Tucker's rabbit hole as it was. "Something's happened that I'd like to discuss with you."

"All right. Let's get into the shade. I'll make us some tea."

When they were settled on the back stoop, Harry brought Tucker up to date on Arthur Kraftmeier's death, Arthur's contact with Ruvin Carter, and Harry's most recent meeting with Riga.

"There was no love lost between Riga and Arthur, and I was witness to one nasty scene between them. I gathered they'd been quarreling ever since Arthur came home," he concluded.

Tucker sipped his tea and sat quietly for a moment, looking out into the patch of slash pine and saw palmetto woods bordering the back of the house, watching a big pileated woodpecker swooping from tree to tree. The bird was calling harshly as it pried and hammered chips of pine bark off the trunks of the trees in search of grubs. Deeper in the woods, another woodpecker answered cry for cry.

"Talking to one another while they work," Tucker said. He smiled at Harry. "It's hard to judge accurately what's going on in a family. They're private spaces. No matter what you think you've seen, the reality is generally something else."

"I'd settle for knowing why Helen Bradley is providing Riga Kraftmeier with an alibi for the night Arthur was killed."

"Until you can prove they weren't together, Occam would tell you to believe Helen."

"Believing her may be the simplest answer, but I don't believe it's the right one."

"Do you think Riga Kraftmeier killed her brother?" Tucker poured himself more tea and raised the pot toward Harry.

Harry declined. The one swallow of tea he'd taken had made him break out in a sweat. "I don't know."

"All right, here's a more interesting question," Tucker said. "Are Arthur and Truly's deaths connected?"

"Ruvin Carter, Riga Kraftmeier, Tom Burkhardt," Harry said. "They're connected to both dead men."

Tucker nodded. "Of course, the police are too. Doesn't mean someone in the Sheriff's Department killed them."

Harry laughed. "Who benefits from their deaths?"

"Not so obvious," Tucker replied.

Harry got to his feet. "That makes it sound more interesting than it really is. When Truly was killed, Riga was given a chance to bid on the Hobson's Choice property. Carter had to begin dissolving the Brown Trust. He doesn't seem to be in a hurry to do that. Is he dragging his feet? If so, why? If Arthur was trying to blackmail Carter, his death eliminates at least one of Carter's problems."

Tucker frowned.

"And if Riga Kraftmeier believed Arthur was capable of breaking her lock on her mother's estate . . . well, maybe she did have a motive for killing him." Harry drank some tea and instantly regretted it. "Did she kill Truly to dissolve the Brown Trust?"

"I believe the Trinity are means, motive, and opportunity," Tucker responded.

"Jim Snyder's not going beyond her quarrel with her brother to look for a motive. He would drop-kick me out of his office, if I was to suggest she killed Truly to get the opportunity to bid on Hobson's Choice in an estate sale. And I think he'd be right to do it."

"Maybe. What about Tom Burkhardt? You passed over him pretty lightly."

"It's possible the quarrel between Riga and her brother

turned nasty enough for Tom to shoot Arthur, but I can't really believe it."

Tucker nodded and gave the subject a quarter-turn. "Has Jim Snyder said anything to you about the investigation into Truly's death?"

"They rounded up half a dozen of those bums Truly hung out with, but so far they don't have a thing. According to Jim, most of them can't remember back as far as Truly's murder. Of course it doesn't mean they didn't kill him."

"Where would they get a gun?"

"Good question. But there are enough guns in southwest Florida to arm a small nation."

"True," Tucker said with a snort of amusement. He stood up with Harry. "You don't know enough yet to reach a decision. Sleep on it. Do some more looking. As for Helen and Riga, I wonder if what you call the alibi has anything at all to do with Arthur's death?"

"Riga could have had a fight with Burkhardt and taken the night off," Harry agreed. He shook hands with Tucker and went back to the Rover by way of Weissmuller's kennel. He said goodbye to Sanchez and Oh-Brother!, marveled again at Weissmuller's transformation, and thought as he left, That dog knows who killed Truly Brown. And by now he's probably told Sanchez and Oh-Brother!.

"Get a grip," he muttered as he hurried toward the Rover.

As he had promised, Harry met Katherine in her obstetrician's office. Esther Benson was small, freckled, and intense. After she had made a brief examination of Katherine, she dropped into her chair as if flung there and said, "How are you holding up?" She ignored Harry. Katherine told her she wasn't sleeping well. Benson leaned forward in her chair, hung her stethoscope around her neck, and said, "It doesn't surprise me. Your pulse is up, your blood pressure is up, and you're tight as a drum head. I could give you medication, but let's try to get along without it. I want you to walk at least two miles every day until I tell you to stop. And make that husband of yours walk with you. Maybe you can shrink that donut around his middle."

Harry put up his hand.

"Yes?"

"Watch it, Benson."

"You watch it, or I'll have you in the stirrups."

Katherine scowled at them.

"It's O.K., Honey," Benson said. She gave Katherine an exaggerated smile. "You've got to keep them down or they'll walk all over you." She turned to Harry. "Out of here. Your wife and I want some privacy."

A few minutes later, Benson came into the waiting room and motioned to Harry. He followed her into an empty examination room. "I don't want to scare you, Harry," she said quietly, "but I'm not happy with Katherine's condition. Physically, there's nothing alarming, other than what I said in my office to both of you. But emotionally, she seems to be running on empty."

"I know. Have you got any suggestions?" he asked.

"Maybe a change of scene. Can you take her away for a while?"

"Probably not. Has she told you about her mother?"

"No."

"That doesn't surprise me. She's developed some heart trouble, may have to stop working, and is not dealing well with the changes. Katherine is worried about her. I've been trying to get her to make a visit."

Benson shook her head. She checked her watch.

"Time's winged chariot," Harry said.

"What?"

"Should she make the trip?"

Benson sighed. "It's her call, but she might be better off going to see her mother than chewing the worry bone. Keep trying. And make sure she takes the walks."

On their way home, Katherine said, "You told her about Ma, didn't you?"

Harry braced himself. "Yes, I did. She asked me why you were so distressed."

"That's not her business." Katherine stared straight ahead as she spoke.

"Maybe not, but you are. And if worry over your mother is complicating your pregnancy and endangering your health, maybe it's better that Benson knows about it."

"Am I to blame for this?" she asked quietly.

"No," Harry said quickly. "But I do think . . ."

"I know what you think, and maybe you're right."

"It's okay," he said.

"Dream on," she answered.

Chapter 16

The morning began badly. The problems between Katherine and Harry had not been solved by a night's sleep, and she went off to work without either of them saying goodbye. For a few moments, Jesse and Minna went on eating their breakfasts in silence. Then Minna pushed away her cereal bowl.

"This place is getting really weird," she said.

"Your mother's not feeling good," Harry said sharply. "We've all got to be patient and helpful."

"What are you two fighting about?" Jesse asked. He carried his bowl to the sink, and Harry passed him his lunch box. Minna took hers and stood, looking up at him with a solemn expression.

"We're not fighting. There's nothing going on here for you to worry about," Harry said. He tried to sound cheerful. "We're all fine."

"Old Man Rabbit gives that a raspberry," Minna replied as she headed for the door.

Jesse looked at Harry. Harry gave up and grinned. Jesse grinned back. Harry went out with them.

"You guys and Old Man Rabbit have a great day," he called after them as they crossed the bridge to the waiting bus.

Harry saw the note on the Rover's hood as soon as he entered the yard. It was held down by a grapefruit-sized rock. The Rover was parked under the big corner oak and, walking across the grass to it, Harry wondered if the note had been there when he left the house with Minna and Jesse or whether Gideon had put it there while he was gone. And if he had, was he still here? Without looking around, Harry shrugged off the question. If Gideon had been waiting for him and had wanted to kill him, he'd already be dead. He tossed the rock into the woods and read the note.

Let's settle this.

The note went on with directions, telling Harry where to find him. He put the note in his pocket, experiencing a sense of relief. He had been freed to act. While getting ready to leave, he thought through what he was going to do. Back in the kitchen again, he wrote Katherine a note.

If I'm not here when you get home, tell Snyder to look for me on the Crawford River oxbow. I love you.

Harry.

He read it over and thought it was a little skinny, but, unable to think of anything else to say, he pinned it on the message board and left. A few minutes later, he drove the Rover over the bridge and turned north. For an instant the thought entered his mind that he might never cross that bridge again, but he pushed it away.

He assumed Gideon wanted to kill him and, although a part of his mind told him what he was doing was stupid, something in him, powerful and unresponsive to argument, was driving him toward this meeting with Stone. He knew that the sensible thing was to call Snyder. But he had no intention of calling Snyder. It was his problem. He would deal with it.

More than anything else, possibly even more than going on living, he wanted Jacob Stone and his death laid permanently to rest. Gideon's arrival on the Hammock had revived Harry's worst memories of Jacob's death and its consequences. He had buried Jacob once. He would bury him again. This time, he intended to drive a stake through his heart. Harry pushed the Rover north.

The narrow dirt tracks finally ran out in front of a cabin half-buried in a tangle of low trees crowding up from the Crawford River. Harry let the Rover coast to a stop under a pin oak and sat for a moment studying the scene before him.

The cabin was a low, weathered, lapstrake rectangle of unfinished boards, with a screened porch at the front and a ragged tarpaper roof sagging under the weight of a profligate jasmine vine. Rusted screening hung in tatters from the porch, and its door sagged open on a single hinge.

Gun in hand, Harry eased out of the Rover. The cabin and the surrounding woods were still as a painting. The air was heavy with the smell of wet pine needles. A twist of blue smoke rose from the chimney, and a flicker of wind brought Harry the oddly domestic aroma of fried bacon. The smell broke his concentration. He paused by the Rover and considered driving away, but he knew it was not a viable choice.

He looked around and saw that the blue Dodge sedan with the Maine plates parked to the left of the cabin was not the car Stone had been driving the night he shot the windshield out of the Rover. Harry walked slowly toward the cabin. He held the gun in his right hand, its barrel pointed at the ground.

"Just keep coming, Brock," a heavy voice said from within the cabin.

The voice failed to startle Harry. The calm that had come with finding Stone's note had continued to grow. Stepping off the porch into the cabin's dimmer light, Harry breathed the musty air and was instantly transported into an older, darker, but hauntingly familiar world. By the light from the two small windows on each side of the cabin, he saw Gideon Stone's hulking form seated behind a table set in the middle of the floor. Stone's broad hands were spread on the table top, and between them lay a heavy revolver.

"Your move, Gideon," Harry said.

"I was about your boy's age when you shot Jacob," the big man said.

"Jesse is my second wife's child."

"Seeing him took me back," Stone said, undeflected. "I didn't expect that."

Harry guessed Stone had seen the boy getting on the bus or coming home. He felt a flare of anger but suppressed it. The gun hung heavily in his hand.

"I came down here to kill you." Stone stood up but left his revolver lying on the table.

His voice was deep and flat. Harry had been prepared for rage, but he couldn't tell whether that was what he was facing or not. In the dim light the big man's face conveyed no message, and his heavy, sloping shoulders and thick arms expressed no obvious tension. Harry was puzzled.

"Just to be sure you know," he said. "I'm holding a gun."

"I see it." Stone seemed to have paused to gather his thoughts. "After you killed Jacob, we lost all we had, not that we had much to lose."

Harry wondered if Stone was working himself up to do what he had come to do. He thought for a moment that perhaps he should shoot Stone and get it over with.

"You just walked away from all that," Stone added.

"Not quite. I lost my job, my wife, and both children. Not that it bears on this."

"You want me to feel sorry for you?"

Harry made up his mind about something. "Just setting the record straight. And while I'm doing that, I'll repeat something you've already heard. Your brother tried to kill me. I tried to shoot him in the leg to stop him. The bullet hit bone, broke up, and a piece went through his heart and killed him."

"Do you care at all about that?"

"For what it's worth, I've regretted it every day of my life since the day it happened. But my being sorry hasn't changed anything."

Stone scratched his chin through the tangle of dark beard. "This hasn't worked out the way I intended."

"No?"

"I planned to kill you."

"So you said. You didn't miss by much."

"I believe I missed on purpose."

"Well, for what it's worth, I'm sorry about what happened to all of you. It wasn't your fault Jacob decided to shoot me."

Stone was fast for such a big man. He swept up the gun and pointed it in a single, fluid movement. Harry jerked up his own weapon and spun away, knowing he was too slow, and already flinched against the shock of a bullet ripping into him. But Stone didn't fire. Instead, he let his revolver sink slowly to his side. Catching his balance, Harry pulled the automatic away from its target. What the *hell* was going on?

Stone frowned at Harry. "Driving down here from Parmachenee Lake must have changed things," he said in a half-apologetic, half-disgusted tone. "I just can't shoot you."

Harry almost said, I'm sorry. That made him want to laugh. He decided instead just to keep quiet and go on hoping his heart would settle back into his chest. It was possible Stone might go for a third try and make it. He didn't ask himself why he hadn't shot Stone.

"What I think is it made a kind of a hill for me to stand on," Stone continued after a pause. "Things began to look different to me." He put his gun back on the table. "Unless you've got some other plan in mind," he said, "I believe I'd like to let this end just as things are."

"It may not be possible," Harry said.

"We don't have to make it any worse," Stone said quietly.

"That's true," Harry agreed. "But there's an APB out on you." He thought a minute. "Of course, they're not looking for the blue Dodge. If you can get out of the state, I think you'll be safe."

"Who knows I'm here?"

"Until about five this afternoon, only the two of us."

"That's what I figured. I drove down here. I guess I can drive back."

"I'm going to put on the safety and slide this gun under my belt," Harry said.

Stone nodded.

"I know the officer in charge. I'll see what I can do to call it off."

Stone seemed perplexed.

"Are you sure you're all right about this?" Harry asked.

"I guess I am. It's like I'm walking on thin ice. I keep expecting to break through."

"The idea is to keep moving," Harry said, and immediately felt foolish.

"Yes, but it don't always work."

"No. Are you married?"

"I was. But there wasn't any kids. I didn't want any. She did."

"I'm sorry."

"You get used to things. But I never expected to have to get used to letting you live."

"Do you think you can do it?"

Gideon rubbed his face as if he was wiping away cobwebs. "I guess I'll have to. Killing you don't seem to be in the cards."

It was over. "I'll be going," Harry said.

Gideon nodded.

Harry started to turn away, then paused. "You might want to shave that beard till you're back at the lake," Harry said, and turned away.

He had reached the door when Gideon's voice stopped him.

"Take care of the boy."

Harry grasped the door frame and looked back. "I'll do that. Good luck, Gideon."

Chapter 17

Harry returned home to find Katherine's Rava and Jim Snyder's CID car in the yard. He jumped out of the Rover and ran into the house.

"Katherine," he shouted from the lanai.

She met him at the kitchen door, white-faced. Jim was behind her, scowling like a judge.

"What's wrong?" Harry demanded.

Katherine held up his note. For a moment he did not remember what it was. Then he did.

"Why are you home?" he asked.

"I wasn't feeling well. I decided to come home. And I came home to this." She shook the note at him.

"Why are you here, Jim?"

"Katherine read the note."

"Shit! Have you sent anybody out there?"

"I was just going to make the call."

"Don't do it." He pushed past Katherine. "It's over. He didn't try to kill me. He's going back to Parmachenee Lake. You'll never hear from him again."

"Hold it." Katherine grabbed Harry's arm. "What are you talking about?"

"Gideon Stone," Harry said, lowering his voice.

"Who?"

"The man who shot out his windshield," Jim said in a disgusted voice.

"He was not trying to kill me," Harry insisted.

156

Jim started to speak but Katherine said, "No!" and stepped between the two men, making a big T with her hands.

"Harry," she said, "talk to me."

"There's nothing to tell," Harry insisted.

Katherine looked at Jim.

"He wouldn't let me tell you. I told him to tell you himself, but he wouldn't."

She turned back to Harry. "You knew all along who took those shots at you?"

"Yes." He gave up. "It was Gideon Stone. Gideon is Jacob Stone's brother."

"That wild man you shot when you were in Maine?"

"Yes."

"Okay. How did you know it was Gideon? He must have been a child when you killed his brother."

"He left me a note." Jim opened his mouth. "Two notes," Harry said.

"I want to see them," Katherine said.

"Look, if you're not feeling good . . ." That was a mistake. "I'll get them," he told her.

Katherine sat down at the kitchen table and opened the manila folder. She looked up at him and said, "After I left for work, you went to meet this man."

Harry nodded.

"My God! Minna and Jesse have been walking alone back and forth to the bus with this idiot loose."

"No," Harry said quickly. "Since the first note, I've walked them both ways. I put them on the bus and I took them off."

Katherine dropped back into her chair. "That's something," she said, "but how did you know where to find him?"

"He left me another note. Probably last night."

She held out her hand. Harry gave it to her. Jim read over her shoulder. "He doesn't sound as angry in this one," the detective said.

"You couldn't know what he was going to do," Katherine insisted. "He might have been waiting out there to kill you."

"I didn't think so," Harry said.

"You took your gun."

"I thought it was the prudent thing to do."

"If you were going to do it at all, it made sense to go armed," Jim agreed.

"Prudent!" she said, shaking her head. "It made sense! Are you both insane?" She suddenly shut her eyes and pushed her hands out in front of her.

"But we settled things between us," Harry protested. "He's going home. It's over."

Katherine opened her eyes and dropped her hands. She looked at Harry. "I'm going upstairs, and if you value your life, which you clearly don't, stay away from me until I say different."

When the bedroom door slammed behind her, Harry blew out his breath. "Can you rescind the APB that's out on Gideon?"

Jim rubbed his head. "Why would I do that? The man tried to kill you."

"No, he didn't."

"He shot out the Rover's windshield."

"He'd changed his mind. It was just that when he picked up the gun, he didn't know that he had."

"Didn't know he'd picked up the gun?" Jim asked, incredulous.

Harry shook his head. "Changed his mind."

Jim's ears were red again. "Let's see. I go to Sheriff Fisher and I say, 'Bob, Harry Brock wants us to pull the APB on Gideon Stone. He says while Stone was picking up and aiming his gun at his head, he changed his mind about killing him and shot out the Rover's windshield instead. He and Gideon have talked it over. There's no hard feelings. Gideon's gone home and we should just forget it.' "

Harry sighed. "Do you have any idea how far it is to Parmachenee Lake?"

"No, but I got an idea trying to check on him. Rangeley was as close as I could get. Okay. He's going all the way back there."

"That's right. All the way. He won't be back."

Jim studied the ceiling for a while. "We're shorthanded and short of money. I'll see what I can do. If somebody falls over the guy, there'll be an arrest," he warned. "Otherwise, not. He probably should lose the beard."

"I told him that."

Harry walked Snyder to his car. Snyder pulled open the door, then stopped. "You feel up to talking about the Kraftmeier murder?"

"Of course."

"Your client isn't being helpful. Do you know why not?"

"No. She isn't all that communicative with me."

"And Helen Bradley's no help either," Snyder complained.

"Did she tell you Riga spent the night with her?"

Snyder nodded.

"Do you think Riga killed her brother?" Harry asked.

Jim shrugged. "Her alibi is obviously phony." He glanced at the house. "I need to ask you some questions. Do you have to go back in there?"

"Eventually, I guess. But we can talk."

When they were settled in Snyder's police car, he said, "By rights this should happen in the office, but I think we can make do here." He put a tape recorder on the dash and turned it on. They went through the routine of identifying the speakers and the date. At first, the questions established Harry's relationship with Riga Kraftmeier. When that was done, Snyder settled into the serious part of the interview.

"Why did Ms. Kraftmeier hire you?"

Harry explained the work he had done for her, and explained that he had always met with her in her house.

"Was Arthur Kraftmeier ever present at these meetings?"

"Once."

"Describe what happened."

Harry described the exchange between Riga and her brother. When he was finished, Jim asked, "Did she ever tell you where she was the night of her brother's murder?"

"At Helen Bradley's house." He gave the times.

"Have you asked Ms. Bradley to confirm what Ms. Kraftmeier told you?"

"Yes. She confirmed it."

"Why did Ms. Kraftmeier spend the night with Ms. Bradley?"

"I don't know."

Snyder checked his watch, made a note of the time, turned off the recorder, and only then said, "Shit."

"That's what I said," Harry responded.

"You asked?"

"Both of them. They refuse to say."

"It may not matter, but if they're lying . . ."

Harry did not miss the way Snyder doubled their names. Snyder turned the recorder on and gave the time the questioning resumed. It went quickly.

"I was afraid I was going to hear just what I did hear,"

Snyder said gloomily when they were finished.

"Have you questioned Helen?"

Snyder nodded. "She's either not cooperating, lying, or I'm missing something I shouldn't be. Why won't they say why Kraftmeier was not home that night?"

"Strong-minded women."

"Is that supposed to make me feel better?"

"Worse," Harry said. "Have you talked to Tom Burkhardt?"

"Oh, yes. He and Riga Kraftmeier must have rehearsed their stories. It's the only way they could be so completely in agreement about what they remember about the night of Arthur Kraftmeier's death."

"How much do you think Burkhardt's involved?"

"My guess is not much. He seems to me to be very much on the fringe of things in that house, even if he is physically in the center of it."

Harry thought Jim was on target, but he also thought it would be easy to misread Tom Burkhardt. "My concern is to protect Riga, as far as I legally can. If I find out she did kill her brother, I'll tell you. But I'm hoping she didn't. And if she's not the shooter, she's in considerable danger. But from where?"

Snyder shook his head and put out his hand. "Stay in touch." He paused and glanced at the house. "Good luck."

"Thanks."

Harry went into the house and slowly walked up the stairs. Katherine was sitting in their bedroom. The door was open. She was looking out one of the back windows. Scrub jays were flickering through the live oaks, making their usual racket.

The floor creaked under his feet and, without turning,

she said, "Come in." She had changed into white draw-string shorts and an orange jersey. When she got up and walked to another chair, her clothes looked a size too big for her. Harry picked up the chair she had been sitting in and put it down facing her.

"Thanks for looking after the kids," she said. She rose from her chair, her gaze averted, one hand pressed against the side of her face.

She looked bruised and miserable and seriously in need of comforting. He half rose to put his arms around her.

"I'm feeling pretty bad," she said, and leaned back to look at him. "You shut me out, Harry. You lied to me. You said you never would and you did."

Her stare reminded Harry of the way Jennifer had glared at him when he came home after shooting Jacob Stone. It was a bad time for that memory to surface.

"I never lied to you," he said. "Possibly I was wrong not to tell you about Stone. I thought I could spare you the worry, which is different from lying to you."

"If I'd known about the notes and that Stone was here, I would have had something to say about your going off alone to confront him," she continued. "Okay, it worked out, but you might have been killed. Were you thinking at all about Minna and Jesse and me?"

"Everything I did, I did after thinking about you three first. Also, I have a history with Gideon Stone. Sure, he might have killed me. But I really thought that if that was what he wanted to do, he would have done it the night he blew out the Rover's windshield."

It was a long speech and Katherine listened. When he was finished, she nodded. "That sounds good, and you may believe it, but I think you did what you did because that was what you wanted to do. I think the rest came afterward."

"And I guess you've decided to believe what you want to believe," he said.

A dog barked. Harry went onto the lanai and found Sanchez at the door, wagging his tail and grinning. There was a message pinned to his blue bandanna collar. Harry read it. Then he checked his pockets for his car keys. "Come on," he said.

"You're not looking too good," Tucker said. "More trouble with Stone?"

They were standing beside Weissmuller's run, looking at the big dog. Weissmuller was watching them with interest. Oh-Brother! and Sanchez were standing close to the two men, their noses pushed against to the wire. Harry told Tucker what had happened. "I think I've got Snyder persuaded to take the teeth out of the APB," he concluded, "but Katherine's pretty upset."

"You sure you ought to be over here right now?"

"I don't think I'll be missed."

Tucker frowned. "Katherine's blaming you for what's happened?"

Harry nodded.

"You've explained why you didn't tell her about the notes."

"It was entered into evidence against me."

Tucker made a face. "Sometimes, there's nothing to do but wait."

"Well, you told me to tell her," Harry replied. "But I didn't listen. What is it you want to talk to me about?"

"Our trustee." Tucker gestured at Weissmuller.

"As long as it doesn't involve me going in there with him, I'm willing to listen."

Tucker laughed. "No. It involves bringing Weissmuller

out here and seeing what happens."

"Oh, no!"

"Now just take it easy," Tucker said. "There's no more harm in that dog than there is in Sanchez. And for a dog who speaks English as a second language, he's about as reliable as they come."

Harry looked down to find Sanchez grinning at him. He looked up and there was Oh-Brother!, ears pricked, studying him. "This is a setup," Harry said. "What have you got in mind?"

"I go in and put a choke collar on him." He walked over to a box and lifted from it several feet of calf chain. "Then I anchor it to this length of wood." Like a conjurer, he reached into the box and came up with a three-foot length of peeled oak limb about four inches thick. "We each take hold of an end of this stick and, with Weissmuller between us, we walk our charge around the yard here for a while. I don't trust to my strength alone to hold him if he decides to bolt. With you on the other end, we might just about hold him."

"And you don't think he'll chew a leg off one or both of us?"

"Never happen. Oh-Brother! wouldn't stand for it."

Harry decided not to go there. "Okay. And if things deteriorate, I want 'I told you so' put on my tombstone." Tucker grinned and Sanchez barked appreciatively. Oh-Brother! merely twitched an ear.

The walk went off without a hitch. Weissmuller trotted between the two men with his head up and his tail erect, taking in the sights with apparent pleasure. When he was released back into his kennel run, Harry laughed with relief. "I expected to be dragged through the saw palmetto and left for the ants."

"He had a certain amount of personal history to over-come, but I'd say love and understanding have done their work well," Tucker said, putting away the chain and the stick.

Harry watched Weissmuller give himself a good shake and then settle down for a nap. "Helen and Katherine both say he knows who killed Truly Brown, and, I suppose, he does."

Both men paused to look at the dozing animal and Tucker asked, "I wonder what Truly would think of his dog now?"

When Harry got home, Katherine was in the kitchen making lunch. She had set a place for Harry.

"Priscilla called. She said Ma is worse. The doctor told her unless she's willing to be treated, there's nothing more he can do for her."

"I'm sorry. Are you still thinking about going to see her?" Harry asked.

"Yes," she answered.

Harry said, "Good," and counted his blessings.

Chapter 18

The following week, Katherine asked Harry to move into the spare bedroom. She said it was because she was sleeping so badly, but Harry thought that was only part of it. Although she had tried to hide it, he knew the business with Gideon Stone had upset her. He filled his hours with work. Fortunately or not, there was more than he could easily handle. He had, however, been able to do very little with or for Riga. Both with him and with the police, she remained monosyllabic on the matter of her brother's death.

But because of the increased pressure of the police presence in her life, she finally took Harry's advice and hired a lawyer. Disgusted with their failure to develop any other, more fruitful leads, and unable to convince the District Attorney they had a viable case against Riga Kraftmeier, the Sheriff's Department turned to other labors. *The Banner* stopped covering Arthur Kraftmeier's murder and moved on to fresher carrion. Riga got Harry's full attention by telling him she planned to put the iron into Ruvin Carter.

"I've filed suit against the bank and named him in the suit," she said.

"Aside from getting yourself fired, what do you hope to accomplish?" Harry asked.

She almost smiled. "They're not going to fire me, Harry. They're vulnerable, and they know it. The terms of the Brown Trust call for a liquidation. Carter's dragging his feet. He knows it. The bank knows it. The suit's not going to trial, but it will light a fire under everybody's tail."

Harry laughed. "Just make sure you're not the one burned."

They were sitting in Riga's back garden. The banana trees and elephant ear philodendrons gave the space a radically tropical look, which contrasted nicely with the rose trellis under which they were sitting. Harry looked from her to the flowers, the manicured grass, and the lacquered hummingbirds darting among the roses. Glancing back at Riga, he mentally gave her the golden apple.

"Are you trying to frighten me?" she asked.

"Two people who have been connected to Hobson's Choice are dead."

"Aside from that?"

"Very funny. I'm not trying to frighten you. I don't want to frighten you. That said, I wouldn't be doing my job if I didn't tell you that I think you're at risk. And it doesn't help that you're telling the police you spent the night of your brother's murder with Helen Bradley."

"It's true." Her blue gaze was steady and calm.

Harry admitted that if she was lying, she was amazingly skilled at it. "Riga, no one believes you."

She smiled very slightly. "Wrong. Helen believes me. Tom believes me. So does my mother, but, unfortunately, she no longer counts."

"Why did you spend the night with Helen Bradley?"

When her silence became too irritating, Harry got up. So did she. He said, "The police know you and Arthur were quarreling before he was killed. You told them. I confirmed it. So did Tom. And Helen. They haven't got anybody else. You're their main suspect."

"There's Ruvin," she answered.

They were walking toward the house.

"Where's the motive?"

"Blackmail."

Harry stopped. "Is there something you're not telling me?" he demanded.

"No, but you heard him call Ruvin a crook. He went to see Ruvin." She looked at Harry quizzically. "Can't you do something with that?"

Harry shook his head. "Arthur can't confirm or deny it. Carter will certainly deny it. It's a blind alley."

"Too bad," she said. "I guess I'll just have to go on being Suspect Number One."

Harry began walking again. A cardinal was singing from the corner of the house roof. Harry suddenly stopped and turned to face Riga. She almost bumped into him. Harry could smell the sun on her and see the faint sheen of sweat on her skin. She made no effort to step back. "Riga, did anything that happened between you and Ruvin Carter give him cause to hate you?"

Standing this close to her, looking into her eyes, Harry had to make a major effort to keep his mind on what he'd just asked her.

"It's not an easy question to answer. Several years ago, Ruvin and I began going out together. He wanted me. I didn't want him. In the end, I had to say so. He had some trouble accepting it."

"Did he threaten you?"

"No. How did you learn about this?"

Instead of answering her, he started to ask why she refused to say what she was doing at Helen's apartment, then changed his mind and turned toward the house.

"How is Mr. LaBeau getting along with Truly Brown's dog?" Riga asked.

The question surprised Harry. She wasn't given to asking casual questions. "He's worked a small miracle there."

"Helen says Mr. LaBeau talks with his animals. Maybe he can get the dog to tell him who shot Truly."

Harry paused to look at her, thinking she'd made a joke, but her face was marked with visible unhappiness. He felt a sudden sympathy and, for a moment, was tempted to take her hand. "I don't think even Tucker could do that."

They had walked around the house. The Rover sat slouched in the driveway, diminishing property values. Its new windshield was no help. "I know you don't want to hear this," he told her, "but be careful. Keep your doors locked. When the lights are on, keep the drapes pulled, and don't drive alone at night."

"I'll consider it," she said and shook his hand, holding it a moment longer than was necessary.

She had started shaking hands with him after her brother was killed. And as soon as Carter guessed he was working for her, she told him to park in her yard. Harry drove away feeling a lot friendlier toward her than was usually the case.

When Harry got home, the phone was ringing.

"This here is Ernshaw Welty. You remember the name?" The voice was high-pitched and penetrating.

"The rustler," Harry said.

"I ain't interested in your smart come-backs," the man replied. "What I've got is a message for that asshole client of yours."

"That would be your neighbor Findlay Jay." Harry thought he might be making a point with Welty.

"This is what you can tell that son of a bitch. I want Jubilee back. You tell him it's gone on long enough."

Ernshaw slammed his phone down. Harry started to dial a number and changed his mind. He had enough years in the business not to be overly influenced by tough talk. But with Ernshaw Welty's pinched and flinty face in his mind and the man's dentist-drill voice still in his head, he decided he had better talk to Findlay Jay.

"What Ernshaw Welty wants and what the little prick of misery gets are two different things," Findlay Jay said. Harry thought the smile accompanying the comment singularly nasty and out of character with the man he thought he knew.

They were standing at the pasture gate, watching the Red Durhams grazing peacefully in the afternoon sunlight.

"You've got your cattle back," Harry said. "You've more than recovered my costs to you in unpaid stud fees from Jubilee. What you do is your business, and I don't even pretend to understand what's going on between you two, but it sounded to me as if Welty was seriously upset."

"He'll get that horse back when he tells me how I stole him."

"How did you steal him?"

The big farmer shook his head slowly. "That's for me to know. What you don't know can't hurt you."

"You mean what I don't know I can't sell to Welty." Harry heard a threat in Findlay Jay's reply and was not pleased.

"No. If I don't tell you, and Ernshaw finds out how I did it, I'll know he didn't learn it from you."

Harry failed to see the difference in the two statements but let it go. "Let me ask you something. What if you were to go to Welty and say, 'I'll give you back Jubilee, if we agree to quit stealing things from one another'?"

Findlay Jay's eyes widened in surprise. "Why would I want to do that?"

"Because what you two are doing is stupid and dangerous."

"It's better than shooting at one another," Findlay Jay said defensively.

"Maybe, but why not put a stop to the whole thing?"

Findlay Jay looked around at the neatly-fenced fields, the house under the live oaks, the barns and outbuildings, and back to his cattle. He shook his head. "Jays and Weltys been fighting for as far back as anyone can remember."

"But you don't know why."

"Don't matter. We've always done it."

Harry gave up in disgust. "Okay, I've passed along the message and said what I think. I'll say this and be done: The past doesn't have to keep repeating itself."

"The past," Findlay Jay said heavily, "reminds us who we are."

Harry caught up with Helen just as she was getting home from work.

"I suppose you want to come in and have coffee," she complained. She was fishing her house keys out of her purse as she spoke, and glowered at him around a thick strand of honey-colored hair that had tumbled across her face.

"It's a good thing I know you," Harry said. "Otherwise, I might think you weren't glad to see me."

"Idiot," she grumbled and stepped into the house.

Mister Johnson shrieked with excitement as Helen entered the kitchen and flung his bean bag out of his cage. Helen let him out and spent a few moments asking him about his day, while he stamped around on the counter, dragging his bean bag and demanding beer. She took an

171

opened Heineken out of the refrigerator, poured some into a heavy green glass, and put it on the counter before tossing her bag and briefcase onto the table and collapsing onto a chair. "God, what a day," she groaned.

"Anything special?" Harry asked. He sat down beside her.

"The bank's turned into a snake pit ever since Ruvin Carter postponed dissolving the Brown Trust. It's as though everyone's underwear has shrunk." She jumped to her feet and began making coffee.

"I could make that for you," Harry said.

"Are you out of your mind?"

"Then while you're working, let me ask you a question."

"Okay."

"First, I was talking with Riga earlier today."

"I wish to God she'd come back to work," Helen snapped.

"She said something about returning in two days. I'm worried about her. The police are not developing any new leads in her brother's death. Snyder tells me the investigation, such as it is, is focusing more and more on her."

"What's the question?" Helen switched on the coffee maker and turned to face Harry, her arms folded. She was scowling.

"The police don't believe that the night Arthur Kraftmeier was killed, Riga was here with you."

"Explaining things to you is a goddamned waste of time," Helen snapped. "You don't seem to understand simple English. Riga was here with me all that night. She couldn't have killed her brother."

"Why was she here?"

"None of your business."

"I'm making progress," Harry said, getting to his feet.

"When I asked Riga the same question, she just looked at me."

Helen sighed and turned to help Mister Johnson, who was trying, a little unsteadily, to drag a roll of paper towels into his cage and swearing because it was jammed behind the toaster. She freed it for him and turned back to face Harry.

"Look, Love," she said in a sudden change of tone. "Riga's not going to tell you. Neither am I. She didn't kill her brother. I sure as hell didn't."

"Two brains as good as yours and hers ought to be able to figure out that the smart thing to do here is to tell the police something—anything—reasonable. Tell them she had a fight with Tom, that she had to get away from her mother for a few hours, that her brother was driving her nuts. Why haven't you figured this out?" He heard his own voice rising and stopped talking.

Helen walked over to him and placed her hands flat against his chest. "It ain't going to happen, fella," she said softly. "Have you talked about this with Katherine?"

"No. At the moment Katherine and I are in Panmunjom, staring across the table at one another."

"Ha. Ha. Very funny. If you're not careful, you're going to be laughing yourself into a divorce court."

"Forget about me. Think about Riga. Unless one of you does something to break this logjam, she may find herself being charged with murder."

"That's ridiculous."

"No. It's a distinct possibility."

She slid her hands around him and held him in a loose embrace, her head against his. The light in the room began to fade. Thunder rumbled, and a rough wind shook the house.

"Hold me, Harry," she said quietly and pressed herself against him. Her pliant warmth wakened him to a hunger he had almost managed to forget. He put his arms around her. She lifted her head and kissed him on the mouth. For the briefest moment an alarm bell rang in his head, but no one heard it. He bent into her kiss, and his hands slid down over the curve of her hips.

If Niels Bohr was right, and an accident is an event the contingencies of which we do not fully understand, then the phrase spontaneous sex is an oxymoron. When Harry eased out of Helen's bed without waking her, the thunderstorm had shrunk to dripping eaves. He dressed and went home.

Chapter 19

That night after Minna and Jesse were asleep, Harry knocked on Katherine's door and asked if he could talk with her. She came out tying her robe, her face impassive. They walked downstairs in silence. Without needing to negotiate the location, they went into the kitchen. The side window was open on the night, and the room was full of its warmth and the sounds of crickets fiddling away in darkness.

"What do you want to talk about?" She looked very tired.

Sitting across the kitchen table from her, Harry felt the breath of winter blowing around him and not only because he had made love to Helen that afternoon. He had not invented fictions to account for what he had done. As long as it had taken them, they aroused and gratified one another's passion until the wells of their desire were dry. He knew exactly what he had done, what she had done. Co-conspirators, mutually consenting adults, adulterers, friends with special privileges. Satiety, not conscience, had finally stopped them.

"Us," Harry said.

Katherine gave a despairing laugh. Harry shifted ground. He asked her how she was feeling about her mother.

She locked her hands and stared at the table. "Harry, I don't know anymore how I feel about anything, especially not my mother."

"Shouldn't we talk about it?" he asked.

"We have, but things don't get any better."

"If this is about Gideon," he said, "I'm going to tell you again that I didn't lie to you. I wasn't trying to deceive you. I'm very sorry you think otherwise."

Katherine sat for a long time staring at her hands. Then, looking a spot on the wall somewhere behind Harry and above his head, she began speaking.

"When I first married Willard, I believed everything he told me. Then I found out you couldn't believe what he said if you asked him for the time. I looked away, too scared and hurt to have to deal with it. When I finally made myself look, I had two kids, no money, and no more hope."

She had a lot more to say. Harry listened to all of it and saw that however much Katherine's circumstances had changed since their marriage, she still regarded him through the filters of her mother's abandonment and her own life with Willard Trachey. As he listened, he also heard Tucker saying that you could try to forget the past, but it wouldn't forget you.

He wondered if Katherine was aware how much her father and Willard Trachey still dominated her life. What about himself? How successful had he been in trying to forget the past? It had not forgotten him. At least Gideon had not forgotten him. He wondered for a moment about his first wife and his children, but that was too painful to endure, and he closed the door to that room.

"So I'm not really sure I believe you didn't lie to me, Harry," Katherine said in closing. "I've got a lot more thinking to do."

"All right," he said. It was not all right and he knew it. Now she had reason not to believe him. "But while you're thinking, will you please also seriously consider going to see your mother?"

"Why is it so important to you that I see my mother?" she demanded.

"Because whether you know it or not, can admit it or not, it's important to you. Take Minna and Jesse to see her before it's too late."

She got up slowly, her face drained of color. "I'll think about it."

Harry sat listening to the night. Until he heard her close her door. Then he shut the window, put out the light, and went to bed.

The next morning Katherine knocked on Harry's bedroom door and, when he opened it, said, "I've been thinking about what you told me last night. I'm going to take the kids and go see my mother and Priscilla. I'll probably be gone a week."

After breakfast she called her office and the school. Then she booked a morning flight out of Avola. By nine-thirty Harry was putting their bags into the Rava and saying goodbye to Minna and Jesse. Katherine came out of the house and kissed him goodbye.

"Good luck," he said to her.

"Thanks," she said and left.

"I've been cutting Weissmuller some slack," Tucker said the following morning, after having expressed his hope that Katherine's going to see her mother would help to settle her mind.

Harry carefully avoided any mention of jumping the gate with Helen. They were walking the big dog around the yard and had stopped to watch Longstreet and his hens scratching for food in their run. Whenever the rooster turned up a particularly juicy grub, he clucked at the hens and gave it to his favorite of the day. That led Tucker to speculate about Longstreet's strengths and weaknesses as a husband.

"What about Weissmuller?" Harry demanded. He did not want to talk about a husband's role in family life.

"I've been letting him out of his kennel without a lead, and it hasn't been a complete success." Tucker paused and moved his hat around on his head and looked uncomfortable with what he was saying.

"Go on."

"Yesterday afternoon he disappeared for a couple of hours and came back with blood on his chest."

"A deer?"

"Probably. But it could have been anything short of an elephant. Anyway, I'm disappointed. Sanchez and Oh-Brother! are not speaking to him. You saw them go off just now."

"I'm surprised he came back at all," Harry said.

"I expect I was overconfident." Tucker reached down to stroke the dog's head. He spoke to him in the soft voice he used when he was talking to one of his animals. Weissmuller looked at him and wagged his tail. "I haven't given up on him."

"What do you think did bring him back?" Harry asked.

They had resumed their walk and Tucker pointed across the yard toward the kennel.

"That's hard to believe," Harry said.

"Not really. He's safe when he's locked in there. He can lay down his sword and rest easy. I expect that's where I made my mistake."

"One of us has been smoking something," Harry grumbled.

"We'll get to you in a minute," Tucker said. "Just bear with me a little longer. Here's what I think happened. He came out of his kennel, felt pretty good for a while, then, with time on his hands and all that space around him, not so good. I was probably in the house. Sanchez and Oh-Brother! were not paying attention, and away he went."

"Tucker," Harry said, "Weissmuller is not a person."

Tucker regarded Harry with a look he usually reserved for weeds in his flower beds. "Do you think animals don't have psychological profiles? Do you think Weissmuller doesn't remember Truly's being shot to death and himself badly wounded?"

The fuse that had been burning in Harry's mind since Helen had lit it finally reached the powder. "Tucker, let's walk Weissmuller up to Ruvin Carter and see if he tries to tear out his throat."

Tucker grinned. "We might even let him."

The next day Harry took Helen to lunch. As soon as they were seated, Helen said, "Okay, Harry, just as a reality check, you and I recently spent the children's hour shagging. And, oh, yes, you're married to my best friend. Do we have anything to discuss?"

"Probably. Katherine's visiting her mother," he replied, a scandalously weak response to her question.

"And you want me to come over?"

"No."

"Then what?"

"Words are not much use here."

"That's true, Harry, but for openers, I don't regret what we did."

"Neither do I."

Their right hands had slid toward one another and met and clasped beside the salt and pepper shakers.

"The thing is . . ."

She squeezed his fingers. "Don't. We both know . . . we both have . . . You were right. Words don't help."

The waitress came to take their orders. When she left, they were no longer holding hands and, to Harry's relief, Helen made no effort to revive the discussion.

Over their meal, when Harry told her about the test he and Tucker wanted to run, bringing Weissmuller and Carter together, she fired her fist into the air and shouted, "Yes!"

As they were leaving the restaurant, the grandmotherly woman at an adjoining table asked, "Did he propose, dear?"

"No!" Helen's face bloomed a bright pink.

"Oh, my, that's too bad," the woman said.

Harry's day was almost made. Once out of the restaurant, she glared at him. "Don't say a word."

Katherine came home the following Sunday. Minna and Jesse were bubbling with excitement over their plane rides and their visit, but Katherine, looking, Harry thought, more rested with more color in her face, kissed him perfunctorily and squeezed out a minimal smile in response to his greeting.

While she unpacked, Harry managed to get an account of her mother.

"Priscilla and I finally prevailed," she told him. "She's going to have the pacemaker implanted. And right now it looks as if she will be able to go back to work. But Priscilla's got a lot to manage. It was a fight, but Ma finally agreed."

"But it's going to work out all right? They don't have to make any drastic changes?"

"No, and I'm grateful."

"How are you feeling?"

"Feeling?" She paused to glance fleetingly at him. "I'm not feeling anything."

Harry took a deep breath. He had thought through what he wanted to say to her, and he decided now was the time to say it. "I knew Willard pretty well."

She continued lifting clothes out of her suitcase. "What's that supposed to mean?"

"On a sunny day, how much of Willard do you see in me?"

"Until you started lying, I didn't see any."

"Are you sure about that? Isn't it what all this is about?"

"I don't know what you mean."

It suddenly occurred to Harry that he had no right to accuse her of anything. He had deliberately not told her about Gideon, and he had no intention of telling her he had slept with Helen. "Neither do I. Let me tell you what Tucker and I are planning."

The next morning Harry ate early, got the kids' breakfasts, and, when Katherine came downstairs, stayed out of her way. About ten o'clock, he finished his desk work and drove the Rover to Tucker's place, making good on his promise to help Tucker divide two hives he suspected were raising new queens and preparing to swarm.

"I'm glad I caught them this early in the season," he said with satisfaction, as he and Harry were taking off their protective clothing.

"What difference does the timing make?" Harry asked.

"New hives need time to hatch new workers and build up their stores for winter, not that we have much winter. But there are a few weeks when they have to feed from their reserves. Further north, if a colony splits and swarms too late in the summer, the migrating bees don't have time to make enough honey to see them through the cold weather."

Harry found comfort in the fact he was no longer living up North, where careless bees seeking a new life died of starvation.

"Are we ready?" he asked when they had Weissmuller in the back of the Rover.

"Our friend looks happy enough," Tucker said, "even if his head is making a bump in the roof."

Weissmuller was sitting up on the back seat, pretty well filling the available space. He was panting happily, his tongue flopped out and his expression benign.

"Hold on just a minute." Tucker turned away from the Rover. "There's one or two things I want to say to Oh-Brother! before we go. He's in charge when I'm away."

Harry sat, trying not to think about the implications of Tucker's giving Oh-Brother! last minute instructions while Sanchez wore his martyr's look. Behind him, Weissmuller's chain clinked quietly and, glancing back at the dog, Harry wondered if something had gone seriously wrong with his mind.

"Let's do it!" Tucker clambered into the Rover wearing a wide grin.

Harry grinned back and released the clutch, his momentary doubts evaporating in Tucker's enthusiasm.

Once they were parked on a quiet side street close to the bank, Tucker said, "I think we ought to walk Weissmuller around here a little and get him used to city life. I don't know that he's had a lot of experience with cars and people and an absence of trees."

"He probably likes it."

"Why?"

"Nothing for the cats to climb."

They coaxed a reluctant Weissmuller out of the Rover

and onto the sidewalk. He had enjoyed the ride and was not pleased that it was over. But he finally jumped down with a deep rumble of complaint. Harry checked his watch, keeping a tight grip with the other hand on the dog's chain. Now that they were in Avola, he was less confident about his plan than he had been on the Hammock.

"We've got a little under five minute before Carter comes out of the bank," he said.

"What are you worried about?" Tucker asked. He gave Weissmuller's collar a tug, to see that the chains were securely anchored. At Harry's insistence, he had put two lead chains on the dog.

"Weissmuller trees mountain lions," Harry said. "And here we are planning to walk him up to a man on a busy sidewalk in the bright light of day, with the hope he will try to turn him into lunch."

"Sounds right to me," Tucker said.

Helen came around the corner from Willet Lane and strode up to them.

"Hey, Tucker," she said. "And here's Weissmuller."

"The one and only," Tucker replied.

She put her hand on his head. "Jesus, Harry," she said. "I'd forgotten how big he is. I never saw him in a Disney movie."

Weissmuller regarded her with what in his world passed for warmth and affection. He even panted at her. Helen looked at Harry and said, "Don't you dare . . . never mind." She patted Weissmuller's head and said, "Good boy," as if she were trying to believe it.

"You know what you're going to do?" Harry asked.

"Of course I do. Give me two minutes. Then follow as quickly as you can. Carter doesn't like talking to me all that much."

183

She turned and hurried away.

"Let's do it," Harry said when the two minutes were up. "Now, Tucker, get both hands on your chain."

"If he starts for Carter," Tucker said, showing some strain, "lean back and pull for all you're worth."

They rounded the corner onto a more crowded sidewalk. With Weissmuller between them and Harry considering the efficacy of prayer as a backup, they started toward the bank. In his jungle, the tiger walks in a silence of his own making. Weissmuller's advance not only created silence but space. Some of the pedestrians even went out into the street to let Weissmuller pass unimpeded.

They were almost on Helen and Carter before Harry saw them. Harry, Tucker, and Weissmuller were splitting the crowd as they advanced like a ship's prow dividing the water, and suddenly there they were. Carter was looking intently at Helen, his face grave. Whatever she was saying had riveted his attention.

"Get a grip on that chain," Harry said. They took four more steps, and Harry said, "Hello, Helen. Hello, Mr. Carter."

Helen turned and stepped away from Carter. Carter and Weissmuller locked eyes. Weissmuller roared and flung himself at the man. Tucker stumbled, and for a very bad moment Harry thought his own arms were going to pop out of their sockets. But Tucker caught his balance and threw his weight against his chain. Harry planted his feet and hauled back with all his strength.

They turned the dog's head. His jaws snapped shut inches from Carter's neck. Yanked sideways, Weissmuller twisted his body violently to keep himself from crashing down on his side. The momentum of his checked leap flung his right flank and hip forward into Carter's chest.

Screaming, Carter was slammed onto his back, arms flailing. Weissmuller landed on his feet like a giant cat.

But before he could launch another attack, Harry and Tucker had dragged the snarling dog away from the fallen banker. With Weissmuller repeatedly trying to turn around and his bellowing scattering pedestrians, they nevertheless kept him moving at a quick trot until they had dragged him around the corner to the Rover. As they wrestled him around the corner, Harry glimpsed the scattered crowd surging back onto the sidewalk and Helen helping a still-yelling Carter onto his feet.

Chapter 20

Harry called the Sheriff's office as soon as he and Tucker had Weissmuller safely locked in his run. For Harry, the ride back from Avola had not been a happy one. Tucker had failed to persuade Weissmuller to sit down, and the dog, deprived of his quarry, kept changing directions on the seat, growling and roaring his frustration at the passing cars.

With a sense of having cheated death, Harry closed and locked Weissmuller's kennel gate. Then he shook it, to be sure it was truly locked. But Tucker was right. Once in his run, Weissmuller took a long drink, threw himself onto to his straw bed with a sigh, and fell instantly into a deep sleep.

"You've got your answer. Now what do you do with it?" Tucker asked when they were seated on Tucker's back stoop, waiting for Jim Snyder.

"Wait and see what breaks loose. It could be a lawsuit for aggravated assault with a man-eating dog."

"Weissmuller did put on a pretty good show." Tucker smiled proudly and got up to bring their tea.

Harry regarded the steaming black liquid in his mug with his usual dread. "I think it's pretty clear that Ruvin Carter killed Truly Brown."

Tucker settled himself comfortably in his rocker and took a pull on the tea. "I don't think there's any doubt about it. Weissmuller walked peaceful as a lamb along that sidewalk until he saw Carter."

Oh-Brother! and Sanchez came around the corner of the stoop, followed by Jim Snyder. Snyder stepped onto the stoop, pulled off his hat, and flourished it at Sanchez and Oh-Brother!. "Who ever heard of a mule and a dog meeting you in the dooryard and taking you around the house to where the other humans are sitting? The scary thing is I found myself talking to them."

"You must be one of the two people left on earth who still calls a driveway a dooryard," Harry replied, "and don't worry, Tucker talks to them all the time."

"Who's the other one?" Snyder asked, shaking hands.

"Me," Tucker said, "but don't mind Harry, he's full of modern notions. How about some tea?"

"Sounds good," Snyder said, glancing at Harry as if he were seeking help. Harry grinned and held up his own mug. "What's so important it couldn't wait?" Snyder demanded.

Tucker got Snyder seated with a cup in his hand and answered for Harry. "We're ninety-eight percent certain Ruvin Carter killed Truly Brown."

Snyder looked at the two men in alarm. "If this is a joke, I don't think it's funny. If it's not, are you out of your minds?"

"As sane as it's possible to be," Tucker said comfortably. "If you don't believe us, ask Weissmuller."

"Weissmuller?"

"Truly Brown's dog," Harry said. He was enjoying watching Snyder's ears turn red.

"Come on! What foolishness am I hearing here?"

"It's simple really," Tucker said calmly. "At noontime today, Harry and I walked Weissmuller up to Ruvin Carter on the sidewalk of Willet Lane, and Weissmuller tried to take Carter's head off. If you had seen it, you would have arrested Carter on the spot."

"Harry," Snyder said. He was not smiling.

Harry took pity on him. "Do you remember my saying to you that whoever killed Truly would have had to go through Weissmuller to get him?" Snyder nodded. "The dog knows who killed Truly," Harry continued. "Well, it took Tucker and me until this morning to figure out how he could tell us. With Helen's help, Tucker and I put Weissmuller and Carter face-to-face."

"Hold it. Where did you two find Weissmuller?"

Harry told him.

"Why am I just hearing this?"

Harry couldn't resist. "You have trouble talking to Sanchez. How much luck would you have with Weissmuller?"

"You'd better see him," Tucker said. The three, accompanied by Oh-Brother! and Sanchez, trooped out to Weissmuller's kennel. Weissmuller was on his feet, the hair on his back bristling and a deep growl rumbling in his chest. He stared at Snyder with obvious suspicion.

"Lord of mercy!" Snyder whispered. "You took that thing into Avola?"

"He's gentle as a lamb," Tucker protested. "Let me get him out here."

"You leave him right where he is," Snyder said. His right hand had automatically drifted toward his shoulder holster.

"See that scar on his head?" Tucker asked. "That's where he was shot. Carter did that. It's healed up nicely, but Weissmuller hasn't forgotten or forgiven."

Oh-Brother! and Sanchez moved closer to Snyder, and Weissmuller relaxed. The hair on his shoulders flattened and his ears relaxed. He opened his mouth and let his tongue loll out.

"They've let him know you're all right," Tucker said with a straight face.

"That's a comfort," Snyder said.

Harry added some explanation. "I think Truly went to Carter and told him that, with the trust money, he planned to launch a large-scale hunt for Tarzan in the Everglades. He had already told Hannah Bridges that was what he intended."

"She owns the Green Thumb Nursery, where Truly was working when he died," Tucker reminded Snyder.

Harry went on. "I don't know how Carter responded, but whatever he said, it got him and Truly onto Hobson's Choice. Once Carter had him out there, he shot Weissmuller and Truly. Remember, we're talking about Truly Brown. He didn't have much to do with what you'd call normal people. But he'd known Ruvin for years and years. His mother had known and trusted him."

"Why would Carter want to kill him?" Snyder was listening carefully.

"A blackjack dealer at the Oconee Casino told me that for some time Carter has been gambling heavily."

"Do you have the dealer's name?"

"I can get it if I have to."

"And you think Carter's been stealing money from the trust?"

"Looks reasonable," Tucker put in.

Snyder stepped back from the fence. "Let me think about this," he said. "Weird as he is, you don't accuse a man in Ruvin Carter's position of murder, unless you're damned sure you can prove it." He looked from Tucker to Harry and raised an admonitory hand. "From right now, you stay away from Ruvin Carter. You hear?"

"Sure," Harry said.

"Suits me," Tucker added. "Anyway, I don't think he's in a hurry to see the three of us again."

★ ★ ★ ★ ★

After leaving Tucker, Harry drove to East Avola to talk with Rafe Juliette about a rash of break-ins at his Wild Turkey Condos. Rafe was a bald, black-bearded, seriously overweight man in his fifties. He sat hunched in his bunker-like office with its dirty, gun-slit windows, at the hub of three narrow streets flanked by rows of gray-roofed condos. He lit a cigarette off the stub of one he had just smoked, and greeted Harry with a growl of complaint.

"This is not a business I'm running, it's a war."

But Harry knew that despite his apparent hostility toward his tenants, and despite the fact they were, one and all, socially and morally challenged, he took enormous pleasure from what he was doing.

"What is it this time?" Harry asked. He looked around in vain for an empty chair to sit in. "Piedra stealing more stoves?"

"Fuck Piedra," Juliette growled, scowling. He waved a thick hand at Harry. "Drop that fucking box on the floor and sit down. People have to be told everything. Helpless. No fucking initiative."

Harry looked in the box before he lifted it off the chair and saw it was half-full of dynamite. "What's this for?" he inquired as he set the box down very carefully.

"One of the tenants didn't want it in the house with the kids. I don't ask what it's for. Never mind the fucking dynamite. You know somebody named Welty?"

"Ernshaw Welty?"

"Sounds right. You know somebody else named Findlay Jay?"

"Why would you think I did?" Harry asked.

"Because one of my *patans,* who thought he was making points with me because he'd seen you hanging around here,

190

said something heavy was going down with those two and I should tell you, if you was my friend, which you're not, to watch your ass. He likes to hear himself talk, but sometimes he gets things straight. You know anything about this?"

"I'm glad to hear you're not my friend. I like not being on the Sheriff's Most Wanted List. Did your co-conspirator say what was supposed to be happening with Welty and Findlay Jay?" He did not want to talk with Rafe about Findlay Jay or Ernshaw Welty. But the news Juliette had given him was cause for concern, despite the suspect nature of its source.

"Rumor is that one or both of them is looking for a shooter. But you did not hear it from me, and I don't remember who I was talking to, if I was talking to anybody, which I wasn't."

"Why did you call me out here?" Harry demanded. "You could have phoned."

"Fuck the phone. I've got trouble. A couple nights ago, some goofy bastards broke into three units and took away a pile of shit the tenants had been storing." Rafe jerked his thumb at a window. "There's two guns for every unwashed body in *este barrio*. You don't rob those people with impunity."

"Who did it?" Harry asked.

"The Jamaicans. Don't sell them life insurance."

"The stuff they took belong to the tenants?"

Juliette shrugged. "They don't have a bill of sale, if that's what you're asking."

"I see. The ownership is contested, origins unknown, probably delivered by boat or plane. And while we're talking about insurance, are you hiring me to cover your ass with the insurance companies? If not, just what do you want me to do here?"

191

Juliette sighed and actually heaved himself back in his chair. The floor groaned under the sudden shifting of his weight. He regarded Harry with an unhappy expression. "Yes, and I don't want you getting killed over this," he said. "These hombres are *peligroso seriomente*."

"These Jamaicans wouldn't be members of that Bible study group affectionately known as *Las Cucarachas?*"

"Possibly."

"I don't suppose the police are being any help."

"Funny you should ask," Juliette answered with a scowl.

"Put me on your payroll," Harry said. He left grinning, but he thought this was one time Rafe was going to get some police help, whether he wanted it or not. And he was certainly not going into Machete Town in search of Rafe's twice-fried beans.

As Harry got into the Rover, he glanced at his watch and groaned. It was his turn to cook dinner, but if he pushed it, he still had time to drive out to Findlay Jay's place. He found the big farmer leaning on the heavy plank fence surrounding the yard where he exercised his bulls. One of his men, a short, brawny Haitian, was just backing out of one of the bull pens facing into the yard. He was pulling on a chain attached to the nose ring of a huge Durham bull. The bull, with immense, down-curving horns, swayed slowly into the yard, its muzzle raised, saliva trailing from its mouth and its heavy dewlap swinging as it walked.

"Don't look like he could get out of his own way, does he?" Findlay Jay asked. Harry had joined him at the fence and braced one foot on the bottom plank.

"No, but as big as he is, he probably doesn't have to move fast."

"Appearances can be deceiving," Findlay Jay replied.

"You might be able to dodge him if he went after you, but you couldn't begin to outrun him."

The bull opened its mouth and bellowed, his eyes rolling up their whites as he twisted his head. From one of the pens came an answering, coughing roar.

"Get him hitched to that walker!" Findlay Jay shouted, pulling himself off the fence. "Keep him moving."

The man redoubled his efforts on the chain and, swearing and grunting, got the bull close enough to the walker to snap the chain onto one of its iron arms. The walker looked like a revolving clothesline made for a family of giants. Once fastened to the walker, the bull settled down and began his slow circling on the slowly-turning arm.

"You want they two?" the man called in a richly accented voice.

Findlay Jay shook his head. "Walk this one, put him back in the pen. Then the other two. If I'm not around, you get Juan to help you. You understand?"

The man nodded. Findlay Jay turned around and braced his elbows on the fence. "What brings you out here?" he asked.

"Have you been trying to hire somebody to shoot Ernshaw Welty?" Harry decided he might as well get it out there all at once.

"Why would I do that?" Findlay Jay asked in apparent surprise.

"You tell me," Harry responded. He sounded braver than he felt. He wasn't exactly afraid of Findlay Jay, but in his company he felt the kind of alert uncertainty he thought he might feel standing in front of one of the rancher's prize bulls.

Findlay Jay looked down at Harry and laughed. Then he lifted his gaze and seemed to Harry to be making a visual sweep over the treed yard in front of him and then across the pastures and wood lots beyond them. Harry let his own eyes take in the same placid scene. At the far, brushy edge of the small creek separating the nearest wood lot from a calf pasture, Harry caught what he thought was a dull glint of metal.

He paused to look more closely and had just made up his mind he was mistaken when Findlay Jay suddenly spun around like a toy top and slammed into the fence. Harry felt something hot and wet spatter his face and heard the sharp crack of a rifle just as the man beside him recoiled from the fence and fell like a tree going down. Then Harry saw the blood on his head and raced for the house.

Chapter 21

Findlay Jay regained consciousness around midnight. His wife was with him. She practically ran out of the room when Jim Snyder came in, followed by a deceptively comfortable-looking nurse who introduced herself as Nurse Thompson. Then she scowled and barked at him like a three-headed dog. "You've got four minutes. If I have to come get you, you'll be sore for a week."

When Jim came out, she partly opened the door for Harry and glared at him as he squeezed past her. "You've got three minutes. As in three blind mice, which is what you'll be if you give me any guff."

Findlay Jay peered up at Harry with one bloodshot eye from a head otherwise hidden by white bandages.

"I won't tell the police, and I'll deny it if you do," the man croaked through the hole they had left for his mouth, "but we both know who did this. Looks like the old times are coming back."

Harry could hear no regret in his voice. "Give him back his horse."

"Jubilee is going to vanish," Findlay Jay said calmly.

"What about your wife?"

"There's a small army guarding her, and the boy's coming home," Findlay Jay said.

"Where is your son?"

"He's in South Carolina working on an advanced degree in horticulture. He wants to make the place into a citrus farm."

"How old is he?"

"Twenty-eight. He's married with two young ones."

Harry thought his time was about up, but curiosity made him ask one more question. "What are you going to do with Jubilee?"

"Ernshaw is going to get a big delivery of hamburger done up in a horsehide."

"Findlay Jay . . ." Harry began, but the rancher raised a big hand off the bed and stopped him.

"The bastard tried to kill me. Considering my other options, I figure shooting his horse shows considerable restraint on my part."

Harry started to say something more, but the nurse had come up on him silently and grasped his arm. "Out!"

"Y'all come back," Findlay Jay called after Harry, as the nurse propelled him through the door.

When Harry came into the house, Katherine was coming down the stairs from her bedroom, tying the belt on her robe.

"Hi," he said. "I'm sorry I woke you."

"You didn't. How is he?"

"He's talking, but they're treating him as if he was in very bad shape. He won't help the police. Jim Snyder's having a fit."

"Doesn't take much," Katherine answered with a pale smile. "Want some coffee?"

"Maybe some cereal."

"I'll make the coffee. You get the cereal. Want anything else?"

He shook his head.

"I heard from Helen this afternoon about the run-in you and Tucker had with Ruvin Carter."

Harry carried the cereal and a carton of milk to the table. "We took Weissmuller to see Ruvin Carter, and we're in agreement. Carter did kill Truly. We told Jim Snyder that, and he groaned out loud. Of course, that was at Tucker's, and what anyone thinks at Tucker's is always subject to later revision."

"Well, about an hour after you conducted your test, Carter was hauled off in an ambulance."

"Nice move," Harry replied.

"What do you mean?"

"It means that if I was in his shoes and wanted to counter that very compromising scene on the sidewalk, witnessed by at least a couple dozen people, I would consider faking a heart attack. I'd do it to lay some groundwork for the lawsuit he's going to file against Tucker and me."

"What scene?"

"Weissmuller tried to tear his throat out."

Katherine stood up and gripped the edge of the table with her right hand. "You mean you pulled this kid's trick, knowing Carter might sue us?"

"He's got no case," Harry said carefully. "The dog didn't touch him. Helen was there. She and others can testify that neither Tucker nor I threatened Carter. And we pulled Weissmuller away before the dog put a paw on him."

"Then why would he want to sue you?"

"Because there's no doubt that Weissmuller was trying to kill him. He will probably decide that his best defense is an attack."

"Your coffee's ready," Katherine said. "I'm going back to bed, but first I want to ask you something. Did you ask yourself what a lawsuit for felonious assault would do to your reputation as a private investigator? Did you ask yourself how it would affect me or the management company I work for?"

She left without waiting for an answer. Harry ate his cereal feeling as if he'd been scrubbed with a wire brush.

"There are things about people I'm never going to figure out," Harry said. He had both Katherine and Findlay Jay in mind.

Jim Snyder rubbed his hand over his face. It was nine the following morning, and the two men were sitting in Snyder's office. The detective was trying to take a statement from Harry about the Findlay Jay shooting. Harry was not being helpful.

"You know it's a crime to withhold information from the police in a case like this?" Loss of sleep had not increased Snyder's patience.

"Do your worst," Harry said. He leaned back in his chair and stretched. "I've told you all the law demands and a little more. If you were to put Findlay Jay and his friends in a book, nobody would believe it."

What he thought about Katherine, he kept to himself.

Snyder was not listening. "Fifteen years ago Ernshaw Welty was charged with illegal possession of alligator hides, but nothing came of it. He was also suspected of running a marijuana transfer point from that little landing strip of his, but nothing came of that either. Then his only child, a boy, was killed in a motorcycle accident, and we haven't heard anything from him since. Until this."

"When was his son killed?"

"A year and a half ago."

"How old was he?"

"I think he was twenty-three."

"How was he killed?"

"We figure somebody ran him off the road. He hit a tree. The crime scene crew estimated he was going about eighty. It happened out on that godforsaken stretch of slash pine and saw palmetto between his father's and Findlay Jay's ranches. The time of death was around midnight, and that's all we ever learned."

"There's your motive."

"What are you talking about?"

Harry had said nothing about Findlay Jay's cattle or Ernshaw Welty's Jubilee, but he had told Jim about the feud and what he'd heard from Rafe Juliette. "I'll bet my last dollar Ernshaw thinks it was Findlay Jay who ran the kid off the road."

Snyder's ears turned red. "I can hear the judge saying how well he liked the idea," he said loudly, "and telling the Assistant District Attorney, 'Press ahead, Counselor. Press ahead. Of course there's no admissible evidence and not a shred of proof, but don't let that stop you.' "

"You feeling better?" Harry asked.

Jim's face had caught up with his ears, and he was breathing heavily. "No. Get out of here before I have a seizure."

Outside the station, Harry met Frank Hodges.

The Sergeant did not look happy. "I'm thinking of transferring to the county sewage treatment plant. I'm looking to upgrade my working conditions."

"What's wrong?" Hodges was always good for a story.

"I just ticketed a man for running a red light and causing a five vehicle pile-up. He was drunk as a skunk, and when he managed to get out of his car he took a swing at the man whose car he ran into, missed, and fell on his face. When I picked him up and cuffed him, he began calling for help and accusing me of using unnecessary force. So I let go of him, and he fell down again. This is a damned poor way to make a living."

"You need to think ahead."

"What do you mean?" Hodges scowled.

It was an expression so foreign to the Sergeant's round face that Harry started to laugh, then forced himself to stop. "You want to let yourself think about how he's going to feel when he sobers up and finds out what he's done."

Hodges grinned. "You're right. And there are the charges: DUI, assaulting a police officer, resisting arrest. I'm already beginning to feel better."

"I've got a question for you," Harry said. "Did you talk with Ernshaw Welty after his son was killed in that motorcycle accident?"

Hodges pulled out his blue bandanna and wiped his face, lifted his hat, and wiped his head. "I remember being out there. Why?"

"You remember what happened?"

"I remember Welty went from being knocked back by the news to being swearing-mad in about seven seconds. His wife was in terrible shape. Had to have the doctor."

"Remember anything Welty said?"

"As I recall, it didn't make much sense. I suppose he was just worked up. Didn't last long. He settled right down and began looking after his wife." Hodges paused. "There was some stuff about killing the son of a bitch who had done this. By the way, are you working for Findlay Jay? He's got a ranch out that way. I heard you were working for him."

"Nothing heavy," Harry said. "Look, Jim isn't listening to me just now. So I'm telling you. Some Jamaicans have been breaking into Rafe Juliette's condos. Of course, he won't report it, but robbing his tenants is right up there with taking a cattle prod to a pride of sleeping lions. There's going to be some major bloodshed if you guys can't cool everybody down."

"Count on Juliette," Hodges groaned. "I'll see what I can do."

That night Boots came into Harry's room and woke him, crying to be let out. That was how he happened to be in the kitchen at three in the morning when the phone rang.

"It's Tom Burkhardt. I'm calling from the hospital. Riga's been shot."

When Harry put down the phone, he went upstairs. Before he had opened Katherine's door enough to let himself in, she hissed at him in the dark, "What are doing? What do you want?"

Harry forced himself to walk to the side of what had once been their bed and answered quietly. "Riga's been shot."

Katherine snapped on the bedside light. She grabbed up her robe. "When did it happen? How did it happen?"

"I don't know. Tom Burkhardt just called me. He would only say she wanted me to know and that the doctors think she's going to live."

"Why would she want you to know? What else haven't you been telling me?"

"It would fill a book. I think her brother's being killed and the police having failed to do anything about it would be two reasons. For a third, I suppose she figures she probably wasn't hit by a stray bullet."

They stood looking at one another across a gulf the Grand Canyon could have dropped into. Katherine looked away, her shoulders slumping. "I wonder if Helen knows?"

"One of us should call her."

"You do it." She paused. "I'm going back to bed now."

He went out of the room, wondering if something between them had broken beyond fixing.

Chapter 22

Harry was still clearing away the breakfast dishes when Snyder drove into the yard. Katherine and the kids were gone. The two men settled down on the lanai. The sun had wakened the cicadas, and the yard was alive with their fiddling.

"I thought you weren't talking to me," Harry said.

"I'm not. This is department business." Snyder checked his notebook. "Kraftmeier was shot twice. Burkhardt says the shooting occurred a little after one forty-five. By five after two, the ER had her. She was probably hit as she walked from her car into the house. One bullet struck her right shoulder and the other her left side. That second shot probably caught her as she was falling."

Snyder flipped his notebook shut and sighed. He looked worn almost smooth. "Burkhardt was waiting up for her. And that probably saved her life. He heard the shots, pulled open the front door, and ran out into that gated area in front of the house."

"Brave man," Harry said.

Snyder agreed. "It took him a moment to get through the gate, and by the time he reached Riga, the shooter was gone. He heard the car but couldn't describe the shooter and couldn't tell us anything useful about the vehicle."

"What does Carter drive?"

Snyder made a face. "I don't know."

"What chance is there of doing a powder test on Carter's shooting hand?"

"None whatsoever, and don't forget he was taken to the hospital the day before the shooting."

"And he was home in time for dinner. I checked. There was nothing wrong with him."

"Harry, the department doesn't have any reason to believe Carter had anything to do with this shooting, or Truly Brown's shooting either."

"At Tucker's you said it was worth looking into."

"That was at Tucker's. And I did do some looking . . . at least some thinking. Then I ran it past the Sheriff. He asked me if I was trying for a demotion and a permanent assignment to road patrol in East Avola."

Harry let it go. "Have you been able to talk with Riga?"

"No. She was still unconscious when I left about three forty-five. We've got a trooper outside her door. When she's responding, I'll be told."

"Did you see Helen Bradley?"

"She was giving the doctor a real bad time."

"Sounds right."

"Did Burkhardt tell you where Riga had been?" It suddenly occurred to Harry that Riga might have been at Helen's. And just as quickly he had that familiar feeling of uneasiness.

"I asked him, but he said he had no idea. And he was huffy that I asked. Now you," Snyder continued, "did you see this coming?"

"I knew she was a possible target."

"How so?"

"She's the third person with a connection to Hobson's Choice to be shot, not counting Weissmuller."

"Weissmuller's a dog."

"And then some."

"What's she got to do with Hobson's Choice?"

There was a sudden outburst of squalling and yelping from under the wisteria vine at the south corner of the lanai. Snyder jumped to his feet. A rolling ball of gray fur exploded onto the lawn and divided into a raccoon and a gray fox, both with all their hair on end, their jaws popping like firecrackers, and hair and dust floating around them in the sunlight like a halo. In the next instant, the raccoon shot back into the wisteria, and the fox sprinted past the two men and vanished around the house.

"What in God's name . . ." Snyder shouted.

"Normally, those two give one another a wide berth," Harry said with a grin. "The fox was Clyde. That raccoon's got four cubs. Looks like Clyde got too close to them."

Snyder blew out his breath. "Well I never . . ." Then he caught himself and dropped back into his chair. "What does Riga Kraftmeier have to do with Hobson's Choice?"

"She's trying to buy it. That's how I came to be working for her. With Truly dead, the Brown Trust will be dissolved, the properties sold off, and the final disposition of the assets made. Who gets what, I don't know. But Riga wants to buy Hobson's Choice. It once belonged to her mother, but she gave it to her husband to settle a gambling debt. Riga, in buying it back, is, I guess, settling some old scores with her father and giving back to her mother what, in Riga's view, should never have been taken away from her. And, by the way, it was Truly's father who won it from Riga's father."

"Buying it back won't do Janet Kraftmeier much good," Snyder observed.

"True, but I think Riga is doing it mostly for herself."

"I hear the bank is holding back on that trust settlement."

"And Riga filed a suit to have the delay terminated."

205

"Against Three Rivers?"

"And Ruvin Carter."

Snyder sat forward in his chair. "Should I have heard this before now?"

"Possibly. But in that world a lawsuit is as common as a runny nose. Riga told me it would never reach court, and wasn't intended to."

"But you think Carter shot her."

"Who else has a motive? Her brother's dead. Tom Burkhardt has nothing to gain, unless he inherits in the event of Riga's death, which I doubt. Knowing Riga, she would make an arrangement to protect her mother and her daughter first."

Snyder got to his feet. "Too bad she doesn't have a dog. You and Tucker could walk it up to Carter on the street. Maybe the dog would try to piss on his shoe."

It was two days before the hospital let Harry visit Riga. He found Hodges leaning on the counter at the nurse's station, talking with Nurse Thompson. The Sergeant pushed himself up when he saw Harry.

"Let's step away from here," he said in a low voice. "This place has more ears than a bat cave."

They walked down the corridor and stopped by an alcove with a bench.

"Jim's talked to her," Hodges said, still keeping his eyes on Riga's door. "She doesn't remember a thing. One minute she was walking toward the house, then nothing."

"Did you see her?"

Hodges shook his head. "Now she's conscious, I'm monitoring who goes into her room. But they're not going to be able to keep me here much after this morning. We're too short-handed. Maybe a deputy at night."

"She getting many visitors?"

"Just hospital staff. Oh, and what's her name. The blonde you were with the day you guys found Truly Brown."

"Helen Bradley. Has she left?"

"Yeah, I think so."

"Anything new on the Brown case?"

"Nothing."

"I'd better see Riga while I can. Anything moving on Rafe Juliette's situation?"

They stepped out of the alcove.

"We're putting something together. I'd better leave it there."

At the nurse's station Harry gave his name to Nurse Thompson, who wrote it down with a scowl but made no threats. Harry crossed the corridor to Riga's room. Thompson had been smiling at Hodges when Harry arrived. He was thinking about that when he opened the door to Riga's room.

He took two steps into the room and stopped breathing. As he stared, the door closed silently behind him. Riga was sitting, propped up with pillows. Helen Bradley was bent over her. She was kissing Riga on the mouth. The reason Riga had not seen him was that her eyes were closed.

Harry eased out his breath and tried to get back out the door, but it was too late.

"Hello, Harry," Riga said.

With a silent groan, he faced the bed. "I'm sorry," he said, with things still clattering into place in his head. "I didn't mean to . . ."

Helen had pushed herself off the bed and was pulling her blouse straight. "Hi, Harry. I was just . . ."

"He knows what you were doing," Riga said.

Helen's face was bright pink.

"I could come back later," he said.

"If you're looking for a punch, Brock . . ." Helen burst out, her face turning scarlet.

Harry ignored her. "Riga, are you up to answering some questions?"

"No!" Helen said loudly. "She's not going to answer any questions about—"

"Put a sock in it, Helen," Harry said. He had no idea why he was angry, and fought to stifle it, but it broke through. "Who you kiss or don't kiss is no damned concern of mine. My interest here is to find out if Riga is feeling strong enough to help me find out who shot her."

Helen glared at him, then snatched her bag off the table beside the bed and strode out of the room. Harry resolutely did not watch her go.

"Are you being altogether truthful, Harry?" Riga asked with a slight smile.

"What?"

"Is it true you don't care who she kisses?"

"I'm surprised it hadn't occurred to you, Harry," Tucker said.

Tucker, with Harry's help, was taking the first honey of the summer out of his home hives. The two men were wearing coveralls and netting.

"I'm not shocked, if that's what you mean."

"I'm relieved to hear it. What did Katherine have to say about it?"

"I haven't told her. What's the matter with these bees? I never saw them so disagreeable."

The two men were surrounded by a swirling cloud of hundreds of bees, all buzzing angrily and trying very hard to sting them. The bees had long since driven Oh-Brother!

and Sanchez to the other side of the house.

"How would you like having your pantry robbed?" Tucker reached into the open super with his frame grip and lifted out a frame heavy with honeycomb.

Harry passed him an empty frame, and Tucker slid it into the super, put the full frame into the bucket at his feet, and put the cover back on the hive.

"It's not just having their surplus food taken," Tucker continued. He and Harry walked away from the hives, each carrying a bucket stuffed with full frames. The heavy smell of sugar-laden nectar from the combs rose heavily around them. "The hives are overflowing with workers, more than they accommodate, and the early summer flowers are setting seeds now. The next wave of flowers hasn't come into full blossom. As a result, the workers are hanging around the hives, stepping on one another's feet. Makes them bad-tempered. What was I saying about Riga and Helen? I do believe my mind's failing."

"You were implying that you knew all along they were in love with one another."

"I didn't go so far as to say they were in love," Tucker replied.

The room in the barn where Tucker processed the honey had a double door and heavy screening on the outer door and the windows. He had to brush bees off the outer door before opening it. "They do love sweet things," he said as he and Harry dodged inside.

"If you had seen them kissing—and there was Riga with an IV in her, lying propped up on pillows and pale as a winter pilgrim . . ." He found he was growing angry again, and stopped speaking.

"I believe things are a little more complicated than that," Tucker said.

He and Harry had put down their buckets and were stripping off their head nets and coveralls. Harry was silent while they hung up their gear.

"Maybe it is," he said finally. "But I don't want to talk about it."

"Good," Tucker replied. He walked to the other side of the room, where his uncapping knife and the extractor tank were located. "Bring those buckets, and let's get started emptying the frames."

When the uncapped frames were spinning in the extractor tank and the honey was being flung out of the honeycomb cells, Harry allowed himself to say something more about Riga and Helen. "At least I know now why Riga wouldn't say why she was at Helen's the night her brother was killed."

Tucker finished steaming clean the uncapping knife. "How much satisfaction do you draw from that knowledge?" he inquired.

Harry scowled. "Not a hell of a lot."

Chapter 23

That night after dinner Harry told Katherine he had seen Helen kissing Riga in a way that left no doubt about what was between them.

"So?" Katherine asked.

"That's it? So?" he demanded.

"What were you expecting?"

The kids had gone upstairs as soon as they finished eating. Harry and Katherine had gone onto the lanai in search of cooler air.

"Jesus, Katherine, Riga's living with Burkhardt. She's got a kid. It's more than a *so*."

Katherine put her coffee cup back in its saucer and watched the new moon shining over Puc Puggy Creek. Somewhere off toward Tucker's farm, a chuck-will's-widow began calling.

"He's close," Harry said. "I can hear the *chuck*. It takes me back."

"To what?"

"When I was a kid in Maine. On early summer nights, there was always a whippoorwill calling from the edge of the woods. Before going to sleep, I used to lie in bed with my window open, listening to it. Sounded a lot like this one, only louder."

"Did Riga tell you anything that might help in finding whoever shot her?"

"No," Harry said. He got to his feet, unable to stay

seated any longer. He wanted to be angry, but couldn't seem to find an acceptable excuse. More frustration.

"Too bad. How upset was Helen when she realized you'd seen her kissing Riga?"

"I started to ask Riga a question, and she threatened to punch me," he answered.

"Anything else?"

"She started shouting at one point, and I told her to put a sock in it." He buried his hands in his pockets. "I could have handled that better."

"Really?"

Harry felt his face getting hot.

"Just how mad are you with Helen?"

"Why would I be mad with Helen?"

"I haven't a clue." Katherine stood up and paused beside him for a moment. They both stared out at the night, neither speaking. The chuck-will's call sounded closer. "I've got work to do," Katherine said and went into the house.

Harry spent the next week trying with little success to make progress on his problems. He and Katherine were still at odds. He and Helen were not speaking. His effort to link Ruvin Carter to Riga's shooting was going nowhere. Despite Hodges' claims to the contrary, the police were doing nothing about the break-in gang at Rafe Juliette's Wild Turkey Condos, and Findlay Jay had gone home from the hospital, still determined to deliver Jubilee to Ernshaw Welty ready for sale to Burger King.

Harry talked three times with Riga, twice with Tom Burkhardt, and then, on the following Monday, with them together. She opened the meeting sitting up in bed. Despite the fact she was pale and her right arm was in a sling, Harry thought she looked stunning. He was just thinking that probably early morning held no threats for her, when she told him the court had set a date for a preliminary hearing on her suit against Carter. She actually smiled while she said it. She said she was way ahead of the doctors' predictions and was looking forward to being at the hearing.

"You might not even be out of the hospital," Tom protested.

Riga lost her smile. "I'll be there," she said.

Tom heard that in silence, but Harry could see he didn't like either the message or the way it was delivered. "Have you thought about how you're going to protect yourself?" Harry asked.

"What do you mean?" Riga demanded.

"When you go home, you're going to be at risk again. I don't want to be melodramatic here, but someone's trying to kill you."

Tom started to speak, but Riga talked over him. "I don't agree. Whoever it was tried and failed. The police are watching the house. He would be a fool to try the same thing a second time."

"Until the Brown Trust is liquidated, you are a target," Harry replied. "If the police won't mount a twenty-four/seven watch on you, I strongly suggest you hire some security."

"We don't even know the person who shot me has any connection with the Brown Trust," Riga said flatly.

"Harry's right," Tom countered. "You're still in danger."

Riga made a point of looking at her bedside clock. "Speaking of risks, I'd feel a lot better if you were home with Cheryl."

Tom jumped up and hiked out of the room. Harry looked at Riga. She appeared to be unconcerned by the manner of Tom's departure.

"Is something the matter?" she asked.

"Yes. There's no way to ease into this, so here it is. I assume you have a will." Riga nodded, frowning slightly. "Does Tom know the terms of the will?" She nodded a second time, smiling a little. "Okay," Harry said, disgusted. "Let's hear it."

She started to laugh and caught her breath. It was a moment before she could speak. "He didn't shoot me for my money, Harry. He wouldn't get any, and he knows it. I don't really want to explain how and how much."

"I don't want to know how and how much. But I have to ask who benefits from your death," Harry said stiffly.

"Cheryl and my mother. Now I have a question. If someone really wants to kill me, can a bodyguard stop it from happening?"

"It significantly increases the odds in your favor. But, no, you can't live a normal life and be completely safe."

"Then I'll think about hiring security, but right now I'm not concerned enough to think very hard about it."

Harry left the hospital and drove east out of Avola. Findlay Jay hadn't been exaggerating. Between the ranch gate and the house, Harry was stopped twice by armed men.

"Are you bird-dogging me?" the big farmer demanded as Harry stepped onto the lanai, where Findlay Jay was sitting in a bentwood rocker with his hat perched on his still-bandaged head.

Findlay Jay's home was a traditional, white-clapboard Florida house expanded to twice the conventional size. It was encircled by a lanai shaded under deep eaves, and the house itself was built around a central, floor-to-roof open space. The space functioned like a huge chimney to pull air from beneath the eaves through all the rooms and then upward to a screened cupola. The steady flow of air in the house cooled the rooms in even the hottest weather.

"Yes, and I smell trouble, not quail."

Findlay Jay grinned. From somewhere deep in the house came an excited yapping. "That would be Willie Nelson. Norma Jean must of put him down."

The yapping stopped. Findlay Jay nodded. "She's picked him up."

"I want to talk. You up to it?" Harry asked.

"You want some of this lemonade? It's damned good even if it's short on wallop, and speaking of that, I believe I've got a jug of something around here."

"I'll take it just as it is," Harry said. He knew trying to hurry Findlay Jay was as useless as trying to hurry a team of oxen.

The farmer reached down beside his rocker and lifted up an old-fashioned brass bell, the kind that teachers in a distant past rang to end recess. Harry had already noticed a lever-action Winchester rifle lying on the floor beside the rocker. Findlay Jay tolled the bell. Harry thought he caught in the echo the faint sound of children's voices. After a while Norma Jean stuck her head out the door, saw Harry, and ducked back inside.

"What y'all want, honey?" she called.

"Bring another glass and some ice for this renegade Yankee," he said. While they waited, Findlay Jay rocked gently and stared out at his pastures, calmly letting the locusts hold back the silence. The glass and the ice first, Harry thought. But a tall young man, unmistakably Findlay Jay's son, brought the glass and a bowl of ice, while Willie Nelson yapped on the other side of the screen door.

"This here's my boy Bradley," Findlay Jay said in a low

voice as he poured Harry's lemonade. "He's running the spread while I heal my head. Bradley, this is Harry Brock. He did a little work for me a while back, and now I can't get rid of him. Watch yourself around him. He's a Yankee."

Harry heard the pride in Findlay Jay's voice and his efforts to hide it. He shook hands with Bradley, liked the young man's straight look and firm handshake. Then he took the glass of lemonade Findlay Jay passed him and sat down. "Is Jubilee still on his feet?" he asked.

"He is," Findlay Jay said.

"What will it take to keep him there?"

The question went unanswered for some time.

"How do you figure it's any of your business?" Findlay Jay asked finally. The rancher's voice was quiet, but the look he bent on Harry had no warmth in it.

"Ernshaw Welty thinks you killed his son."

"There's no way my father could have done it," Bradley said in a younger version of Findlay Jay's voice.

Findlay Jay put down his glass very slowly without taking his eyes off Harry. "He tell you that?"

"No. He didn't have to. I checked and found out where and when the boy was killed. I'll give you all the odds you want on this. He thinks you ran the kid off the road and into that pine tree. Did you?"

"No. And why should I believe you?"

"Put your hand up to your head. Why else would he want to kill you?"

"He can't figure out how I stole Jubilee."

"Not good enough. I talked to the man. He is walking around fully-cocked. I think Jubilee just gave him the excuse he was looking for."

"Pa," Bradley said, "I thought we agreed that the Jubilee business was going to be settled."

Findlay Jay leaned slowly back in his rocker and raised his hand to silence his son. "Wouldn't you say what Ernshaw Welty believes is his problem?"

"I'd say it belongs to both of you. Then I'd go a step further and say that if you don't tell him you didn't do it and make him believe it, then you're as much in the wrong as he is."

"I don't owe Ernshaw Welty one goddamned thing."

They were interrupted by a young, yellow-haired boy three or four years old, who burst out of the house. He was followed by his mother, a tall, dark-haired woman in dungarees and sleeveless white blouse, who grabbed him from behind and hoisted him into her arms, where he wriggled and kicked, trying to escape.

"Hi, I'm Pam," she said, thrusting out a hand to Harry as he got to his feet. "This here's Wainfleet the Terrible, and I'm going to take him out to see the bulls, and while I'm doing that, I'm going let him run until he drops."

"Good luck," Harry said, shaking her proffered hand.

"I'll need it." She strode off the lanai and set Wainfleet on his feet. As predicted, he ran.

"He goes like that from dawn 'til dark," Findlay Jay said approvingly.

"Pa," Bradley put in, "why not think about what Mr. Brock is saying? What's to be gained by keeping this feud running? It's way past the time when it should stop. Ma is . . ."

"We'll leave your mother out of this," Findlay Jay said in a hard voice.

"Yes, sir," Bradley replied, "but what do we gain by keeping that Jubilee horse?"

Harry caught the *we* and thought, The young man is a step ahead of his father.

"What *we* gain, Brad," his father replied, "is the satisfac-

217

tion of knowing we've bested Ernshaw Welty."

Bradley set aside his lemonade and leaned toward his father. "Is it worth dying for?"

"I'm a long way from being dead," Findlay Jay replied.

Harry did not want to be caught between these two men, if a struggle between the generations was going to break out. But he didn't have to resign his position either.

He stood up. "Findlay Jay, start thinking about what you owe yourself."

"What does that mean?"

"One thing it doesn't mean is making Jubilee into hamburger. I think Bradley's making sense. It does mean moving beyond where you are now with Ernshaw Welty." Harry picked up his hat. "Thanks for the lemonade. Think about what I've said. But don't try to go over there on your own. This isn't a John Wayne movie."

Bradley grinned.

"He was a good man," his father said calmly.

"Yes, he was. But after they shot him, he got up and walked off. That's not how it will work with you."

"I'm still walking."

"Only because he shot you in the head. Call me. Nice meeting you, Bradley. You've got your work cut out for you."

On his way home, Harry stopped to talk with Rafe Juliette. The condo owner was in his office, hunkered over his desk like a fat spider.

"You had any more break-ins?"

"Two. One down."

"Dead?"

Juliette nodded. "One of the burglars."

"The police know?"

"Hell, no."

"The body?"

"It went into the Seminole River on an outgoing tide."

"You looking for a war out here, Rafe?"

"I may not have a choice. A couple of deputies from the Sheriff's department came out, looked around, cited me for inadequate handicapped parking, warned me about running a disorderly house, and left. Couldn't put a night patrol out here, too short of men."

"I'll try again," Harry said and left. He was beginning to think he was in for a rerun of the previous week.

That night after dinner, Katherine said she wanted to take a walk.

"We were so busy I worked straight through lunch," she told him.

"That's not so good," he said. He knew he shouldn't make a criticism, but lately with Katherine what he knew and what he did were not always connected. And the list of things he wasn't supposed to say to her was getting too damned long to remember.

The moon was up, and as they walked toward the bridge, they had it and the creek glinting through the trees for company. The early summer night orchestra was tuning up. Katherine usually walked with the same explosive energy she put into everything else she did, but tonight that energy seemed to have all drained out of her. The doctor was giving her good reports on the pregnancy, but she was concerned about Katherine's weight loss. Katherine, however, seemed too preoccupied to take the issue seriously.

She had let his comment pass without acknowledging

it. He tried again. "How are you feeling?"

"Fireflies," she said.

They were passing a tongue of mangrove swamp that bordered the road to their right. The dark understory of the swamp was winking with pale, greenish lights. Harry thought briefly how mysterious the lights were, but his mind wouldn't stay on the fireflies.

"Katherine, how much longer is this going to go on?"

"About five months."

"Try again."

"I don't think so."

"Then I will. Can we end this stand-off? It's not doing either of us any good, and I think it's harming the kids."

"Are you trying to use the kids against me?"

"No. But Minna's stopped talking about Old Man Rabbit. She's not reading, and even Boots can't make her laugh. Jesse does nothing *but* read his science books, and I can hardly get him outside to rake a leaf."

"Minna's not a baby anymore and neither is Jesse. They can't be happy all the time. Life isn't cut that way."

She had picked up her pace as she spoke, and Harry lengthened his stride. "Now that's cleared up, how about if we try talking to one another?"

She stopped. In the moonlight, Harry saw that her face was wet with tears. She reached out and let her fingers brush the front of his shirt.

"You'd be better off talking to the moon," she said in a choked voice as she pushed past him and strode back toward the house.

Chapter 24

"You can't hurry Katherine on this thing," Tucker told Harry. They were in Tucker's citrus orchard, scything the grass. Weissmuller, Sanchez, and Oh-Brother! were supervising.

Harry swore silently at himself for having brought up the subject. He stopped working and tried to turn the conversation in a new direction. "You need either a ride-on mower or some sheep."

Tucker leaned on his scythe and regarded Harry critically. "Sheep belong on a mountain. A power mower belongs under a landslide on the same mountain."

"Or you could rig a one-horse mowing machine."

Oh-Brother! was nibbling a patch of clover. He lifted his head and stopped chewing to stare at Harry. Harry, awash in guilt, immediately recanted. "I mean a one-mule mowing machine." God, he asked himself, what am I doing?

"Never mind that," Tucker said. "You've got two women mad at you and with good reason. So do some creative listening. You cut Katherine all the slack she wants. As for Helen, call her, and keep calling until she's convinced you really do want to talk to her and not just make her feel worse than she's already feeling."

"Why should she be feeling bad? I'm the one she threatened to punch, and now she won't speak to me."

"She didn't want it known that she and Riga Kraftmeier are having an affair. If that's what it is."

"It's a duck all right."

Tucker made a face. "Get over it."

Sanchez was grinning. Weissmuller had stopped listening and was staring off into the woods. Oh-Brother! was nodding.

Jesus, Harry thought, and turned his back on them. "I could give it a try," he said with considerable reluctance.

"Then let's get this hay down." Tucker unlimbered his scythe.

That warm-up was what put Harry in front of the Three Rivers Bank at noon. He was uncomfortable but ashamed to cut and run, which was what he wanted to do.

"I'm buying lunch," he said, falling in beside Helen when she came out of the bank.

"The Pig's Tail," Helen said without looking at him.

They were taken to a table at the back of the restaurant. Helen looked around, still wearing a scowl.

"I'll get us another table," Harry said.

"Sit down and listen," Helen snapped and pulled out her chair as if she was giving it a stress test. Harry sat down. "I don't know why I'm even talking to you," Helen began.

"Maybe you just can't turn down a free lunch," Harry suggested, pretending to look at the menu.

"Idiot," she said and snatched the menu out of his hands.

Harry felt better. As long as she was calling him names, there was hope. "Helen, it's none of my business. It really isn't." He started to say he didn't care what she and Riga were doing, and stopped himself.

Quite suddenly Helen's eyes filled with tears. "Shit!" she said, and swept them away.

She tried to glare at him, but instead of the glare, Harry saw the black smudges under her eyes. He also saw how pale and drawn her face was. "What's wrong?" he demanded. "And don't say, *'Nothing.'*"

She sighed and slumped back in her chair. "Nothing. Everything. I don't know."

Their waitress arrived. Harry ordered for both of them. Helen let him do it.

"Give it a shot," he said.

"To begin with, you were never supposed to see us kissing."

"Somehow, I guessed that."

She laughed. Then she went quiet. Harry waited.

"I guess your seeing us made it real for me," she said finally.

She left it there and began shredding her napkin. Harry risked pushing her a little. "Is that good or bad?"

"Bad." She balled the torn paper in her hand and squeezed it until her knuckles turned white.

"Why?"

She unclenched her hand and, in a gesture Harry couldn't read, dropped her elbows onto the table. "How do you feel about me now?"

"I'm not sure. I guess I should have known, but I didn't."

She sighed. "That's not an answer, but I guess I don't deserve one. Your seeing us together like that has changed things."

"Helen, I don't have any claims on you."

"Yes, you do, Harry. You sure as hell do."

"How much difference does it make?"

The waitress brought their orders. When she was gone, Helen gave Harry a straight look and said, "A lot. As long as no one knew . . ." She stopped, apparently stuck.

Harry tried another tack. "How long have you and Riga been together?" He hated the euphemism, but couldn't say more directly what he meant.

"Almost two years."

Harry did some counting that located it just after he and Katherine married. He allowed himself to wonder briefly if Helen had been in love with Katherine and then stifled the thought. "I understand now why you've been so protective of Riga."

"Don't feel sorry for me, Harry Brock." She dropped her fork in her plate and flashed him an anguished look.

"Forget I said it. Tell me where we are."

"How mad at me are you?"

"I'm not mad at you, Helen. I'm jealous."

He was astonished he had said that. Her eyes brimmed again, and she reached across the table and grabbed one of his hands and then snatched her own back as if she'd touched a hot stove. "Oh, Harry," she said in an unsteady voice. Then she bent her head and snatched up her fork. "Now shut up and let me finish my lunch."

An hour later after he got home, Harry had a call from Findlay Jay.

"I've been turning over what you said about Ernshaw thinking I killed his boy. Norma Jean reminded me we were in Columbia, South Carolina, when he died. We were seeing Bradley through an appendicitis operation. I'd forgotten about it. Probably being shot in the head didn't help my memory."

"Why wouldn't Welty know that? Despite your troubles, you can throw rocks into one another's wood lots."

"We come and go without a lot of fuss."

"In your own planes."

"That's about it."

"What do you want me to do?"

"First, stop thinking I might be such a back-shooting, snake-eating bushwhacker as to have run that poor boy off the road and killed him, even if he was a Welty."

"What else?" It was worse than trying to pull a turtle out of its shell.

"If you was to tell Ernshaw where I was when his boy was killed, I'd be obliged."

"Anything else you want me to say to him?"

"I can't think of anything."

Harry wanted to say a number of things, but he limited himself to one. "What about using this message I'm delivering as the occasion for opening up the Jubilee issue?"

After a long pause, Findlay Jay said, "Brad had the same idea, but no. One thing at a time."

The drive into Ernshaw Welty's place made Harry's scalp crawl. The ranch seemed deserted. He stepped down from the Rover into a silent yard with only a dusty white rooster for company. The bird was pecking at something in a patch of dry grass near an upended wheelbarrow and took no notice of Harry's arrival. Harry looked at each of the three barns. Then he turned to the house. It stood a couple of hundred feet to his right in a small grove of pecan trees. There was no one in sight.

Harry was considering driving on to the house, when Welty stepped out of the black shadow of an open barn door not more than thirty feet from him. A moment later, four more men appeared from other doors. Three of them were carrying rifles and the fourth had a revolver stuck in the waistband of his jeans. Welty appeared to be unarmed. Harry studied the rancher as he approached and concluded he looked more than ever like a strip of dry leather.

"What do you want, Brock?"

"Hello, Welty," Harry replied, ignoring the man's slit-eyed hostility. "I don't want anything other than to give you some information."

"Let's hear it."

Harry decided not to be fancy. "Findlay Jay didn't kill your son. He and his wife were in Columbia, South Carolina, when your boy was killed. I checked. You can go to the bank with it."

"You know you're trespassing?" Welty demanded.

The men with the rifles had drifted out of sight, but Harry assumed somebody with a gun was watching the two of them, as others had probably watched him drive in from the gate.

"Yes, and it would be a real downer to be shot for it, but I figured it would be worth the risk. I wouldn't take much pleasure out of shooting you either." Harry was not carrying his gun, but he figured this exchange was a pissing contest and decided to take his turn.

Welty gave a sour grin. "Let's step out of the sun," he said. He gestured toward a live oak shading a space between two of the barns. Under the tree was a split log bench with a watering trough beside it.

"Nice spot," Harry said. He sat down on the bench and took off his hat. A cool breeze stirred the leaves over his head and brought him the smell of drying hay. The water in the trough bubbled quietly.

"The horses like it." Welty eased himself onto the bench and put his elbows on his knees. "Why are you telling me this bullshit about Findlay Jay being in Columbia when Henry was killed?"

"He didn't do it. Couldn't have."

"I hear he had an accident himself."

"Yes. You interested in getting your stallion back?"

"Getting shot weaken Findlay Jay's mind?" Welty gave a

short laugh that Harry did not like.

"No. And I'm all that's keeping him from sending Jubilee back to you as hamburger, done up in a horsehide wrapper."

Welty straightened up and shot Harry a hard look. "You like your work?"

"No. Sometimes I have to spend too much time with damned fools like you and Findlay Jay."

Harry thought he had stretched that worm about as far as it would go, possibly a little beyond. Welty's eyes squeezed almost shut and his dark face grew blacker.

"Just what do you mean, Brock?"

Harry leaned back on the bench and ran his hand over his head. "I mean you two could stop this right here, right now. Jubilee could come home. Your men could go back to ranching instead of carrying guns. You could start sleeping nights."

"This is none of your fucking business."

"Wake up, Welty. The way this is going, there's a good chance of one or both of you being killed."

"Like my boy," Welty said quietly.

It sounded to Harry like a threat.

"Why didn't Findlay Jay come over here, if that's what he wants?" Welty demanded. "Why send you?"

"Somebody put a bullet into his head. Remember? And I wouldn't let him come, even if he could."

Welty pulled off his hat and slapped it down on the bench between them. Harry pretended not to pay any attention. But he thought it might be a good sign. The rancher stared out across the yard and blew out his breath. Harry took a chance.

"I'll say to you what I said to Findlay Jay. You may hate one another's guts, and probably God himself couldn't change that. But you could set aside those feelings long enough to ask if you've got any interests in common. I could start the work by giving one."

"And that is?"

"Jubilee. You want that horse back, and Findlay Jay doesn't want to kill him. But he will if this goes on. And if he does, you'll do something back."

"That's for damned sure."

Harry nodded. Then he took another chance. "Nothing's going to bring your son back, but Findlay Jay didn't kill him. Neither did Norma Jean. They were with their boy in a Columbia hospital while he was having a ruptured appendix taken out the night Henry died."

Welty looked off across his yard. He hadn't called in his SWAT team. Harry breathed a little easier. He thought he might have found in Jubilee the kingpin he'd been looking for. He stood up and pulled on his hat.

"Where are you going?" Welty demanded.

"Home."

"Hold on . . ."

"Think it over what I've said. You've got my number, if you want me."

Welty got to his feet, facing Harry squarely. Harry looked at his deeply-scored features and saw with a sudden shock of understanding that suffering, more than the sun, had worn the furrows in that face.

"Henry was my only son, our only child," Welty said. He seemed ready to say something else, then changed his mind.

"I'm sorry," Harry said. "It's a terrible thing to lose a child."

"What would you know about that?"

"They're not dead, but I lost two."

Harry put out his hand. Welty regarded him in silence

for a moment, then took it. "Don't let this chance slip, Ernshaw," Harry said. "If you want me, call. Never mind the time."

When Harry got home, he knew Minna and Jesse were there ahead of him. From upstairs came the sinister throb of music Minna wasn't supposed to be listening to. An equally disturbing silence from Jesse's end of the hall meant he was holed up again in his room. Harry thought for a minute, then went upstairs.

"This won't take long, so stop complaining," he told the two of them as they trailed out of the house in his wake.

Grumbling and protesting that they were hot in the dungarees and long-sleeved jerseys he had insisted they wear, they followed him toward Tucker's farm until they reached a tangle of white columbine vines on the creek side of the road. The vines had smothered the low hillock of sand separating the road from the water, but Harry, not to be denied, pushed his way into the coffee bushes and Brazilian peppers crowding against the columbines.

"If I've got the time right, this will be worth the effort," was all he would say as he dragged the two laggards after him.

They had almost reached the edge of the creek when something big flung itself off the bank into the water with a loud splash and vanished in a muddy swirl of brown bubbles.

"Alligator!" Jesse shouted.

"I want to see it!" Minna demanded.

They pressed past Harry, forgetting their boredom and resentment at being forced outdoors.

"Has that alligator got a nest here?" Jesse asked.

"No, but something else has," Harry answered. He had

turned away from the water and was pushing branches aside for a look at the sand pile.

"What?" Minna asked, hiking after him.

"You tell me," Harry said.

"What are we looking for?" Jesse asked. He came after Minna and began helping Harry pull back the branches.

"Baby turtles!" Minna shouted.

And she was right. One after another, quarter-sized painted turtles were digging themselves out of the sand and scuttling toward the creek.

"How did you know?" Jesse asked Harry. He was grinning and Minna was on her hands and knees, pushing sticks and rocks out of the way of the scrabbling turtles. Both were showing more enthusiasm than Harry had seen either of them exhibit in a month. A weight lifted off his spirits.

"I knew female turtles had been laying eggs in this pile of sand. I checked the calendar and figured there was a good chance we'd see some hatching about now."

Jesse laughed. "That alligator must have been checking his calendar."

"It's not getting these ones!" Minna shouted and herded a new cluster toward the water.

An hour later the hatch ended. Once back on the road, the two youngsters lost most of their rejuvenated spirits. Minna stopped hopping and Jesse walked beside Harry, staring glumly at his shoes. He glanced back at Minna and asked in a low voice, "Are you and Mom breaking up?"

Harry's first impulse was to tell the boy he was too young to understand and that it was none of his business. But, of course, it was his business. And even if he was young, it was still his business and also Minna's. He stopped and waited for Minna to catch up with them.

"Minna," he said, "Jesse asked me if Katherine and I

were breaking up. Are you thinking about that?"

She looked up at him and her brother with a slight frown. "I want things to be happy again."

"That's not what Harry asked you," Jesse said angrily.

Harry put his hand on the boy's shoulder. "If things were okay with your mother and me, you wouldn't be asking if we were breaking up. Right?"

Jesse nodded.

"You already know some of what's wrong. Katherine has been worried about your grandmother. Also, she's not feeling as well as she should. She's not really sick, but the pregnancy has been hard for her."

"Why?" Minna asked.

"I don't know," Harry said. "Sometimes it goes that way. She's also angry with me because I didn't tell her about Gideon Stone being down here, and my going off to talk to him frightened her. That made her mad. She had a right to be. I should have told her about Gideon and what I was going to do."

"But it turned out all right," Jesse protested.

"Mom didn't know that till he got home," Minna countered.

"Okay," Harry said. "You're both right."

"Are you two breaking up?" Jesse asked again.

Harry looked at the boy and wondered what he could say that was both true and hopeful. "No matter what it looks like or how it feels to you two, your mother and I love each other, and we're working on the problem."

"What problem?" Minna asked.

Harry's heart sank a little. "I guess she's not sure right now that she can trust me to take care of the three of you the way I should."

"Can you?" Minna asked.

"Don't be dumb," Jesse exploded. "Of course he can."

"Wait, it's a fair question," Harry said. "But it's your mother who has to answer it."

Chapter 25

"Where the hell have you been?" Katherine demanded from the lanai door.

"Hi, Mom," Minna called out when they were halfway across the lawn. "Harry took really good care of us. Old Man Rabbit would have given him five." She ran forward with her arms out.

Katherine bent forward and lifted her with a groan. "I'm not going to be able to . . ."

"We were watching baby turtles dig out of their nests," Jesse said loudly. "We didn't drown. The alligator didn't eat us. We weren't lost in the swamp."

He pushed past his mother and disappeared into the house. Harry winced. It occurred to him he might have made another mistake. Katherine kissed Minna and put her down.

"What's all this?" she asked Harry when Minna had run into the house after her brother.

"We caught a hatch of sliders at the sand pile," he said. "How was your day?"

"Busy. Why didn't you leave me a note? I came home to an empty house."

He could hear the fear in her voice and see it in her face. "I'm sorry. I guess the time got away from us."

"What have you been telling them?"

He could have said, "Nothing," but he didn't. Saying what he had to Minna and Jesse seemed to have clarified something for him. "Jesse asked me if we were breaking up. I said we were working on some differences. Also, there were issues of trust you were thinking about."

"What issues?"

"That's what they wanted to know. I told them you weren't sure you could trust me to take care of the three of you properly."

"Harry!"

He kept talking. "I also told them why you were angry with me. I said I hadn't told you about Gideon Stone and that you had a right to be angry."

"You had no right to tell them anything about our problems. They're kids, Harry."

"Katherine, they're worried about us, and they're frightened. Kids are always right when they say something's wrong in their lives. They're not so good about understanding what it is. That's where we come in."

"Maybe," she said.

"Maybe," he admitted. "But what they heard from me wasn't as scary as whatever they've been imagining. And for an hour they were just kids again. We can thank the turtles for that."

"Thank you, turtles," she said. She looked at him with an expression he couldn't read. "Help me set the table. If the dinner's dry as a stick, we can thank the turtles for that too."

At nine that night Ernshaw Welty called.

"I figure to call his bluff," Welty said.

Harry waited. The line crackled faintly, then went quiet. "Welty?"

"Your move."

"What do you want to do?"

234

"I already said it. If Findlay Jay wants to talk, it's your move."

"All right. I'll get back to you," Harry replied.

Welty hung up. Harry went upstairs and knocked on Katherine's door.

"Welty wants to talk," he said.

She was sitting up in bed reading. Her hair was falling loose over her shoulders, and in the soft light Harry thought she looked beautiful.

"About what?" she asked, a little less impatiently than usual.

"Jubilee."

"Why are you talking like that?" she demanded.

"Like what?"

"As if words were rationed."

"It's the way Ernshaw Welty talks, and it's catching. Never mind. I'm all right. I've been trying to get Findlay Jay and Ernshaw Welty together. I think it's going to happen."

"Mr. Fix-It," Katherine said. She dropped her book onto her lap and looked at him skeptically.

"It's a start," he said.

"If I were you, that's what I'd be afraid of."

"Why?"

"Because those two families have been fighting for a hundred years. Do you really think you can stop it?"

"I've got Jubilee."

"The horse?"

"Yes, and neither one of them wants that horse dead. I'm counting on that to get them past this bad patch—that and the fact that Findlay Jay didn't kill Welty's son. I think I've got a shot at getting it fixed."

"Bad patch! Welty shot Findlay Jay, and if you're asking

me, you've got an equal to better chance of getting yourself shot," Katherine said in a burst of anger. "You don't know anything about these people. You're a Yankee, Harry. I left out the *damned,* but they won't. You don't know how they think."

Harry felt his own anger climbing. He had come to her to share some good news. Now she was . . . He stopped the voice. "It's worth a try," he said, trying to rescue his optimism. "I'm sorry you think otherwise."

He closed the door and went back downstairs.

The next morning over breakfast, Katherine said, "Harry, about last night, there's nothing wrong with what you're trying to do, but for God's sake don't do anything that would let them blame you if things go sour."

Harry was pleased by her shift in attitude, but instead of encouraging him, it made him wonder what she was seeing that he wasn't. He decided to run it by Tucker.

"Well," Tucker said, "as Katherine said, they've been scrapping a long time." He put a plate of oatmeal cookies on the table between the mugs of tea and motioned to Harry to sit down. Weissmuller and Sanchez were lying on the back stoop, and through the screen door Harry could see Oh-Brother! cropping grass under one of the big live oaks. Cicadas were filling the yard and the kitchen with their fiddling. Tucker's gingham curtains billowed gently in the morning breeze.

"Katherine thinks I'm painting a bull's eye on my back if I go on trying to bring those two together. What's your opinion?"

"They used to shoot one another, and they've started doing it again. The prognosis is clouded. Have another cookie."

Harry took one, to be polite, he told himself, but when he finished it, he found himself taking another one without making an excuse. "Between them they've got enough fire-power to invade Avola."

"Don't mind the crumbs. Sanchez and Weissmuller will suck them up." Tucker leaned back in his chair and frowned at the ceiling for a moment. "The guns worry me. I agree with Katherine. You don't want to be halfway between those two if they start shooting at one another."

"If I get them together, they're going to be unarmed."

"Harry, you've got more hope of disarming a rattle-snake."

Harry took another cookie. He did not like what he was hearing, and got up and walked to the door and stared out at the sunlit world beyond the stoop. Peaceful kingdom, he thought. Then he noticed Weissmuller was on his feet staring into the woods.

"What's Weissmuller looking at out there?" he asked.

"He's been doing that for a while now. Whatever it is, it doesn't interest Sanchez or Oh-Brother!."

Harry came back to the table and reached for his tea. There was no point in putting it off. "So you think I'm at risk here?"

"Hard to say. Just don't give them an excuse to shoot you."

"That's a joke, right?"

"No, they've been wearing the same spots for a long time now."

Harry went over and over his plan as he drove to Findlay Jay's. Although he couldn't find anything wrong with the plan, he couldn't shake his uneasiness. Findlay Jay or Welty might turn it down, but what more could go wrong?

Nothing. He pulled the Rover into Findlay Jay's yard and stepped out into the blazing afternoon sun, ready to make his pitch.

The big rancher and his son were on the porch. He did not get up to welcome Harry, but Bradley did. He shook hands and gave Harry a smiling welcome.

"The wad of bandages on my father's head has shrunk since you last saw him," Bradley said with a broad grin.

Harry agreed it had and asked Findlay Jay how he was feeling.

"Middlin'," the rancher answered.

His hat hung on the back of his chair and a pitcher of lemonade stood sweating on a folding table beside him. To Harry's relief, the rifle was missing.

"Rest your feet," Findlay Jay said when he finished shaking Harry's hand. "What's your plan?"

Harry told him. The rancher listened quietly, his hands folded across his stomach. When Harry stopped talking, Findlay Jay carefully filled a glass with lemonade and passed it to Harry. He held the pitcher toward Bradley, who shook his head.

Harry asked, "What do you think?"

Findlay Jay took a drink of his lemonade and put the glass down carefully, as if he was doing it for the first time. "And you want Ernshaw to come over here?" He had begun to smile slightly.

"That's my idea. I didn't think you ought to be banging around over the roads."

"We'd hear from Norma Jean on that one," he agreed. He paused again. "You figure I should let Ernshaw take Jubilee home with him." Another pause. "As a gesture of goodwill."

"Yes."

"And what am I getting in return?"

"No more getting shot in the head or having your cattle rustled," Bradley said patiently.

"That the way you see it, Brock?" Findlay Jay asked.

"That's what we're aiming at," Harry said.

A long pause followed. "We're going to do this without guns?"

Harry nodded, mentally crossing his fingers.

"It makes me uneasy that Ernshaw has agreed to this, but I'll give it a try."

He stood up so quickly Harry jumped to his feet, startled. Findlay Jay looked down at him, studying him or something else. His smile had been replaced by a frown that was no more than two lines between his eyebrows. Harry thought he was about to say something, but the moment passed. The frown vanished, and Findlay Jay thrust out his hand.

"Let him set the time."

"All right."

"My family won't be here on visiting day," Findlay Jay added.

"I'll be here," Bradley said.

Harry nodded. "However you decide. I'll set it up."

"You'll let me know if the dog won't hunt," Findlay Jay said.

"Oh, I think he'll hunt," Harry said.

Findlay Jay smiled just enough to crinkle the skin at the corners of his mouth, but Bradley said in a voice full of feeling, "Lord, I hope you're right."

Harry drove out through the guns with his uneasiness for company. Something in Findlay Jay's manner had troubled him, but he couldn't say just what it was. He pushed the

Rover down the road, leaving a plume of dust behind him, and turned in at Welty's gate. Once again, he drove through apparently empty ranch land with only cattle in the scattered pastures. But he knew he was being watched, and Ernshaw Welty was waiting for him under the pecan trees.

"That's right," Harry said after he had filled Welty in on his conversation with Findlay Jay, leaving out what he thought it best not to tell him, "if this thing goes right, you get Jubilee back." He wanted to add, And you both get to grow old, but decided Welty was in no mood to hear it.

The rancher kicked the dirt with the toe of his boot and studied the results. Harry took the opportunity to look around. Not a soul in sight. The barns soaked in the sun, the trees stirred quietly in the feeble breeze, and on every side the fields and the woods lay stiff and still as a painting. It made Harry's skin crawl.

"What persuaded Findlay Jay to give me Jubilee?" Welty raised his head and his eyes flickered across Harry's and slid away.

Harry could have said, Maybe getting shot in the head had something to do with it, or maybe he's sick of playing these stupid and dangerous games. He didn't. Instead he concentrated on trying to understand what Ernshaw Welty's question was really asking. When he thought he knew, he said, "If you mean, what's he getting out of this that you don't see, the answer is nothing. He gives you back the horse, and then both of you quit stealing things from one another."

"Wrong, Brock. He's doing this for his boy." Welty's eyes darted back to Harry and his mouth stretched into a thin and bitter grin.

"Maybe, but when you've got Jubilee, it's over. You could shake on it or not. Suit yourselves."

Harry had not intended to add the part about shaking hands, but the expression on Welty's face had rattled him. The rancher made no comment on the optional handshake. His grin faded into the grimness from which it had emerged.

"If we're doing this, let's do it. Day after tomorrow?"

"Okay."

"Around noon?"

"Fine."

"No guns."

"No guns."

"Then it's day after tomorrow."

"Your horse is coming home," Harry said.

Welty pulled his hat lower over his eyes. "You'd better hope so."

Chapter 26

Katherine showed no enthusiasm for what she darkly called the Jubilee Project. "I wouldn't trust either one of them as far as I could throw the Rover." She said this while she savagely chopped vegetables for the salad. "And I would like to throw it a long way."

It was a fairly good gloss on how things were between them that Harry felt encouraged by her response. Jesse, who was sitting in the rocker reading a book on the ecological history of North America, lifted his head. "I like the Rover," he said.

"So do I," Harry said, but Jesse dove back into his book again. "I think that in two days Welty's going to have his horse back, Findlay Jay's men will be looking after the cattle, and . . ."

"And Shane can ride off into the hills," Katherine said. She swept the salad into a colander and rinsed it under the faucet as if she was drowning it.

"And becomes a legend in his own time," Harry added.

"If you live," she said. She gave the colander a shake and stuck it into the refrigerator.

"Welty thinks Findlay Jay is ready to bury the hatchet because of his boy," Harry replied. "He may be right."

Katherine stopped. "What did he say?"

"He had asked me what Findlay Jay was getting out of the settlement. I said nothing but an end to the fighting.

Welty said I was wrong. He was doing it for his boy. Perhaps he's right."

"Was he pleased?"

Harry remembered the expression on Welty's face. "I wouldn't say so."

"Must be hard after having lost his only child." She walked to the door and paused in it long enough to look at both Harry and Jesse. Jesse was buried in his book. Harry was gathering up the files he had piled on the table. She appeared to be preparing to say something, but if she was, she changed her mind.

Riga Kraftmeier was still in the hospital, but just barely. She was prowling the corridors when Harry found her, dressed in blue silk pajamas and a flowing blue silk robe, her hair spread over her shoulders. She was not exactly rejoicing to run a race. Harry guessed she was in a lot of pain, but he knew better than to say so.

"How about our sitting down?" he asked. "I've been rowing a galley since first light, and I'm pooped."

She eased herself onto the nearest bench, leaned her head back against the wall, and closed her eyes. Looking at her, and it would have been impossible not to look at her, Harry suddenly remembered with a wrench of his heart another woman who had loved flowing clothes. In what part of the world was Abigail Blakeley wandering? He put the memory back in its box.

"How bad is it?" he asked. She was the color of skim milk.

"I'm not used to walking yet," she said. "I get lightheaded. I'll be all right when I get home."

"Speaking of your going home, have you or Tom done anything about security?"

She leaned forward slowly and opened her eyes. They were dark with pain. "No," she said. "I'm not even sure . . ."

"I am." He pulled a pair of business cards out of his shirt pocket and passed them to her. "Here are the names of a couple of reliable companies. Unless the police promise to cover you full-time when you leave here, hire one of them."

"Why should I bother?" she asked. "You're always around." Her attempt to smile collapsed. She shut her eyes again.

"I'll get a chair," Harry said and stood up.

"No," Riga snapped. She forced herself upright. "I'll be fine."

When she had driven off the nurses who had put her back into bed, scolding her as they gave her pills and a shot, and propped her up on a stack of pillows, Riga asked Harry if Helen was in any danger.

The question startled him. "Do you think she is?"

"I pulled her into this mess. I just don't know how far. If whoever's trying to kill me can't get to me, is there a chance he'll try to harm her?"

"Riga, if you have any reason to think that might happen, tell me now."

"I don't know. All I do know is that I can't seem to stop worrying that . . ." She stopped and dropped her head back onto her pillows. "If anything were to happen to Helen because . . ."

A line of poetry suddenly ran in his head. "Who would have thought my shrivel'd heart/Could have recover'd greenness?" She lay with her eyes closed, beautiful even in pain. Only love, he thought, or some comparable agony, could have made it happen. Then he pulled himself together. "There's no certainty in any of this," he said gently, "but unless there's something you haven't told me, she's probably safe."

There was some space between his words and the truth, because he was aware that only the murderous bastard who had tried to kill Riga knew the full answer.

Harry drove away from the hospital still thinking about what Riga had said. The burden of beauty, he thought, is nothing compared to the burden of love. Well, her pain was hers, but he intended to do every last thing possible to make sure neither Riga nor Helen came to any further harm. Riga may have been telling the truth when she said she was not keeping anything from him, but Harry was taking no chances.

"A lot rides on this, Helen," Harry said.

They were in Shell Mound Park, sitting beside the Seminole River under a huge willow on a bench he had once shared with Abigail Blakeley. In front of them a gleaming white thirty-two-foot Catalina, its paint and brass glistening in the sun, was idling past on the ebbing tide, on its way to Oyster Pass and the Gulf. He remembered another boat passing . . . The old willow swayed its long, drooping branches in the breeze. Deep in the tree, a ring dove was calling.

Helen put up a hand. "Are you the turkey club?" she asked, interrupting him to forage in the large, brown paper bag that held their lunches. A pair of stubby Perrier bottles were open between them with Helen's straw stuck in one of them.

"Yes."

Helen passed him a stack of napkins, and while the lunch was set out between them, Harry gave up trying to talk and looked around the park. It was three years since his last visit, but coming here was still a bad idea. It had not been long enough. A tall, elegantly-dressed woman, swinging a parasol, was walking toward him. She took off her hat and, seeing him, began to smile . . .

"Harry, stop daydreaming. Take the sandwich. I'm giving you half of it because if I give you all of it, sure as hell, you'll drop it." She looked up at him and froze. "Oh, shit, Harry," she said. "It's Abigail Blakeley, isn't it? I'm sorry. I forgot." She started to put things back in to the bag. "Come on. Let's get out of here."

"It's okay. It was a long time ago. I want my lunch, and I want to talk to you. Give me back the sandwich. All right, half the sandwich."

"Are you sure?"

"Yes. Here's your water. Now listen."

When he was finished, Helen leaned back on the bench and sighed. "I probably don't know as much as you do about Riga's affairs," she said. Her discontent was obvious. "In fact, what I don't know about her life would make a fat book."

"In this case, it's probably a good thing."

Helen let that pass. "She's going to leave the hospital pretty soon. She's not ready, but she's going just the same. She listens to me about as much as you do."

"Are you worried?"

"Of course I'm worried, Harry. He'll come after her again. And this time he won't stop shooting until she's dead."

"Do you think it's Ruvin Carter?"

"Who else could it be?"

Harry crumpled his sandwich wrapper and dropped it into the bag. "I think it has to be him, and I'm worried."

"Why?"

"Because he could be thinking that you know everything that Riga knows."

"He'd be wrong."

"That may not matter, but I don't think he'll trouble you as long as Riga's alive."

"It's amazing how much better that makes me feel."

"This might help. I think I've persuaded her to hire some private security."

"How much good will that do?"

"It's better than nothing, and you've got mayonnaise on your chin."

Harry drove into Findlay Jay's yard and saw that he'd timed things right. Findlay Jay and Bradley were on the lanai and Ernshaw Welty had not yet arrived. Harry got down from the Rover and looked around, squinting in the sun's glare. He was a little uneasy about the coming meeting, but the peacefulness of the scene restored some of his confidence. Aside from Findlay Jay, rocking meditatively in the lanai's deep shade, and Bradley standing quietly beside him, the yards were empty. A deep, truculent bellow from one of the herd bulls broke the stillness and startled Harry. Then the silence drifted back.

"This here's a day I never expected to see," Findlay Jay said. He stood up when Harry stepped onto the lanai and shook his hand.

Bradley shook Harry's hand as if he was just coming out of church and being greeted by the minister.

"Let's hope things go as planned," Harry replied, slightly awed by Findlay Jay's turnout. The rancher was rigged out in what looked to Harry like dress westerns. From boots to hat he was brand new. His belt and his maroon vest had enough silver trimmings to make a Navajo envious. Bradley was wearing stone-washed jeans and a green T-shirt.

"Is Ernshaw going to show?" Bradley asked.

"I think so." He turned to Findlay Jay. "Where are your men?" It occurred to Harry that Welty might read a sinister intent into their absence.

"Here and there. Jubilee's in that second barn. When it's time for the turnover, I'll ring this bell. I figure Ernshaw will come with his horse van."

"It sounds right. But before you walk Jubilee out, I'll repeat the terms of the agreement. Is the handshake still on?"

Findlay Jay nodded. "Tell him about the bell. When I reach for it, I don't want anybody to think I'm going for a gun."

Before he finished speaking, they heard Ernshaw Welty's truck rumble over the cattle grate leading into the ranch's central compound. Welty's silver pickup and matching horse trailer rolled to a stop about twenty yards from the porch. Welty got down slowly from the truck. His turnout was much like Findlay Jay's, except for a loose jacket. Everything he wore was a somber black.

"There'll be a gun in there somewhere," Findlay Jay said quietly. Harry swore under his breath. Findlay Jay did not seem disturbed. In a louder voice, calm and without urgency, he said, "Come and set, Ernshaw. There's whiskey. There's lemonade. There's water."

As the invitation was being made, Welty strode across the yard, his boots kicking up puffs of dust as he advanced. After his initial look around him as he swung down from the truck, he had not taken his eyes off Findlay Jay.

"Where's my horse?" he demanded, ignoring Harry. He stepped onto the lanai, his narrow face stiff with some harsh emotion.

Harry started to speak, but Findlay Jay said, "Jubilee's in that second barn. He's right as rain and curried and brushed to a five-dollar shine. Let's have a little of that whiskey, to rinse the dust off our tonsils."

Harry wanted to say he didn't have any tonsils, but he knew that was only nerves and suppressed the impulse. Welty seemed to relax a little. "All right," he said.

Findlay Jay turned slowly and bent toward the low table beside his chair. He paused and looked at Welty. "Ernshaw, how will you have it?"

"Just as it comes."

"I like a little ice."

"None for me."

"Brock?"

"Show it to the brook."

Findlay Jay laughed easily. "I believe a brook has water in it."

"It's what makes it a brook," Harry answered.

"Bradley?"

"I'm fine as I am."

While Findlay Jay made the drinks and passed them around, Welty looked at Bradley and said, "It's been a while since I last saw you. I believe Henry was alive."

"I think he was," Bradley replied.

Findlay Jay raised his glass. "Here's to the girl up on the hill." He drank.

Welty said in a strong voice, "Here's to her sister," and followed Findlay Jay's lead.

Harry said, "Here's to all the black-eyed women." Findlay Jay gave Harry a pleased smile, and even Welty managed a thin, short-lived grin. Bradley said nothing, but he was watching Welty as if he expected him to explode. The whiskey burned all the way to Harry's belt buckle, and he struggled not to make a face. God, he thought, I'd rather drink gasoline.

"Will you set a spell?" Findlay Jay asked Welty.

"No. Let's get to our business."

"All right," Findlay Jay said.

Harry turned to Welty. "I'll just go over a couple things. Findlay Jay is going to return Jubilee to you, no strings attached. Then you and Findlay Jay are going to agree to stop stealing things from one another." He thought that sounded dumb enough to get him state aid. But he forged ahead. "You're not going to shoot at one another any more." Jesus. "And from this time forward you're going to live as neighbors."

Harry stepped back from between the two men and looked from Welty to Findlay Jay. "You may want to shake hands on it." He waited. Nothing happened. "Hold it," he said. "I'm supposed to say that pretty soon now Findlay Jay's going to lean down and pick up that old school bell and ring it to tell one of his men to bring Jubilee out of the barn."

Welty's mouth trembled, and Harry did not think the man was on the verge of tears. He swore a little more to himself. But Findlay Jay took a long step forward and put out his hand. Welty, stiff as a piece of dry oak, jerked forward and grasped the proffered hand. Harry began to breathe a little easier.

"Let's see the horse," Welty said.

Findlay Jay backed up, keeping his eyes on Welty, and picked up the bell. He raised it and swung his arm downward. The bell's clear, strident note rang out across the yard. And at that same instant, the sound of gunfire ripped through the celebratory chiming of the bell.

In less than a breath Harry, Findlay Jay, and Welty had guns in their hands.

"Son-of-a-bitch," Bradley said between his teeth.

"I'm surprised at you, Harry," Findlay Jay said with an easy grin.

"I'm not," Welty added. He looked as fully wired as a switchboard.

Harry felt himself sweating. Welty and Findlay Jay were pointing their guns at one another. Harry wasn't pointing his at anybody, and he felt foolish just standing there threatening to shoot the woods. Another crackle of gunfire rattled along the fence line beyond the pasture.

"Somebody's made a mistake," Harry said. "Who's out there?"

There was more shooting.

"Some of my people were out there," Findlay Jay said sheepishly, "kind of keeping an eye on things."

Welty shifted nervously. "Three or four of my men were coming in from that direction in case anything went wrong."

There was an exchange of fire that sounded like a whole string of firecrackers going off.

"How many?" Harry asked.

"Well, six or seven," Welty said.

Harry looked up at Findlay Jay. The tall man's face darkened. "There might be that number of my people out there."

Two men carrying rifles came running out of the barn and skidded to a halt when they saw the standoff on the lanai.

"Go back into the barn and bring out the stallion," Harry shouted.

"What are you playing at?" Welty demanded, the muzzle of his gun wavering slightly in Harry's direction.

Even Findlay Jay looked less benign.

Harry took a deep breath. He thought of Katherine as a widow and then moved on. "The three of us are going to put these damned guns away. Then, along with Jubilee, we're all going to take a walk across that pasture and stop the shooting before somebody gets killed."

Harry held his breath and watched Findlay Jay and Welty decide whether or not to shoot each other and maybe him, to round things out. Findlay Jay moved first. He eased the hammer on his .44 Magnum and shoved the gun into the waistband of his trousers. "I always admired General Pickett," he said, recovering his smile as he looked toward the new outbreak of gunfire.

"Why take Jubilee?" Welty asked.

"Because nobody's going to shoot the horse," Harry answered.

Welty hesitated. Then his .357 vanished under his coat.

"Bring him out," Findlay Jay called to the two men.

The shooting dwindled as they advanced, and when they reached the last gate, it stopped. In ones and twos, men began standing up and moving cautiously out of the trees, edging toward the three men and the horse. Harry was just beginning to feel good about being alive when the howl of sirens drifted brokenly across the fields.

Chapter 27

"Don't look at me," Harry said.

Findlay Jay and Welty had found their guns and were looking at him.

"Let's all stay real calm," Bradley put in.

Welty and Findlay Jay exchanged glances, and then Findlay Jay turned to face the men advancing on them. "Git out of here!" he roared.

"Go!" Welty shouted.

A moment later, only four men and a horse were left in the field, watching five Sheriff's squad cars pour into Findlay Jay's yard, dust spiraling behind them.

"Well, shit," Welty said as he and Findlay Jay, Bradley, Harry, and Jubilee began their walk back to the compound.

"You had me worried," Snyder said. He and Harry were standing beside the Captain's cruiser as Snyder unfastened his body armor. Harry had just given him a deeply sanitized account of what he had been doing with the two ranchers.

Welty and Findlay Jay had put Jubilee in the horse trailer while Bradley and Harry looked on. Findlay Jay had shaken Welty's hand a second time and Welty said, as he climbed into the cab of his truck, "It must be good to have your boy at home."

"And the grandson," Findlay Jay replied.

Welty froze for a moment, then nodded. Harry thought Findlay Jay might have left that out, but Welty started the

253

truck and Findlay Jay took off his hat and waved Welty out of the yard.

While Snyder and Harry talked, Bradley was taking Sergeant Frank Hodges and a small group of interested troopers to look at the bulls.

Harry wiped the sweat out of his eyes with his sleeve. "You damned near got me shot."

"I didn't see any signs of trouble," Snyder replied. "What were you all doing out there in the field with the stallion?"

Harry had not mentioned the skirmish. "Ernshaw Welty wanted to be sure Jubilee was in good working order before he trucked him home."

"Beautiful horse," Snyder said, tossing his gear into the trunk of the cruiser.

"What brought you out here?" Harry asked.

Snyder looked embarrassed. "Well, actually, Rafe Juliette called it in. I got the call. I figured if Juliette is calling the cops, it's got to be serious. He swore a shooting war was going to break out. And when it did, you were likely to get killed and he couldn't afford to lose another low-bid rat catcher. And Sergeant Hodges claimed he heard shooting while we were driving in here, but he's got an overactive imagination."

"Well, things were a little tense, but nobody came close to shooting anybody," Harry lied blithely.

"How do you suppose Juliette knew you were going to be out here?" Snyder asked.

"He gets a little help from his tenants."

Snyder nodded. "Say hello to Katherine and the kids for me." Harry said he would, and the detective got into his car and drove out of the yard.

When the last of the troopers had left, Harry followed

Findlay Jay and Bradley onto the lanai. "Is this truce going to hold?" he asked.

Findlay Jay shoved his hands into his pockets and looked out over his fields. His face was as solemn as Harry thought it could get. "Maybe," he said. He stood in silence for a while. Harry waited. "Yesterday, I would have said that by this time today one or all of us would be in the undertaker's hands." He looked down at Harry and smiled. "You did all right, Brock. I'd be proud to drink with you."

"And so would I," Bradley echoed.

Jesus, Harry thought, the things I have to do to make a living, but he was grinning when he took the glass from Findlay Jay. "To peace and prosperity," he said.

"To the end of feuding," Bradley said.

The big man raised his glass and said, "One thing at a time."

Harry drove home and found two calls on his answering machine, one from Helen and one from Riga. Riga was home. He called Helen first and made arrangements with her for lunch. He got Riga's answering service and left his name. He thought it was odd that no one answered the phone. Who was looking after Janet? But he was feeling too good about the Jubilee Project to worry about Riga's babysitting arrangements.

"You did a good job, Harry," Katherine said.

They were standing on the bridge over the Puc Puggy, watching the sun set in a salmon sky, streaked with feathery wisps of gray and vermilion clouds. The colony frogs had begun their evening chorus, and under the bridge a contingent of pig frogs were carrying the bass.

"Thanks. I don't know what Welty thinks, but Findlay Jay seemed satisfied."

Katherine nodded. "He should be." She was leaning on the top plank of the bridge railing, her face bathed in the fading light. She looked tired to Harry and sadly worn.

"How are you feeling?" he asked.

"I'm all right," she said.

"Try again."

"I'm tired. More tired than I should be at this point in the pregnancy. And I don't like what I'm hearing from Priscilla. Our marriage is beginning to smell like week-old fish. Otherwise, everything's great. Is that better?"

"Do you want to stop working for a while?"

"No."

Harry recognized the tone of voice and did not argue. "What's happened with your mother?"

"She's working and trying to do too much. The doctor tells her to slow down, but she won't listen."

"Call her or go up there again. Try to change her mind. She probably stopped listening to Priscilla a long time ago."

"No."

"Blessed are the peacemakers," he said.

"Spare me," she replied and turned away from him.

At ten o'clock he was working in his study, bringing his reports up to date. He kept brief narratives of his cases and how they were developing. He had finished writing up Findlay Jay when the telephone rang.

"This is Riga. I need to . . ."

The phone went dead. Harry listened until the service signal returned and dialed her number. There was no answer. When the answering machine picked up, he put the phone down. He suddenly had a bad feeling. But what was there to be worried about? Janet must be a constant source of interruptions and small crises. She hung up, dealt with the situation, someone called, and she answered. She'll call back.

He finished filing the folders piled on his desk. No call. He picked up the phone and called her. Again, there was no answer. Harry went upstairs and knocked on Katherine's door.

"Something may be wrong at Riga's. I'm going to take a look. If everything's all right, I'll just turn around and come home."

Katherine sat forward in the bed and put her book down. "What could be wrong? Are you babysitting her now?"

Harry told her about the call.

"I don't like you going there alone."

"It's probably nothing. I'll be right back."

He closed the door. In that almost unconscious way of married couples, they had been speaking quietly to keep from waking the kids. Harry thought how strange it was that they were so badly at odds. He wanted to say something conciliatory, but the words hadn't come. Stubbornness and resentment, as he well knew. On his way to the stairs, he went into his room, buckled on his shoulder holster, and pulled on a light jacket.

Harry parked a block away and out of sight of the house. He walked up Riga's front path without being challenged. There was no security. And he saw with a slight stir of alarm that the patio gate was open. He did not go through it. Because of her mother, Riga kept the gate closed and locked. He thought about that, and decided to walk around the house, to see if anything else was open.

The only light he found was a faint, yellow glow showing around the drapes in her father's study. The rest of the house appeared to be in darkness, either because there were

257

no lights on or because shades and drapes were tightly drawn. He saw no signs of a forced entry and began to feel more comfortable.

He returned to the front of the house, thinking that perhaps he should just go home. But the open gate niggled. He walked through it into the courtyard and heard voices. Now and then one of them became louder than the others, but he could not tell who was speaking or what was being said.

He hesitated at the door with his hand raised to knock. Then, instead of knocking, he grasped the door handle and pressed down slowly on the thumb latch. The door was unlocked. Harry stepped into the hallway. The hall was dimly lighted by the small Tiffany lamp on the side table and the light over the oil painting.

Now he identified Riga's and Tom's voices. Both sounded angry, but the heavy study door still made it impossible for him to understand what they were saying. Shit, he thought, I've walked into a family quarrel. He was turning to make a silent escape when the door to the study opened and Tom stepped into the hall.

"Harry," he said, "what's going on?"

"I'm sorry about this," Harry began lamely. "Riga's call and the unlocked gate made me think . . ." He stopped himself. "Are you and Riga all right? I thought—"

"What are you doing here?" Riga demanded. She stepped into the hall in front of Tom, as if he had not been there. She was wearing a jade green silk robe. The light from the study fell across her at a dramatic angle, and Harry thought, despite his embarrassment, that outside of the movies he had never seen anyone look the way she did at that moment.

"Never mind," she said. "Come in here."

She whirled around and vanished into the study. Tom,

dressed in a gray sweat suit, looked at Harry and shrugged his shoulders. Harry braced himself, and walked into the dreaded study.

"I'm not breaking and entering," Harry said. He felt as if he has been caught stealing apples.

"I'm not interested in hearing what you thought you were doing," Riga said icily. As in their first interview, she was standing stiff as a statue behind the polished desk.

"It's not a gripping story," Harry agreed, "but I'm going to tell it." Anger had suddenly flooded through him.

"Get on with it then. It's what, eleven o'clock? And don't correct me."

"You and I were talking and the connection was broken. I decided to come and have a look to see if everything was all right. You've got no security, and the gate is open. I tried the front door, and it was open. I heard voices and stepped into the hall. That's when Tom found me."

Riga did not relent. She went on staring at him as if he was one of the lower and more disgusting life forms.

"Thanks," Tom said. He came forward to stand beside Harry. "It was damned good of you to make the effort. And no, we don't have any security." He sounded aggrieved. "The police said they were stretched too thin to provide it, and Riga wouldn't let me hire anyone."

"Are we surprised?" The voice came from behind Harry.

Harry spun around and saw Ruvin Carter standing in the door holding a gun. It was pointed at Riga. Carter stepped carefully into the room and took up a position slightly to the left of the door. "Tom," the banker said, "walk around the desk and stand beside your lovely companion. Brock, I'll have you on the floor, face-down, spread-eagled."

Harry did as he was told, slowly, keeping his hands where Carter could see them. Tom was staring at Carter, his face dark with anger. "Don't even think of it," Harry told him. "Do as he says."

"That's good advice," Carter said.

Tom backed around the desk. On the floor, Harry could no longer see Riga and Tom, but he had a good view of Carter. Instead of his usual western regalia, he was dressed in black, including his sneakers. Harry realized that Carter had probably seen him arrive and could easily have watched from the shadows while Harry circled the house. Then Carter simply followed him inside. There's one born every minute.

"What do you want, Ruvin?" Riga's voice was calm and clear. Harry cheered silently. It was the right gambit. She was signaling a willingness to negotiate.

"I've already got what I want, Riga." Carter's voice was equally calm. He took a step forward.

"If I get my hands on you, you son of a bitch," Tom shouted, "I'll—"

"Stop it, Tom," Riga said firmly.

Carter laughed. "You won't get your hands on me, Toy Boy, because I'm going to blow your stupid head off."

"Ruvin, why did you shoot me?" Riga asked the question as if they were having an ordinary conversation.

Brains and guts, Harry thought while at the same time trying to figure out how to get to his gun. Lying the way he was, the only way he could get it was to roll onto his back, drawing it as he rolled. Fat chance, unless something broke Carter's concentration.

Carter gave a bark of incredulous laughter. "I want you dead, Riga. Isn't that obvious?"

This one is loony as the March Hare, Harry thought.

"I know that, Ruvin, but why?"

Harry was trying without success to think of some way

to distract Carter long enough to make the roll.

"Nothing personal. Your name just came up." He broke into violent laughter and then stopped, as if his mind had shut off a faucet. "Come on, don't you remember the line? *Peanuts*! Charlie Brown is lying in bed. He says, 'Sometimes at night I lie here and ask, Why me?' and a voice answers, 'Nothing personal. Your name just came up.' "

"Tom! No!" Riga shouted. Then Harry saw Tom's legs coming over the desk. Carter fired. Tom's feet hit the floor, his knees buckled, and he fell into a shapeless heap on the floor. He lay perfectly still.

It was over before Harry could respond. He cursed himself silently.

"Don't either of you move," Carter said. "The Toy Boy is not moving. He has acquired wisdom." He smiled at Riga. "Is your question still in play?"

"Yes," she said. Her voice was weaker but steady.

Keep doing it, Harry urged. Sprawled as awkwardly as he was, he was beginning to stiffen. He tried make some small adjustments in his position, but Carter took a step forward and kicked him in his right side. It hurt like hell.

"I said, don't move."

"Right," Harry gasped.

Carter stepped back. "Now, where were we? Oh, yes. Why did I shoot you, Riga? The answer is simple. I had made some unauthorized withdrawals from the trust. Of course, I planned to return the money. Then that fool Truly went to work and, before I could put it back, two years had passed. Of course, I had to kill him, to stop the clock, so to speak."

He smiled affably. "Then you began pressing the bank to liquidate."

"And you felt you had to kill me."

"Exactly." He seemed to lose track of his story and scowled down at Harry. "The dog thing, Brock, that was cute, but not as cute as what I'm going to do to you. I think I'll start with one of your legs. I'll save the head for later."

He smiled again at Riga, then began slowly lowering his gun just as Janet Kraftmeier rushed into the room, her long, white nightgown billowing out behind her.

"Are you having a party?" she cried in an excited voice. Startled, Carter raised his head and swung his gun toward her. She had been looking at Riga, but now she noticed Carter and ran toward him. "Arthur! Where have you been? I've been worried sick over you. Oh, it's so good to have you home."

She reached out to wrap Carter in an embrace. Harry began his roll just as Carter shouted, "Stay away from me."

"Don't be silly," she said with a laugh.

Carter lowered his gun to shoot Harry, but Janet was too close, and he shot her instead. The impact of the bullet knocked her off her feet. As she fell, Carter swung the gun toward Harry, but before he could fire, Harry shot him in the chest, slamming him into the door frame. His gun flew out of his hand and skidded into the hall. As Harry got to his feet, Carter slid down the door frame to his knees, groaning.

Harry turned to see if Riga was all right. She was holding an automatic in both hands. It was pointed at Carter, and there was no doubt about what she was going to do with it. She had stepped to the center of the desk to get a clear shot past Harry.

"Riga," he said. "Don't do it. It's over."

"Not yet it isn't."

Harry stepped between her and Carter. "Riga, if you love Cheryl, don't kill him."

She hesitated, then her shoulders slumped. She let her breath go and lowered the gun.

"Pick up the phone," he told her and turned toward Tom.

Chapter 28

Janet was dead. Tom was unconscious but still alive. So was Carter. As soon as the ambulances left, Harry called Helen. He told her what had happened and said Riga had gone to the hospital with Tom.

"Where's Cheryl?" she asked.

"Asleep. She slept through it all. One of the troopers is keeping an eye on her."

"I'll be there in ten minutes."

Then he called Katherine. "There's been some trouble at Riga's. Jim and his people have Ruvin Carter in custody."

"Was there any shooting?"

"Yes."

"Who's dead?" Her voice was flat calm.

"Carter killed Janet and wounded Tom. I shot Carter."

"Wonderful. Are you all right?"

"Yes."

"And Riga?"

"She's all right."

"That's just great. Three down and two still standing." She hung up.

"Sorry to rush you, Harry," Snyder said at his shoulder, "but I need to ask you some questions."

Harry put the phone down. Troopers were everywhere. Crime scene people were swarming over the study, taking pictures, making notes, and putting bits and pieces into bottles. Chalked outlines on the floor showed where the bodies had been lying. Beyond the door, lights from the other rooms were streaming into the corridor. Troopers kept passing the door.

"Where the hell were you guys when she needed you?" Harry demanded. "There must be twenty people here. If just one had been watching this place an hour ago, none of this would have happened."

"You're probably right," Snyder said. He regarded Harry critically. "It's shock. Your system's overloaded. It's only natural."

"I guess," Harry said. He took a deep breath.

"Let's go over it again," the detective said. "I tried to talk with Riga Kraftmeier, and she just shoved me out of the way and climbed into the ambulance with Burkhardt. He was out and so was Carter. That leaves you."

Harry took him through it.

"Damn," Hodges complained. He approached them gingerly, picking his way over the blood-soaked carpet. "This place looks like a slaughterhouse." He came to a stop and mopped his face with his blue bandanna. "That Kraftmeier woman surely did not want her mother being taken out of here in a body bag. She made one hell of a fuss."

"Strong-minded woman," Snyder said.

Harry agreed. He was remembering how she had looked with the automatic in her hands. "But her mother was the real hero here."

"It's too bad she had to die," Snyder said. He had put away his notebook and was looking around the room. His expression was still pained.

"Did you ever meet her?" Harry asked.

Snyder shook his head.

"She was an Alzheimer's victim," Harry said for Hodges' benefit. "She thought Carter was her dead son. She tried to hug him. He shot her and that gave me the chance to shoot him." Harry had not mentioned Riga's part in the action to Snyder and did not now. The police had taken away the gun she had been holding. But it had no relevance. It had not been fired.

"Well, maybe it was a mercy," Snyder said uncertainly.

"Of course it was," Hodges put in. His face got redder as he said it.

"Don't be too sure," Snyder replied sharply. "She was still a person, and she's dead."

Hodges bristled. "At least three people are still alive because she took the bullet. And who the hell would want to go on living when you can't even remember your own son is dead? If I get the damned thing, I hope somebody shoots me." He turned stiffly and stalked out of the room.

"Once in a while he gets like that," Snyder said. Then he asked if Carter had said why he was trying to kill Riga.

"He's been dipping into the trust money and couldn't put it back. He interrupted his explanation to say he was going to shoot me. Then Janet came running in, and you know the rest."

"The wheels of God," Snyder said.

"I'm going home," Harry said. He was exhausted. He still had to face Katherine. He did not want to discuss God's wheels because he thought one of them was about to run right over him.

Katherine was asleep. The house was quiet. At the edge of the woods, the chuck-will's-widow was calling. Harry was too wired to sleep. He went out onto the lanai and watched the moonlight in the oaks. Then he called the hos-

266

pital. The surgeons were still working on Carter and Burkhardt. He was surprised when Helen came on the line.

"Cheryl's with me," she said. "I'll take her to my place in a few minutes and let her finish her sleep. Tom has lost a lot of blood, and they're still working on him. I don't know about Carter. One of the nurses said he's not too good, but I don't really know anything."

"How's Riga?"

"She's okay. She said you were great. She said you saved her twice. What does that mean? She won't tell me."

"It's nothing. She's probably still in shock."

"That will cost you, Harry."

"All right, Wonder Woman, how are you?"

"Not so good."

"What's wrong?"

"A bunch of things. But I don't want to talk about it."

"Right. I'll talk to you later."

"Harry."

"What?"

"I'm glad you're okay. That both of you are okay. Thank you."

She hung up before Harry could reply.

When he did finally sleep, he slept so deeply and so long that when he woke, the sun was over the trees, the cicadas were fiddling, and the house was empty. He felt disoriented and abandoned, as if he'd missed a train. After a sketchy breakfast, he called the hospital. Both men were alive and out of danger. He tried to work, but he felt so strange and restless that he gave up and went to talk to Tucker.

Harry hoped the walk on the dusty road with the sun hot on his back and the life of the Hammock surging around him would settle his mind. Instead, he began by reliving the shootings and then settled with a thump on Katherine. Why hadn't she wakened him this morning? The answer he came up with was that she didn't want to talk to him. So, what else was new? By the time he reached Tucker's place, he was in a thoroughly sour mood.

"You look like something the cat dragged in," Tucker said. The old farmer was working with his hives and was not wearing his protective clothing. Sanchez and Oh-Brother! stopped with Harry at a respectful distance from the clouds of bees. The two animals had met Harry when he turned in off the road and led him to Tucker. Part of the way, Oh-Brother! had carried Harry's hat in his mouth.

"Don't ask me about it," Harry said to Tucker when the mule gave it back to him. "What are you doing?"

"Adding supers," Tucker replied. "This morning the bees began fetching the honey in rivers. They're going to need more storage space. Basically, the supers just add another story to their houses. By August, they'll have filled them with honey."

He added the last super and walked slowly out of the humming cloud.

"Daniel emerging from the lion's den," Harry said.

"Well, we scrape along," Tucker said with a pleased smile. "I believe there was some trouble at Riga Kraftmeier's last night."

"That's right. Where's Weissmuller?"

"We'd all like to know that," Tucker said.

Harry noticed that Oh-Brother! was nodding his head toward the woods, and Sanchez was looking in the same direction with a glum expression. Harry quickly looked away. "How long has he been missing?"

"Two days. Day before yesterday he was sitting the way he does, the way he often did," he corrected himself, "staring into the distance. Then he got up and just trotted away in the direction he had been staring without a word of explanation. When Sanchez and Oh-Brother! noticed he was missing, they went after him. They came back without him."

Tucker waved an arm at the woods. "He's out there somewhere. Now, let's have some tea and carrot cake, and you can tell me about last night."

"So it was Carter," Tucker said sadly, when Harry finished the story. "I'm glad you're still with us. And Tom, of course. Too bad about Janet."

Harry thought of Snyder and Hodges arguing about Janet's death. "Is her dying a deliverance or a tragedy?"

"We can't find out."

"What do you mean?"

"The only person who can tell us is dead."

"Janet."

"Yes." Tucker paused to pour more tea. "I'm not a prophet," he continued, "but I suspect that Helen, Riga, and Tom Burkhardt, when he recovers a bit, have some hard days ahead of them."

Harry found he had nothing to say. Tucker looked at him with a slight frown and moved on. "How are things with you and Katherine?"

Harry shrugged. "About the same, I guess."

"How bad is it?"

"She hasn't forgiven me, and I've given up thinking she will."

"The kids doing all right?"

"Kids are like sponges. They soak up all the spilled feelings around them, good and bad. Our troubles aren't helping."

"Bring them over. The raspberries need picking."

"I'll do that," Harry said. He got up. "I'd better get back. I've got work to do."

"Any chance of my getting you and your family over here for supper some day soon?"

"We'd like that," Harry said. "I'll mention it to Katherine. I hope Weissmuller comes back."

Tucker shook his head and followed Harry onto the back stoop. "He's looking for Truly. Of course, he knows he's not going to find him. That's the part that worries me. He can't come to terms with the past."

"It's not easy," Harry said sourly.

Harry arranged with Katherine to take the kids raspberrying. Minna lasted among the savagely hooked canes for about fifteen minutes. Jesse braved them for an hour. But then they both turned to riding Oh, Brother!. Sanchez grinned so much even Katherine was laughing. But when the day was over, she and Harry were as estranged as ever. She had added to her list of complaints the near-fracas at Findlay Jay's and the shootings at Riga Kraftmeier's.

Although the chill between them was deepening, they did go to Janet Kraftmeier's funeral together. There was a huge turn-out. Florence Herrick and Jason Bryde were there.

"Our generation is becoming an endangered species," the Judge said cheerfully after shaking hands with Katherine. "Amanecida doesn't like me to say things like that, but I assert myself in the few remaining ways I can."

Funeral or not, he was flirting with Katherine.

"You only say that because she's not here," she said.

"That's true." He turned back to Harry. "Congratulations, Harry. You saved Riga Kraftmeier's life."

"Janet deserves the credit."

"No. You do," Florence Herrick insisted. "Janet was a leaf blown by the winds of chance. I'll grant her arrival probably saved your life, but it was left to you to act on the opportunity."

She turned to Katherine. "Your husband's a brave man."

"No man's a hero to his wife," Harry said quickly.

"Bravery, like charity, begins at home," Katherine replied without smiling.

After leaving the cemetery, they drove back to the Hammock and picked up Minna and Jesse from Tucker. The children were full of their adventures among the bees and the rabbits.

"The little ones are the spitting image of Old Man Rabbit," Minna said. "I 'spect they're his grandchildren."

"And great-grandchildren," Tucker added.

Jesse groaned loudly, then asked Harry if he'd ever seen the bees do their honey dance. Before Harry and Katherine left, they agreed with Tucker on a time to come for dinner. The kids' bubbling enthusiasm lasted all the way home and even made Harry feel better. But when he and Katherine were finally alone, she said, "I think that after our dinner with Tucker, I'd better take the kids and move into town."

"You don't have to do that," he replied. "If you don't want to be around me, I'll go."

"How would that work, Harry?" she demanded angrily. "What about Minna and Jesse out here alone? For God's sake, use your head."

"I was just trying to . . ."

"To get away from me as fast as you can."

"That's not true."

"Isn't it? That's how it looks to me."

And that was where they left it.

271

★ ★ ★ ★ ★

Two days later Helen called and asked Harry if he could stop by the house. He went, dragging his feet. He told himself he did not want to see her. But that was not true and he knew it. He actually did want to see her, but he did not want to deal with that, and not seeing her was the easiest way to avoid having to.

"I've got to talk to someone about this," Helen said, bringing the coffee to the kitchen table.

Mister Johnson shrieked at his bean bag and threw it off the counter onto the floor. Then he whistled shrilly at Helen.

"No," she said. "That's the third time you've done that in the last hour. It can stay there."

Muttering imprecations, the gray parrot began hauling himself up the front of his cage.

"God, he's worse than a kid," she said.

"What's wrong, Helen?" His uneasiness made Harry abrupt.

She dropped into a chair and planted her arms on the table. Her hands were trembling and she locked them together when she saw that Harry had noticed. "Tom is leaving Riga. It's awful, Harry. I don't think I've ever felt worse about anything in my life." Her eyes brimmed with tears. "Oh shit!" she said, brushing them away.

"When did this happen?"

"Hold on." She blew her nose loudly on a piece of roller towel. "Yesterday. He told her that when he was discharged from the hospital, he was moving into a furnished apartment at the Hawkswood Beach and Tennis Club. That was where he worked before he began living with Riga. He had made the arrangements before he was shot. The Club's giving him his old job back."

"You must have seen it coming."

Helen nodded. "I thought it was what I wanted."

He waited, but she sat staring at the table. "But?"

"Now I don't feel the same."

"Why not?"

"Christ, Harry, they were in love. And there's Cheryl. I've just wakened up to the fact that I've done something terrible."

He wanted to put his arms around Helen and comfort her, but he stepped down hard on that impulse and settled for being angry with Riga. "Two things," he said gruffly. "You're being too tough on yourself here. If something hadn't been wrong between Riga and Tom, Riga wouldn't have turned to you. And if anybody's going to feel bad about wrecking that relationship, it should be Riga."

"I've told myself all that, Harry, but it doesn't help." The tears came back.

"What are you going to do? What do you want to do?"

"I don't know."

"Do you love Riga?"

"Of course I do. That is, I must, but I'm pretty sure I'm not *in* love with her. Maybe I never was. And now I'm so ashamed I want to crawl into a hole somewhere and die."

"You didn't force Riga . . ."

"Don't be dumb, Harry, I've wrecked . . . well, not a marriage, but they have a child. What was I thinking of?"

"Maybe thinking didn't have a lot to do with it. But beating yourself up isn't going to help." He thought about where he was with Katherine and knew he was in no position to be giving Helen advice. "What about you and Riga?"

"I don't know." She sighed and blew her nose again. Then she straightened her back, as if she had suddenly reached a decision. "I know I don't have any right to ask

273

this, but I'm going to. Harry, can you forgive me and be my—" she stumbled and then finished in a rush "—friend again?"

This time Harry stood up and strode around the table. She jumped up and threw herself into his arms.

"What's this *again* stuff?" he demanded.

Chapter 29

The next morning Harry was on the phone with Rafe Juliette when Jim Snyder knocked on the lanai door and called, "Anybody home?"

Harry covered the mouthpiece with a hand and shouted, "Come in."

"It's me," Snyder replied.

"You know the little problem we had out here?" Rafe asked.

"You mean the shooting war?"

"Whatever. That's all over now. My people found out who was doing it. They arranged a meeting and settled the problem. Only three went down and, except for immediates, nobody'll miss 'em. Hey, I'm glad you're still on your feet."

"So am I. Thanks for placing the call."

"*De nada.*" He hung up.

Harry found the detective sprawled on a lounge chair, looking like a rainy Sunday. "What's wrong?"

With obvious reluctance, Snyder pulled himself up in the chair. "I've got some bad news."

"Is Katherine . . ."

"No, no," Snyder said, clambering to his feet. "It's not about Katherine or the kids."

Harry began to get his breath back. "Okay, let's hear it."

"It's about Findlay Jay. This morning he and his wife took off for South Carolina. From the way things look, they

275

had no more than gotten into the air when something went wrong. He tried setting down in a pasture and hooked a fence with the landing gear and cartwheeled. Killed him and his wife."

"And Willie Nelson," Harry added bitterly.

"Willie Nelson?"

"Norma Jean's dog."

"That wasn't in the report."

Harry rubbed his hand across his face. "Did it burn?"

"No."

"Then get a mechanic you can trust to go over the plane."

"You're thinking Ernshaw Welty."

"I'd bet my last nickel on it."

Snyder nodded. "We're on it. I'm sorry, Harry. We all hoped you'd won that one."

"So had I." He felt as if he'd been kicked in the stomach.

Snyder grabbed his hat off the chair. "I've got to go. I left Hodges trying to sort out an armed robbery over on South Avola." Snyder put on his hat and dropped a hand on Harry's shoulder. "I'm sorry about Findlay Jay."

"He was a good man," Harry said. Long after the dust from Snyder's car had blown away, Harry stood staring out the door, thinking about Findlay Jay and Norma Jean and about their son, who had inherited a lot more than a ranch.

By the time Katherine came home, Harry had made a decision. After dinner he asked her if she could give him a few minutes. The children had gone upstairs, and he and Katherine were clearing away the dishes.

"What do you want to talk about?" she asked. There was no enthusiasm in her voice.

"Findlay Jay and his wife are dead. Snyder came out this morning to tell me."

"I'm sorry," she said. "What happened?"

"It looks as though Ernshaw Welty killed them."

With a deeply-banked fury that had been slowly building since Snyder's visit, he told her what he had learned from Snyder. When he was finished, she said, "I think things between them would have come to the same end with or without you. And from where I'm standing, it looks as if you put yourself and us at risk for nothing."

"Maybe," he said. He started the dishwasher. Katherine put the bowl of fruit back on the table and turned to leave.

"There something else," Harry said. "I saw Helen today."

Katherine swung around. "And?"

"She said Tom Burkhardt is leaving Riga."

"Is that it?" Katherine asked in a flat voice.

"Just about."

Katherine paused and then said, "Are you in love in Helen?"

Harry felt as if he'd been speared. "What kind of question is that?"

"A reasonable one. She's been in love with you for years."

"She loves Riga."

"Probably. But it's why she told you and not me that Burkhardt is leaving Riga. The snake is loose in paradise."

Harry's head spun. "I thought you were her friend."

"I thought so too, but lately she's been avoiding me like the plague."

"Are you avoiding her?"

"Maybe. And you're giving up on us. Is that what you're leading up to?"

"No, Katherine. What I want is for us to stay together.

But if you've decided that isn't going to happen, I want you to tell me now."

"And put you back in control of this runaway train?" She gave him a grim smile.

"Not likely. You haven't answered my question."

The phone rang. Katherine picked it up. Harry could hear a woman's voice speaking loudly and rapidly. Katherine listened carefully.

"Not now, Priscilla," she said. "I can't take the kids out of school again this soon. Can you handle it?" She listened some more. "Okay, I'll call her. Yes. As soon as I can."

She hung up the phone.

"Is your mother worse?" he asked.

She nodded. "Either her heart's weakened or she's having a bad reaction to her new medicine. Priscilla wants me to come back as soon as I can. You heard what I said."

"Do you want to leave Minna and Jesse and just go yourself?"

She looked at him with a hard, flat stare and said, "No."

Two days after Findlay Jay and Norma Jean's funeral, Harry got a call from Snyder asking him to stop in at his office. He had been unwilling to say why.

"What's the mystery?" Harry demanded, dropping into a chair in front of Snyder's desk. Hodges was sitting beside Harry, looking as somber as his face allowed.

"The gasoline in Findlay Jay's plane was doctored. He had probably climbed only a few hundred feet when the engine stalled out. There's no question. We're looking at murder. We've made a preliminary check of the people who had access to the plane. It turns out that about a month ago, Findlay Jay hired a drifter who called himself Dooley Barnes as a kind of fill-in man and general fetch-and-carry person. One of his jobs was to check the inventory in all the working segments of the ranch. He was in and out of the hanger on a daily basis."

"And he's turned up missing," Harry said.

"That's right," Hodges said.

"Maybe it's coincidence, but I doubt it," Snyder added, completing Harry's thought.

"The money came from Welty," he said bitterly, "but even if you could find Barnes, which you probably can't, and if you could prove he salted the plane's tank, which you probably couldn't, you would never be able to trace the payment back to Welty."

The anger he had felt when he heard of Findlay Jay's and Norma Jean's deaths surged back, strengthened by his own and Snyder's words.

"Well, I suppose there's some consolation in knowing the worst is done. The feud's over," Hodges said.

"It's not over," Harry said, and added with a sudden shock of recollection. "I should have seen it coming." He repeated for Snyder and Hodges what Welty said to Findlay Jay about how nice it must be to have his son at home and Findlay Jay's saying with that mean grin, "and the grandson."

"Welty won't rest until they're all dead," Harry concluded.

"And what do we do about that?" Snyder asked with a scowl and threw his pencil onto the desk.

"We could shoot the son of a bitch," Hodges said, planting his elbows on his knees.

"That's not helpful, Frank," Snyder complained.

"Are Bradley Jay and his family still at the ranch?" Harry asked.

"Yes," Hodges said.

"Then they're at risk. Does Bradley know about the doctored gasoline?"

"I had to tell him his father and mother's deaths were
now regarded by the police as homicides. He didn't take it
well," Snyder said.

"Angry?"

"Very."

When Harry got home, he had a message from Bradley
Jay asking him to call. Harry did.

"You know about the plane?" he asked, sounding years
older than when Harry had last talked with him.

"I'm sorry. It's a bad thing," Harry responded.

"I had pretty well sold myself the story that their deaths
were quick and clean. But their being killed takes away the
clean part. Of course, we both know who killed them."

"I should say there's no way of knowing for sure until
the police complete their investigation, but it wouldn't be
an honest answer. It puts you in a bad place."

"I know what you're really asking, am I going to go
hunting Ernshaw Welty? Well, the answer is no. When I
was about twelve, I promised myself that I would never do
one thing to continue this stupid feud, and I plan to stick to
my position. But I can surely try to find out if there's some
way to prove that Welty did kill my parents. I owe them
that, wouldn't you think?"

"What are you planning to do?" Harry had silently
cheered Jay's decision.

"Ask you to go to work for me, to find out everything
you can. I know the police are on it, and I think Captain
Snyder's a fine man, but I also know there's limits on what
they can do."

"If you want me to," Harry said, "I'll do what I can, with

the understanding that everything I find that might contribute to an arrest and conviction of whoever killed your parents goes to the police."

"Sounds right to me."

"Then I'll draw up a contract. And one other thing. Beginning right now, I want you to take every precaution you can to protect yourself and your family. Take half a dozen of your most trusted men and set up a schedule of twenty-four-hour protection. Neither you nor your wife drives alone to town. Wainfleet doesn't play outside unattended. You do not walk or ride on the ranch without an armed escort. Better yet, take yourselves back to school."

"Pam and I are not going to begin the rest of our lives by being run off our land. We'll stay, but I will make sure we have protection."

"All right," Harry said. "I'll be talking with you."

"That's just great, Harry," Katherine said when he put down the phone. "What the hell do you think you're doing?"

Chapter 30

Harry turned to face Katherine. She looked as angry as she sounded.

"Has Jay hired you?" she demanded.

"Yes."

"You're going to go out there and try to prove that Ernshaw Welty killed Jay's mother and father. That's it, isn't it?"

"The shortest answer is yes."

Katherine turned away with her fists clenched.

"Katherine," he said and reached out to put his hand on her shoulder.

She jerked away and faced him again. "No!" she shouted. "No! You're not going to stop until you get yourself killed, are you?"

There was no use in pretending he didn't know what she was talking about. "I have a personal stake in this case, Katherine. Findlay Jay was a good man. If Welty isn't stopped, he's going to kill Bradley Jay and his son."

When he finished, she planted her fists on her hips and said, "That's a great speech, Harry, but as soon as Welty finds out you're investigating him, he will begin hunting you."

"Possibly," he admitted. Something tugged at his mind, then slipped away.

"Quit now, while you're still alive," she said.

He pulled his attention back to her. He could agree, step

back from this, give her what she wanted. It was possible that *was* what he should do. The errant thought nudged him again, but he ignored it. "No," he said.

The moment he spoke, the idea he had been dodging flooded his mind. Of course, that was the way to begin the investigation. Something Katherine said had triggered it. He had to tell her, maybe she would see . . . He started to speak, but she pushed her hands at him.

"I don't want to hear it," she said and stalked out of the room.

The next morning Harry talked with Tucker about Bradley Jay's call.

"What did Katherine think of it?" Tucker asked as he and Harry walked through the citrus orchard, looking for signs of fruit fly. Sanchez and Oh-Brother! trailed after them, looking to Harry, unnaturally subdued.

"It fails her test for appropriate work."

Tucker shook his head. "How serious is her objection, comments like that last one aside?"

"This business with Bradley Jay has upset her a lot. We're in a Mexican standoff as to whether or not I'm going to go on making my living doing what I do."

"I'm sorry to hear that."

"So am I."

"I assume you've made up your mind to go on working for Jay."

"Yes."

"Then there's not much for me to say." The old man stopped and looked squarely at Harry. "You do know how dangerous Welty is."

"I should."

"And you've thought carefully about whether or not you

might be paying too high a price for putting some salve on your conscience?"

"I don't know about my conscience," Harry said, a little huffed, "but somebody's got to stop Welty."

"Does it have to be you?"

"I have to try."

Tucker nodded and changed the subject. "There's some more bad news. Guy Bridges, the game warden, stopped by this morning to tell me he'd shot a big dog that's been killing deer in the Stickpen. From the description, I'd say it was Weissmuller. I guess he's found Truly."

"I'm sorry," Harry said. "I've been hoping he'd come back. Is that why Sanchez and Oh-Brother! . . ."

"Yes," Tucker said in a low voice. "They're feeling bad. And they've been acting like that since about midday yesterday. I believe they knew he was gone long before Bridges got here. And, like you, I was hoping he'd come back, but what we want and what we get in this life don't always coincide."

Harry drove to the Sheriff's office.

"I'm working for Bradley Jay," he told him.

"Why am I not congratulating you?" Snyder asked sourly. "What have you contracted to do?"

"Try to prove that Welty killed his mother and father."

"You know we're working on it."

"Another warm body might help."

"What's your plan?"

"That's what I came to talk to you about."

He laid out for Snyder what he wanted to do. When he finished, Snyder shoved his chair back and said, "Jesus, Harry, have you got any idea . . ."

"I know," he said and waved his hand dismissively.

"Will you help me or not?"

"Since trying to talk you out of it would be a waste of time, I guess I'll have to."

For the rest of the week, Harry talked with everybody who had any contact with Findlay Jay's plane. He knew Snyder's people had already interviewed most of them, but he slogged along, putting in the hours, hoping Welty would find out what he was doing. On Thursday night, he interviewed the last person on his list without developing any new leads. The next morning he caught up on some desk work. At ten-thirty, he took a folder out of his file drawer, opened it, read it, thought for a moment, then dialed a number.

A gritty voice answered. "This here's Ernshaw Welty."

"Hello, Welty."

There was a pause.

"Well, well. Brock. I hear you're asking questions about that airplane crash that took off the Jays. You working for young Jay?"

"That's right. I called to ask if you can tell me where to find Dooley Barnes." Harry felt his dislike of the whipsaw voice and man behind it rise in him like an icy tide.

"You're a joker, Brock. I might just surprise you by saying I do have something to tell you about that crash, but I'm not going to do it over the phone."

Harry allowed himself a slight buzz of satisfaction. No, you bastard, of course you're not. "Where would work for you?" He kept the tone of his voice just short of insulting.

"Well, my wife's kind of upset about the Sheriff's people coming out here and all," Welty said. Harry noted the rasp of anger had suddenly slid out of the rancher's voice. "So I don't want her to know you're dogging me. Let's try this:

after you come over the first cattle grate off the county road, there's a track on your right just beyond a big lignum vitae tree. You know where I'm taking about?"

Harry said he did.

"Good. Down that road a few hundred yards, there's a pond with a chiki hut and a barbecue pit and some picnic tables by the water. We used to use the place more than we do now. The fishing's good. My boy liked fishing. You think you can be there in an hour or so?"

"I can be there."

"That's fine and dandy, Mr. Brock."

Harry could almost see Welty's wolfish grin.

Harry found the tree and the road and let the Rover idle its way along the narrow track. He was wearing chinos and a short-sleeved shirt that was not tucked in. His 9mm was holstered under the waistband of his chinos, slightly in front of his left hip, and hidden by the shirttail. He rocked along the track, studying the woods ahead of the Rover, aware of a faint prickle of fear stirring the hair on his neck.

He knew Welty was a bushwhacker. He or one of his men had shot Findlay Jay. Harry thought there was a chance he might die before he ever got to Welty's picnic place. If it happened, Katherine could say, "I told you so." What kept him easing the Rover forward was his guess that if Welty was going to kill him, he would want the pleasure of telling him first and watching him sweat. But he admitted the argument had sounded more convincing when he made it in Snyder's office.

He turned a final brushy corner into a clearing. There was the pond, the barbecue pit, and the picnic tables. Sitting at the table closest to the water was Ernshaw Welty. He was wearing the same outfit he had on the day he came to collect Jubilee, and Harry remembered how the gun had come out from under that coat like a snake striking. He expected it to come out the same way today. On the table in front of Welty was a large, brown paper bag, lying on its side, the open end facing him. A blue plastic cooler stood beside him on the bench.

"Come and set," Welty called when Harry climbed down from the Rover. "I've got us some cold beer." Then he reached into the sack and pulled out a stack of sandwiches wrapped in waxed paper. "Thought we could eat while we talked."

"Sounds good to me," Harry replied. "I'd given up on lunch."

As Harry settled himself at the plank table and Welty went on talking about what else there was to eat in the sack, Harry, pretending to admire the area, took a good look around. He didn't learn much. The usual crowding in of brush and saw palmetto against the edge of the clearing formed a green wall. Who and how many were watching him and Welty from its shadows was anybody's guess.

"This here's a ham and cheese with some green chili dressing. That sound all right?"

"Fine," Harry answered and pulled the tab on his can of beer.

Then he sat and waited until Welty's line of talk ran out.

"Eat up," Welty said. He took a bite from his sandwich and laid it back on the table. "What good do you plan to do talking with Dooley Barnes?"

Harry put down his beer and unwrapped his sandwich without picking it up and, like Welty, kept his hands in sight on the table. "I figure it was Dooley Barnes who salted the gas tank in Findlay Jay's plane. Somebody paid him to do it. He knows who that is."

"And if you knew that, you'd have solved the crime," Welty grinned.

"I've already done that, Welty," Harry said in a calculated sneer. "Barnes' testimony is for the District Attorney."

"Too bad, Yankee boy, Barnes won't be able to help you. He's sunk in the mud of that pond at your back. And that's where you're going."

Harry was watching for Welty's left hand to move toward his coat. Instead, he pulled the revolver out of the bag.

"By Christmas," he said, pulling back the hammer, "there won't be a Jay left standing."

Harry threw himself to the right and yanked out his gun just as Welty fired, and the bullet burned like a hot iron through the flesh of his left shoulder. Welty's second shot ripped splinters out of the top of the table.

Welty tried to stand, lean across the table, and fire down on Harry, but the bench caught him behind the legs and stopped him. Harry swung the automatic under the table and fired straight into Welty's stomach. The impact of the slug folded Welty and threw him backward onto the ground, his boots banging the table as his feet flew over his head.

Harry rolled to the ground under the table, his gun pointed at Welty's sprawled body, and waited for the shooting to start from the woods. But the only sound was the startled and rapidly fading cawing of a crow, frightened by the noise. Harry lay still. His left shoulder burned like a fire. Very slowly, he crawled out from under the table and stood up. Welty lay face down, motionless, his back and the ground under him drenched in blood. The soft-nosed slug had torn a path straight through him and out his back, shattering his spine as it exited.

Now Comes Death

★ ★ ★ ★ ★

Harry pulled off his shirt and wrapped it as best he could around his shoulder. The pain blurred his vision. When he had done all he could to stop the bleeding, he leaned against the picnic table and waited until his head cleared enough for him to drive.

At the Avola Community Hospital Emergency Ward, Harry called Snyder's office and got Hodges. He told him what had happened.

"You know, Brock," Hodges said, "it's about time you got yourself a cell phone."

"Maybe so," Harry said, but the shots he'd been given put an end to that line of thought.

Around two-thirty he woke up in the recovery room. Katherine was sitting beside him. She did not say anything. The nurse came in and went out. The doctor came in.

"You're going to be sore," he said, "but the bone wasn't damaged. It was mostly muscle and cartilage and some of your hide that got torn. I sewed you up pretty well, if I do say so. We may have to do a skin graft, but you can go home as soon as you feel like it. Keep the arm in a sling. Come back and see me in a couple of days. You can tell me what happened."

He handed Katherine a prescription for Percocet and left. Snyder met them leaving the hospital and said he was relieved to see Harry walking.

"Have you got the tape?" he asked.

Harry reached into his pants pocket and passed it to Snyder. "The wire's in the Rover, if you need it."

"Nope. You were right. Welty's dead. Tomorrow, we'll start dragging the pond for Dooley Barnes' body. Katherine, your husband deserves a medal. He really does."

"Don't ask me for a donation," she said.

289

★ ★ ★ ★ ★

Three days later, Harry saw the doctor. He put on a new dressing, and told Harry to come back in a week. Harry was back on the Hammock by noon and found Katherine there ahead of him.

She was sitting at the kitchen table when he came in. "Are you okay?" she asked.

"Yes, are you?"

"No, but I will be," she said. She spoke again before he could ask what was wrong. "I'm leaving you, Harry. I'm taking the kids and moving back home with Ma and Priscilla."

"Because I won't give up being a private investigator."

"That's right."

"Let me see if I've got this straight. You're afraid I'm going to be killed or crippled, and that will put you and the kids at risk."

"That's about it."

"So you're going to hurry things along by leaving me and putting yourself and the kids in the same position you would be in if I was dead."

Her face flamed and she said, "I hoped you would help out with their support."

"And I will, that is, until someone kills me."

"I'm still going, Harry. My mother needs me."

"And I don't?"

"Not really. Not enough anyway. You lived alone too long. You don't need me, Harry. There are days when I think you don't need anybody."

"You're wrong, Katherine."

He could already taste the loneliness.

"That's possible, but I've got to do the only thing that's really ever worked for me. I've got to trust myself."

"Can't we talk about this? What about Minna and Jesse?"

"I've done all the thinking I need to do, and all the talking. I've told the kids we're going to visit Grandma. I picked them up at school. They're at the office with Bob Arnell. I've worked out my notice. When I finish here, we'll be on our way."

"How long have you been planning this?"

"I thought I knew a month ago. Your getting shot made me certain."

Harry couldn't think of anything to say. He couldn't even claim to be surprised. He knew what was coming when she stopped sleeping with him. He knew they were finished when he got into bed with Helen Bradley.

"Do you have enough money?" he asked.

"Yes. I'll call in a few days and we can begin to deal with what has to be dealt with." She stood up. "Goodbye, Harry."

"Katherine," he said, but the door was already closing behind her, and he did not make any further effort to stop her.

She drove away. The sound of the Rava faded until he could no longer hear it. He stood, still listening, as the silence flowed back, bringing with it the grief he had expected and a relief which he had not.

About the Author

Kinley Roby has published several nonfiction books, including *The King, the Press, and the People: A Study of Edward VII*; and *Arnold Bennett: A Writer at War 1914–1918*. He is also the author of the first Harry Brock mystery *Death in a Hammock*. Roby lives in southwest Florida with his wife Mary Linn Roby, a writer and editor.